DUST OF THE TRAIL

DUST OF THE TRAIL

BENNETT FOSTER

THORNDIKE
CHIVERS

LIBRARY OF CONGRESS CATALOGING-IN-PUBLICATION DATA

Foster, Bennett.
    Dust of the trail / by Bennett Foster.
      p. cm. — (Thorndike Press large print western)
    ISBN-13: 978-1-4104-1344-4 (alk. paper)
    ISBN-10: 1-4104-1344-6 (alk. paper)
    1. Large type books. I. Title.
    PS3511.O6812D87 2009
    813'.54—dc22
                             2008049071

BRITISH LIBRARY CATALOGUING-IN-PUBLICATION DATA AVAILABLE

Published in 2009 in the U.S. by arrangement with Golden West Literary Agency.

Published in 2009 in the U.K. by arrangement with Golden West Literary Agency.

U.K. Hardcover: 978 1 408 43305 8 (Chivers Large Print)
U.K. Softcover: 978 1 408 43306 5 (Camden Large Print)

Printed in the United States of America
1 2 3 4 5 6 7 13 12 11 10 09

CAST OF CHARACTERS

Rusty Shotridge . . . gun-slinging 'puncher, born to the saddle.

Bud Sigloe . . . outlaw, on the rampage.

Tom Flanders . . . one-time marshal of Abilene, a giant of the Kansas trail.

Ellen Watrous . . . a red-haired hellion.

Colonel John Watrous . . . he bought the LM steers.

Leonard Carlisle . . . his two-fisted partner.

Marcia Carlisle . . . Leonard's lovely dark-haired sister.

Scott McBride . . . an angry trail boss.

Honey Yates . . . smooth-faced rider, he made his own rules.

Gil Travis . . . young, devil-may-care 'puncher, a swaggering rider.

CHAPTER I

Rusty Shotridge could not avoid falling in with the stranger. The two roads came together, and just at their juncture the stranger sat a tall bay horse. Rusty, coming from the south, leading his bed horse, saw the tall man waiting and, as he came up spoke a greeting.

"Evenin'."

The stranger returned that word, thin lips smiling tightly beneath his gray mustache. Rusty halted his horses, and the two men surveyed each other. The stranger's blue coat was rolled behind his saddle, and he wore blue trousers and a white shirt that was neatly adorned with a small black bow tie. So much bespoke the townsman. On his feet were tight shop-made boots and on his head a Stetson. These said "cattle." About the stranger's middle was a wide belt, innocent of cartridges but supporting a heavy gun in a holster, and the stranger's saddle and gear showed well-cared-for use. Amazed at the contradiction of clothing, Rusty studied the stranger's face. It was pleasant, firm jawed, clean shaven, tanned and with sun wrinkles at the corners of the eyes. To Rusty it seemed that the face threw in with the hat and boots. Cattle had the edge over townsman. Rusty grinned.

"You headed for San Marcial?" the stranger asked, his inspection finished.

"Headin' that way," Rusty agreed, and then, because he was young and had not talked with anyone for a day, he amplified: "I'm goin' to catch on with the Watrous trail outfit."

The stranger nodded slightly, his smile broadening beneath the mustache. "Your first trip north, I take it," he said. "You seem mighty sure that Watrous will take you."

"Watrous was our neighbor. . . ." Rusty began and then, refuting any implied criticism that the stranger's words might have carried: "Everybody's got to make a first trip sometime, ain't they?"

"Sure," the tall man agreed pacifically.

"You been up the trail?" Rusty ventured after a small pause.

"I have," the stranger agreed. "I . . ." He broke off and stared at Rusty questioningly. Apparently satisfied with what he saw, he spoke again. "Would you take word into San Marcial for me?"

"It isn't much further, is it?" Rusty asked. "I thought I'd get in . . ."

The stranger's gesture was impatient. "You'll get in," he interrupted. "The thing is I ain't goin' to San Marcial . . . yet. I want to send word in. Will you take it for me?"

"Sure."

The tall man considered briefly, forming his message in his mind. "You find Bud Sigloe," he directed. "You tell him that I'll be there."

Rusty nodded, his eyes brightening. Bud Sigloe was known up and down the land. Trail boss, fighting man, Bud Sigloe's stature was on a par with that of Blocker and Flanders and Pierce and those other giants of the Kansas trail.

"I'll tell him," Rusty assured. "Who'll I say sent the word?"

"Tom Flanders," the tall man drawled. "Just tell him I'll be there."

Rusty stared at his companion with renewed interest. Tom Flanders! This was Tom Flanders talking to him! Tom Flanders was an immortal, a legend, one of those who topped the Olympus of public fame. Flanders had been with Billy Dixon at the Adobe Walls fight; he had been a sergeant

9

of Rangers, had served as night marshal of Abilene when that Kansas town was the lusty throat through which the first of the Texas cattle flowed to fill the belly of the North. Wherever men went in the vast reaches of the frontier, wherever peace and law needs must be enforced, there surely Tom Flanders appeared.

"Yeah," said Rusty Shotridge, and touched his horse with the rowels of his spurs. "I'll tell him." The horses — saddle horse and pack animal — moved ahead. A hundred yards Rusty rode, then looked back. Flanders still sat there at the forks of the road, tall and straight upon his bay.

The road wound down from the higher country toward the bottom land of the Puerco. Debouching from the mesquite after a mile of riding, Rusty passed an adobe building. Another house was passed, and then another until, rounding the corner of a particularly long and squat building, Rusty Shotridge found himself in town. San Marcial sprawled before him, the Puerco a dirty thread of water at its western limit, dust and buildings spreading toward the river. Horses dozed at hitch rails, and in front of the post office a little knot of men stopped their talk to survey Rusty as he passed. There were stores and warehouses, a blacksmith shop, a courthouse, saloons; and on one corner a church, white painted, sturdily occupied its place and made no compromise with its surroundings. Beyond the church, across the street from it, was the livery barn. In the dim recess of its alleyway Rusty Shotridge dismounted.

The lanky hostler chewed a straw and languidly informed Rusty that the stalls were filled but that he could put his horses in the corral and his bed and saddle in the grain room. The charges, the hostler said, would be four bits a head, one dollar in their entirety. Rusty pulled off bed and saddle, and the hostler led the horses away. When he returned Rusty had stowed away his belongings and was knocking dust from his trousers.

"Where," Rusty demanded, "will I find Bud Sigloe?"

The hostler's eyes widened. "What do you want Sigloe for?" he returned.

"I want to see him."

In the hostler's mouth his straw twitched as he chewed its end, and the hostler's eyes searched Rusty, surveying him from his small-rimmed, battered hat, on down past red-brown hair and tanned face, past powerfully sloping shoulders and slim waist girded with a heavy belt and weapon, past denim

11

Levis to the toes of his brush-scarred boots. Then, lifting his gaze, the hostler met Rusty's gray-green eyes. "You don't want to see Bud Sigloe," the hostler said.

"You're mistaken, friend. I do."

The hostler twitched his straw again. "Bud Sigloe's on the rampage," he announced. "He's raisin' hell. He's took in the town. The marshal's scared of him. They sent to Dulcina for Tom Flanders to come over an' talk to Bud."

"So?" Rusty prompted.

"So," the hostler said with finality, "you don't want to see him unless yo're lookin' for trouble. Bud heard that they'd sent for Tom an' he's down in the Bank Saloon now, waitin' for Tom to come. He sent Flanders a message hisse'f. He told Tom when he come to come a-shootin'. Bud says that Tom Flanders nor nobody can curry him. Bud an' Tom was friends, too, but they ain't now. There's goin' to be a killin'. You stay away from Bud Sigloe, kid."

Rusty's eyes grew bleak at that last word. Young he was, but certainly he was no kid. "The Bank Saloon?" he drawled. "Thanks, friend." Wheeling abruptly, he left the wide-eyed hostler chewing on his straw.

The Bank Saloon was down the street beyond the church and opposite a store.

There were no horses at the hitch rail in front of the Bank Saloon, nor were there men loitering under its awning. A little knot of men occupied the church corner, and farther down the street there were more men. Rusty noted these as his boots stirred up the dust of the street he crossed. The Bank Saloon had double doors, half shutters that swung easily. Rusty pushed the shutters aside.

Inside the shutters all was quiet. There were three men at the upper end of the bar talking to the bartender. At the far end of the bar one man stood alone, squat, dark and unshaven. He put down his whisky glass and watched the door as Rusty entered. The bartender stepped away from his associates, and these paused in their conversation. Rusty walked past them and stopped. "Mr. Sigloe?" he said.

Small brown bloodshot eyes searched Rusty's face. "An' what of it?" the owner of the eyes snapped. Bud Sigloe was drunk and ugly but not incapacitated. Looking at him, Rusty Shotridge could well believe the stories he had heard about this man. There was power in evidence, power in the body, power in the face. Drunk as he was, Bud Sigloe could still be reckoned as a whole man.

"Not much," Rusty answered quietly, "except I've got a message for you."

"What is it?"

"Tom Flanders said to tell you he'd be here."

Sigloe digested the words. "He'll be here, huh?" he snapped. "Are you a friend of Flanders?"

"Would you ask a better man to be a friend to?" Rusty answered. He was not at all afraid. Indeed, in Rusty Shotridge some of that same combativeness that possessed Sigloe welled up and made itself felt. He liked Sigloe, would, he knew, have given a good deal to have Sigloe as a friend, and yet at the drop of a hat Rusty Shotridge would have gone to war with the trail boss. Sigloe, angry and drunk as he was, paused to consider the question Rusty had asked.

"No," he answered finally. "Tom Flanders is all right for a friend."

"Well then," Rusty returned, "I brought his word to you." He wheeled, turning his back to Sigloe. The bartender was moving his head from side to side in little significant jerks. It was almost as though the barman spoke, saying: "Lay off. Lay off." Up at the end of the bar, close to the door, one of the three men shifted away from his fellows.

"It's right at six o'clock," the man stated

14

meaningly.

Six o'clock then was the time that had been set. Bud Sigloe had stated that he would be waiting for Tom Flanders at six o'clock, and Tom Flanders had sent the word that he would be on hand. A challenge had been given, and Rusty Shotridge had brought the answer to that challenge. Wheeling from the bar, Rusty stepped across to the wall opposite and sat down upon a bench. Sigloe watched him, as did the bartender and the other three. His status was undetermined. If he was a friend of Tom Flanders he would bear watching. Relaxing on the bench, Rusty produced his tobacco and papers. His hands, forming the cigarette, were steady and adept. Finishing the smoke, Rusty lifted his eyes from his fingers and coolly met Sigloe's belligerent stare.

"I met Flanders at the forks of the road," Rusty drawled. "I'd never seen him before but I was glad to accommodate him."

Sigloe continued to stare, then with a grunt he turned back to his empty glass and the whisky bottle. Rusty lighted his cigarette and addressed the bartender. "Is Colonel Watrous in town?"

The bartender said: "Uh . . ." and stopped suddenly. Under the push of a hand the shutters swung open and the doorway darkened as a man stepped through. At the bar end Sigloe set down his whisky glass and squared around. The three men at the front of the bar stepped swiftly back toward the wall, and the bartender, hands spread flat on the bar top, poised himself. Tom Flanders was inside the Bank Saloon, standing to the right of the door.

"I got your word, Bud," Flanders stated flatly.

"I got yours," Sigloe said. "The kid brought it."

Tension, hard and stretched to the breaking point, hung all along the length of the bar. The quiet that followed the briefly spoken statements was ominous, yet in the quiet and the tension there was a reluctance. Temper and pride had brought these two together as enemies. Hot words spoken in haste had done this damage. Rusty Shotridge could feel the reluctance. He was on his feet, not realizing that he had risen, and now he moved forward to the bar. From the end of the bar one man threw out a short exclamation, and then the quiet held again. At the bar, between Bud Sigloe and Tom Flanders, Rusty Shotridge stopped.

"I've come a far piece today," he said quietly, looking at the bartender. "I'd like a glass of beer."

The bartender did not move. Rusty turned his head and apparently saw Tom Flanders for the first time. "Will you take a drink with me?" he asked Flanders.

"I . . ." Tom Flanders paused briefly then moved forward. "Why, yes. I'll take a drink." The words were reluctant and hesitant. This interruption was a break in the set pattern Tom Flanders had formed in his mind. He could not cope with the broken pattern. From Flanders Rusty turned and looked at Bud Sigloe. Sigloe's eyes were wary, and there was a question in them. For Bud Sigloe, too, the pattern had been broken.

"Would you take a drink, Mr. Sigloe?" Rusty drawled.

Sigloe did not move as Rusty spoke. He was crouched at the end of the bar, tense, ready.

"A drink, Mr. Sigloe?" Rusty said again.

Tom Flanders stopped a half step beyond Rusty. There was a moment of breathless waiting, and then Bud Sigloe's heavy shoulders relaxed. "Why . . ." Sigloe said. And then: "Yeah. I'll take a drink."

The bartender let his breath go in a gusty sigh, and Rusty drawled: "Make mine beer," and turned casually so that his shoulders were against the bar. Sigloe was approach-

17

ing warily, taking the short steps that would bring him to Rusty's other side. At the end of the bar the black-haired man who had spoken of the time shifted and spoke again.

"False alarm. I thought they'd back down when the time come."

Rusty could feel Sigloe tighten once more. Flanders stared across Rusty's body at Sigloe, his face becoming a bleak, expressionless mask. Rusty did not move. Simply he stared at the black-haired man, his gray eyes, more green than gray now, blank and agate hard.

"Friend," drawled Rusty Shotridge, "yore mouth is considerably bigger than yore brains." He continued to stare. The black-haired man could not meet those gray-green eyes. His own eyes lowering, he shifted nervously, looked at his companions for support and, finding none, wheeled and made toward the shutters. They closed behind him, and Rusty, turning smoothly, faced the bar again. "Where's the beer?" he demanded.

Wakened to his duty, the bartender reached down for glasses. Sigloe's heavy shoulders had relaxed, and from the corners of his eyes Rusty could see the beginning of a grin on the beard-stubbled face of the trail boss. Flanders rested his elbows on the bar

18

and was looking into the back-bar mirror. Flanders, too, had relaxed.

"Kid," Bud Sigloe drawled. "Yo're a damned fool. Make mine beer, Slim."

Flanders nodded his head gently, corroborating Sigloe's statement. "A damned fool," he murmured. "Right now I can like a damned fool. I'll take beer too."

Slim, the bartender, set out three foaming glasses. Rusty, the hard bleakness erased from his face, reached out his hand for his glass. Slim was looking at him, and there was awe in the barman's eyes.

Flanders sipped his beer and made drawling comment: "San Marcial is too big a town to hurrah, Bud. You got 'em treed. Don't you reckon it's time you let 'em come down?"

Sigloe turned the stem of his glass between broad, spatulate fingers. His voice was apologetic. "There wasn't nothin' to do, Tom."

"Uh-huh." Tom Flanders understood. The energy in Bud Sigloe had demanded an outlet, and there was nothing to do. An apology had been given and accepted. Flanders spoke again. "I been called to Dodge City. They want me to take over the marshal's job up there. I'd like to have a man along that I could trust, Bud."

Sigloe drank his beer, emptying half the glass at a gulp. "There's no man I'd sooner side, Tom," he said. "But I'm contracted to Ad Marble. I've promised to take a herd north for him." Sigloe paused, and now the grin broke frankly all across his face. "How about takin' the kid here?" he asked. "I think he'd do."

Tom Flanders looked at Rusty. "How about it, kid?" he asked quietly.

Down deep in Rusty Shotridge pride welled up. These men did not even know his name, but to them he was an equal. To these two actions were more than names or words. "I'd like to go," Rusty said. "Thanks for the offer, Mr. Flanders. But I always wanted to go up the trail. I . . ."

"Yore man, Bud," Tom Flanders interrupted. He lifted his glass of beer again. "Here's how."

Rusty's glass was in his hand. Together the three drank.

The beer finished, Flanders and Sigloe moved from the bar. Rusty would have remained, but Sigloe's hand upon his arm urged him to accompany them. The Bank Saloon was busy now. Men were coming in, lining the bar, their curious glances following the three as they seated themselves. Word of what had happened had left the

Bank, and now the curious came to see for themselves.

Flanders squared his chair around, and his eyes were bright with curiosity as he looked at Rusty Shotridge. "What's your name, kid?" Flanders asked. "Whereabouts are you from?"

"I'm Rusty Shotridge. We got a place down close to Arroyo Grande." Oddly the appellation "kid" coming from Flanders did not anger Rusty. Sigloe put his hands on the table top and leaned back in his chair.

"Dan Shotridge's boy?" he asked.

"Yes."

Flanders nodded, and Sigloe's smile, ever close to the surface, began to form once more, the wrinkles appearing so slowly at the corners of his eyes that Rusty, watching, could almost hear them crackle. "That accounts for it then," Sigloe stated. "I knew your daddy, Rusty."

"I've rode with Dan Shotridge," Flanders seconded. "How's the country down that way? Dry?"

Rusty could sense that these men were using him. They made conversation with him so that they might gain ease with each other. He rose to the occasion. "No. We've had some rain," he said. "The grass is pretty good."

Neither Flanders nor Sigloe, Rusty could see, was paying a great deal of attention to his words. They watched each other. Rusty went on talking, utilizing commonplaces, grass and season, water and cattle, for his subjects. He could feel his companions relax as he talked, could feel the tension, still present, drain out of them. Exhausting his topics, Rusty stopped. Both his companions were leaning back in their chairs, and their faces had settled into placid lines.

"A good year then," Flanders said. "Are there many cattle comin' out of that country?"

"There's been some bought."

"How come," Sigloe drawled, "that you didn't tie on with a herd goin' north from there?"

Rusty looked at Sigloe. "Colonel Watrous used to be a neighbor of ours," he answered. "He promised me a job whenever I undertook to make the trip up the trail."

Both Sigloe and Flanders nodded understandingly. An awkward silence fell. He had served his purpose, Rusty knew. Sigloe and Flanders were at ease now and wanted only their own company. Rusty got up slowly.

"I've not had supper," he said, "an' breakfast is a long time ago. If you gentlemen will eat with me . . ."

"I've got to hunt a barbershop an' clean up," Sigloe announced. "I'm dirty as a hawg. Tom, you an' Rusty . . ."

"I'll go with you, Bud," Tom Flanders interrupted and smiled at Rusty. "Suppose we meet here after supper, Rusty? That suit you?"

All three had risen. Rusty grinned and nodded in answer to Flanders's question. "That suits me," he said.

"An' we'll celebrate," Sigloe announced.

They moved off from the table, Flanders and Sigloe toward the door, Rusty following. He paused at the bar to let the other two go on alone. The shutters swung closed behind Sigloe's back and the bartender hurrying up, stopped and faced Rusty Shotridge. There was admiration in the bartender's eyes.

"You sure done it!" the bartender pronounced. "I never seen the beat of it."

Rusty disregarded the bartender's adulation. "Who," he drawled, "was the black-haired fello' that gave up so much head?"

"Slippery Smith," the bartender answered and busied his hands with bottle and glass. "Here. Have a drink. This one is on the house."

Chapter II

The lobby of the Stockman Hotel was not so grand a place as the lobby of the Delhi in Austin, but it was grand enough. Rusty Shotridge, pausing just inside, surveyed the lobby's brass chandeliers, its red plush and its deep-piled carpet before advancing. Across from him, at the desk, cowmen were standing talking to the clerk, and some of the chairs and sofas were occupied. Making his way toward the desk, Rusty passed by a chair and hesitated. There was something familiar about the back of the red head that showed over the chair top.

"Sorrel-top," Rusty murmured softly as he paused.

He had always been able to get a fight out of Ellen Watrous by using that name. This occasion was not an exception. The red head turned swiftly, and Rusty found himself looking into angry blue eyes. For an instant he was chagrined, believing that he had made a mistake; then his grin broadened as the blue eyes lost their anger. "Rusty Shotridge!" Ellen Watrous exclaimed and came up from the chair.

She was slight, not so tall as Rusty by a full head, but there was a wiry strength in her hands as she put them on Rusty's shoulders and shook him. "What are you doing here?" Ellen Watrous demanded: "Why didn't you let us know you were coming? Have you seen Dad? When did you leave the ranch?" The questions were shot out, one following on the heels of the other. Rusty's grin was affectionate as he looked down at the girl and, lifting her hands from his shoulders, held them.

"Easy," he commanded. "There wasn't any use in writing when I was comin', was there? I haven't seen the colonel yet but I'm lookin' for him. How are you, Ellen?"

Recollection flooded Rusty. This was the girl he had taught to ride. This was the little redhead that had followed him about the ranch, dogging his footsteps. Little redheaded nuisance. "You haven't changed much, Ellen," Rusty commented. "You still ask questions. You haven't grown up too much."

Ellen tugged at his hands. "Come here and sit down," she commanded. "Dad's in the bar with Leonard Carlisle. They've bought the LM steers. Come and sit down, Rusty."

Obediently Rusty allowed himself to be led to a seat. Beside the chair Ellen had occupied there was another, and across from the two chairs there was a sofa. Rounding the chairs, Rusty stopped short. A dark-haired girl occupied the second chair, her eyes showing her amusement as she looked up.

"Uh . . ." Rusty said. "I didn't know . . . that is . . . I didn't see . . ." His embarrassment was apparent, and the dark-haired girl smiled. Ellen, five and a half feet of impatience, made introduction.

"Marcia, this is Rusty Shotridge. I used to play with him when we had a ranch at Arroyo Grande. We were neighbors. Rusty, this is Marcia Carlisle."

Rusty's hat came off and was clutched in both his broad hands. He cleared his throat again and was desperately conscious of the size of his hands and of his awkwardness. "Pleased to meet chu," Rusty stammered. "I didn't know . . ."

"Won't you sit down, Mr. Shotridge?" Marcia Carlisle asked gently.

Rusty found himself seated on the sofa. Ellen was ensconced in her chair, asking questions, making demands on his attention. Rusty could scarcely take his eyes from the dark-haired girl. He had never seen anyone like Marcia Carlisle before, had never seen anyone so beautiful. She smiled at him gently and, lost in her smile, Rusty made perfunctory answers to the queries

Ellen flung at him.

The folks were all right, Rusty said. Things were just the same down along the Arroyo Grande. He hadn't seen Bess Walther. Walther had moved. No, he didn't know where. Yes, his mother was fine. They'd built a new house. The questions were endless and a little annoying. Rusty wanted to look at Marcia Carlisle, not answer Ellen's questions.

Interruption came when Rusty heard his name boomed. He got up. Colonel John Watrous, big, beginning to pack a stomach, his thick mane of hair just beginning to show a little gray, was looming over him. Beside Watrous was another man, dark, smooth, almost as big as Watrous himself. Rusty shook hands with the colonel and looked expectantly at the dark-haired man.

"Mr. Carlisle, Rusty," the colonel introduced. "Leonard, this is the son of my old friend, Dan Shotridge."

Rusty shook hands with the dark-haired youth. The colonel drew a chair over and sat down. Rusty occupied the end of the sofa once more. Carlisle took the other end.

"And what brings you up north, Rusty?" Watrous demanded.

Rusty twisted his hat, turning it around and around in his fingers. "You told me to come an' see you," he answered. "You said for me to do that whenever I wanted to go up the trail."

The colonel's laugh boomed. "Got the fever, have you?" he demanded. "Want to go up the trail. Well, you've come to the right party, hasn't he, Leonard?"

Carlisle was watching Rusty intently, his dark eyes questioning, not friendly, but searching. He nodded slightly.

"Leonard and I have bought the LM steers," the colonel continued. "We're driving them north. You're just in time, Rusty."

Rusty looked from Watrous to Carlisle and back again. Colonel Watrous had never before had a partner. He had always operated alone. The colonel answered Rusty's unspoken question. "Carlisle wants to be a drover," he said. "I needed a pardner." The colonel's hands finished the explanation with a little gesture. Rusty nodded.

"How are things down south?" Watrous asked. "How did you leave Dan and your mother?"

"They're fine," Rusty said. "Dan had a horse to fall with him last winter, but he's all right now. Are you going to have a place for me, Colonel?"

"For Dan Shotridge's boy?" The Colonel laughed. "Of course I've got a place for you.

I'll see McBride in the morning. Now tell me . . ."

Carlisle's smooth voice broke in. "I hate to interrupt, Colonel, but weren't you supposed to see Mr. Boyce?"

"That's right!" Watrous came ponderously to his feet. "I am supposed to meet Boyce. Right now too. You stay here with Ellen, Rusty. I'll be back."

Watrous took his bulk across the lobby toward the desk. Carlisle had risen with the colonel. Now he seated himself again, his eyes on Rusty. Ellen was watching Carlisle, Rusty saw. Since his advent she had done nothing but watch Carlisle. Her blue eyes were soft. Marcia Carlisle was looking first at her brother, then at the other girl. The silence was awkward.

"You're in the cattle business, Mr. Shotridge?" Leonard Carlisle asked.

It was Ellen who answered. "Rusty was raised with cattle, Leonard. His father had a ranch next to Dad's when we lived at Arroyo Grande. Rusty is a real hand. You ought to see him ride!"

Dull red came up across Rusty's cheekbones, and Ellen's voice went on: "Rusty taught me to ride. Do you remember old Paint, Rusty?"

Rusty nodded. There was an undercurrent

here, a thing that he could feel but not place. An antagonism. Ellen's voice was hurried, a little high, a small note in it that was not quite true. Looking from the red-haired girl to Marcia Carlisle, Rusty could see the amusement in Marcia's eyes, the tiny curl at the corners of her lips. Something existed between the girls, some cross-purpose. Ellen chattered, recalling past occurrences. Marcia was quiet. Both girls watched Leonard Carlisle. Rusty said "yes" or "no" as Ellen referred to him, using him for corroboration. Unease filled Rusty Shotridge, and with it came a feeling, almost of pity, for Ellen Watrous.

Ellen's chatter slowed. Marcia, with the check in the talk, arose gracefully from her chair. "Will you take me upstairs, Leonard?" she asked. "I'm tired. I know Ellen and Mr. Shotridge will excuse us. They're old friends and they have a great deal to talk about." She smiled flashingly at Rusty.

Carlisle came to his feet. Rusty arose when the other man got up. Carlisle's voice was pleasant when he said that he had been glad to meet Mr. Shotridge. There was warmth in it when he spoke to Ellen. Brother and sister crossed the lobby toward the stairs, and Ellen, leaning back in her chair, watched their progress. Rusty sat down again. The two Carlisles disappeared up the stairs.

For a time Rusty sat watching the spot where Marcia and her brother had disappeared. Marcia Carlisle was gone, but her memory remained, an ineffable presence.

Ellen Watrous's voice was bitter as she broke into her companion's thoughts. "Has she got you too?"

"What's that?" Rusty demanded, turning quickly to the girl.

"Her brother, you, every man she meets," Ellen said. "That's the way she affects all of them."

Uncomfortably Rusty met Ellen's eyes. There was sorrow in those eyes, and something else that Rusty could not fathom. He shifted uncomfortably in his chair.

"Look here, Sorrel-top," Rusty ordered, changing the subject. "What's all this about? How come the colonel to take a greenhorn into pardnership with him? What's happened, Ellen?"

"Dad had bad luck last year." Ellen's voice was abstract. "He lost money on the herds he sent up the trail. He needed capital and Leonard wanted to go into partnership with him. They . . ." The words trailed off. Ellen rose from the chair. "I think I'll go upstairs, Rusty. I'm tired."

31

She did not wait for Rusty's answer but walked toward the stairs. Rusty followed her with his eyes. There was something wrong with Ellen. Plenty wrong. He put on his hat, pulling it down. Ellen was trailing up the stairs, a small figure, her shoulders drooping a trifle. Rusty Shotridge grunted. If there was anything wrong with Ellen Watrous and he could fix it . . . He turned and, straight-backed, his shoulders swinging, made toward the door.

Bud Sigloe and Tom Flanders were waiting for Rusty in the Bank Saloon. Rusty had not been expecting to find them there, and his face showed his surprise when he saw them. Sigloe left the bar and greeted Rusty, while Flanders, leaning against the bar, smiled his welcome.

Bud Sigloe was a far different man than he had been when Rusty first saw him. Sigloe was clean, shaven to the quick and almost sober. The fine thin edge of excitement still clung to him as he accompanied Rusty back to where Flanders stood.

"What happened to you, Rusty?" Flanders demanded. "Bud an' me been waitin' here. Didn't you know there was a celebration comin' an' that you was in on it?"

"I went up to the hotel," Rusty answered.

"I wanted to see Colonel Watrous."

"See him?"

Rusty nodded. The sober mood he had brought from the hotel clung with him. He could not shake it off. Flanders seemed to sense Rusty's depression.

"We're drinkin' beer, Bud an' me, but you have what you like," he invited companionably. "Then we'll put out an' see what holds San Marcial together."

"Beer suits me," Rusty said absently.

They had their drinks and left the Bank, going on from the saloon to see what other attractions San Marcial might offer. In the Tivoli they played roulette. In the Mint Sigloe bucked the blackjack dealer while Flanders stood by. There was an air of high hilarity about Flanders and Sigloe. They were on the town, and San Marcial seemed to sense it. Gradually as the trio went from place to place they collected sycophants, a little crowd of satellites gathering about them. Everywhere they went they were welcome, and Rusty, in company with Flanders and Sigloe, accepted by them as a friend and equal, was swept up and carried along. Still he could not entirely turn loose and enjoy himself. Still the depression gained in the Stockman's lobby stayed with him.

At midnight Rusty had had enough. Sigloe and Flanders were going strong, just beginning the night, but Rusty, with a week of steady riding behind him, wanted to sleep. Despite the protests of his friends he left them and went back to the Stockman.

Before he left he had a final word with Bud Sigloe. Sigloe, throughout the evening, had introduced Rusty to all those he met as a member of his trail crew. Nor had Rusty demurred. He would ask nothing better than to go north with the herd Bud Sigloe bossed. Still there had been Watrous' promise of a job with the Watrous trail outfit, and Rusty spoke of it to Sigloe.

"Don't forget," Bud Sigloe said as the three parted. "Yo're goin' up the trail with me, kid. I'm goin' to learn you the business. You see Watrous in the mornin' an' tell him."

Rusty agreed, said good night to Flanders and, leaving the Mint where they happened to be at that moment, started up the street.

There was a long porch across the front of the Stockman Hotel and, entering it from the side, Rusty found a chair and sat down. He wanted to smoke and relax before he went up to his room. Leaning back in the shadow, he found his tobacco and papers and rolled his smoke. He was exploring his pockets, searching for a match, when two people came down along the porch and stopped close by. So preoccupied and intent were they on each other that they did not see him there in the shadow. Rusty shifted in his chair, preparatory to rising and making his presence known, but Ellen Watrous's voice stopped him. Ellen's voice was as bitter as her words.

"You don't care," she said. "If you did you wouldn't let her tell you what to do."

"But, Ellen . . ." the man protested. Rusty recognized the speaker as Leonard Carlisle.

"She never leaves us alone," Ellen declared passionately. "Never! Tonight for instance: She wanted you to take her upstairs, so you left me and went with her. You do everything she says. You tell me that you love me, and then she calls you and you run to her."

"You don't understand, Ellen," Carlisle said. "Marcia's my sister. I . . ."

"I understand that you think more of her than you do of me," Ellen interrupted angrily. "I understand that she's got you under her thumb completely. I'm going in."

The girl turned, and Rusty could hear her heels venting her anger in small staccato clicks as she went to the hotel door. Carlisle, having taken but a single step to follow, stood motionless. Ellen disappeared into the doorway, and Carlisle groaned and walked to the porch rail. Rusty moved a trifle and his chair squeaked.

Instantly Carlisle turned, his voice hoarse as he demanded: "Who's there?"

"Shotridge," Rusty answered uncomfortably, damning the squeaking chair in his mind.

Carlisle came from the porch rail. "You were spying!" he accused angrily. "That's what you were doing. You heard us."

"Well," Rusty said slowly, "I ain't deaf. But I wasn't spying. I sat down here to take a smoke and before I could say a word you and Ellen were talkin'. I'm sorry. . . ."

"Spy! That's what you are!" Leonard Carlisle paid no heed to Rusty's explanation. "Run and tell if you want to, but if you do I'll give you the whipping you deserve."

Rusty got deliberately to his feet. His intentions had been entirely pacific, but no one had ever promsied Rusty Shotridge a licking without having the opportunity to make good. "I'm right here," Rusty drawled. "I wasn't spying on you an' I'm not going to tell anybody, but if you think you can take it out of my hide, go ahead."

He was entirely ready to fight at the moment, but he was not ready for what followed. Leonard Carlisle said nothing more. Instead his hand lashed out, swift as the strike of a snake and straight and forceful as a piston. The clenched hand collided with Rusty's cheek, and Rusty, braced as he was, sat down with a thump on the porch floor and banged his head against the chair. Bright lights filled Rusty's eyes. He reached out his hand for support, found the floor and pushed himself up. When he reached his feet Carlisle was going through the lighted doorway of the Stockman Hotel. Tenderly Rusty felt of his eye, groped behind him and, finding his chair, sat down again.

"Well," said Rusty Shotridge. "What do you think of that now?"

Up early the following morning, through habit, Rusty dressed and left the Stockman. Breakfast over, he wandered along the street before returning to the hotel. San Marcial in the morning was briskly alive with traffic along its streets. Rusty loafed along, savoring the bustle and vigor of the town. Now and then he met men who glanced at him keenly. Occasionally a passerby smiled. Rusty touched his eye tenderly. It was swollen almost shut from Carlisle's blow. He was keenly aware of the eye and of his appearance and touchy concerning both. That damned Carlisle!

At the post office Rusty inquired for his mail. Receiving none, he stood outside the building, listening to the familiar talk of the loafers, talk of grass and water, cattle and horses. To these subjects was added another: the trail north, its condition and the location of the herds that were being put up the trail.

Returning by way of the livery barn where he inspected his horses, Rusty entered the Stockman's lobby. Watrous and Carlisle, with Ellen and Marcia, were in the lobby. Rusty spoke a good morning to them and would have passed, save that Watrous stopped him.

"Come over here, Rusty," he commanded. "By George! What happened to your eye, boy?"

"I got hit," Rusty answered shortly.

Watrous grinned broadly. "Fight or celebration?" he asked. "No matter. I want you to meet Scott McBride. Scott, this is the boy I spoke to you about. He'll go up the trail with you."

Rusty looked at the short, square-shouldered, gray-haired man that Watrous introduced. McBride was Watrous' trail boss, and he looked the part. Bud Sigloe's parting injunction flashed into Rusty's mind, and he cleared his throat awkwardly.

"I was goin' to speak to you about that, Colonel," he said. "I've kind of changed my mind. I . . ."

Carlisle gave a contemptuous snort, and Rusty stopped in mid-speech and looked inquiringly at the man.

"I thought so," Carlisle said, glancing significantly at Watrous.

"What did you think?" Rusty asked quietly.

Carlisle faced him squarely. "I thought," he announced evenly, "that you would back out. You don't want to go north with a herd. All you want to do is to make an impression."

"Now see here, Leonard," Watrous began. "You've no right to say that. I know this boy and . . ."

Rusty interrupted his old friend's defense. His voice had dropped a tone and slowed a beat as he spoke. "You think I was four-flushin'?"

Carlisle shrugged. That was in itself answer enough, but he chose to amplify it. "It takes a man to make the trip."

"You're a man?" Rusty asked quietly.

Carlisle said nothing. Rusty was angry clear through. He had been insulted gratuitously, he thought. His voice drawled on. "I reckon yo're goin' to make the trip, Carlisle? Or had you ever thought of it?"

Carlisle stared at his questioner. A sudden gleam came into his eyes. "I'll go north with the herd if you will," he challenged. "How about it, Shotridge?"

"Leonard!" Marcia Carlisle snapped the word. "You can't. You know you can't. I . . ."

Glancing at Ellen, Rusty saw that the red-haired girl's eyes were eager. There were a good many things in Rusty's mind, but cold anger was uppermost. He threw his soft drawl into Marcia Carlisle's words, checking them. "I got to quit a job with Bud Sigloe to take you up, Carlisle. But if you mean that an' won't back out, I'm your huckleberry."

Chapter III

Scott McBride, entering the door of the Tivoli, nodded briefly to the bartender on morning shift and asked a question: "Slippery in back?"

"Him an' Yates," the bartender agreed, and then, stifling his natural curiosity behind a yawn: "Want me to call him?"

"I'll call him myself," McBride grunted and stalked on toward the door in the rear of the barroom.

Passing through that door, he entered the private card room of the Tivoli. There was a big green-covered poker table, chips stacked at the slot and two decks of cards beside the chips. Chairs were placed in some semblance of order about the table, and in two of these chairs men sat. Both looked up quickly as the door opened and then, recognizing their caller, relaxed once more. McBride came on back to the table, pulled out a chair and sat down.

Slippery Smith, black eyes curious, turned his smooth bulk to face the newcomer, rubbed his hand down the length of his face from nose to chin and made comment.

"I didn't hardly look for you, Scott. You think it was all right for you to come back here?"

"I wouldn't of come if I hadn't had to," McBride said morosely. "It's all off, Slippery. I come to tell you that."

Smith glanced quickly at his other companion and returned his gaze to McBride. "Why?" he demanded. "Watrous bought the LM steers, didn't he?"

McBride nodded.

"I've still got them LM cattle I bought last year," Smith continued. "I'm puttin' up a herd an' I've got my boys hired. Why do you figure it's off, Scott? You gettin' cold feet?"

"My feet ain't any colder than anybody else's," McBride retorted testily. "But it's all off, just the same. You heard what happened in the hotel yesterday, ain't you?"

A smile appeared on Smith's face. "Oh, *that!*" he commented. "Yeah. I heard. Seems like yo're goin' to have more crew than you counted on."

McBride nodded again. "Carlisle, damn him," he rasped. "He's bound he's goin' with me, an' so is Shotridge."

"Well . . ." Smith's drawl pulled lingeringly on the word. "You ain't worried about Carlisle, are you? Look, Scott. You hired the boys I sent for you to hire, didn't you?"

Again the morose nod of McBride's head. Smith drawled on: "Then what you worryin' about? Carlisle can't count cattle. He'll believe any count you give him."

"It ain't Carlisle I'm bothered about," McBride replied. "It's that damned Shotridge. Look here, Slippery. Shotridge an' Carlisle had an argument in the hotel this mornin'. Shotridge was goin' to back out an' not go with us, an' Carlisle called him a quitter. Shotridge bristled up an' said he'd go if Carlisle would. Carlisle took him up on it. Shotridge is packin' a black eye, an' I think Carlisle give it to him. They're sore as hell at each other. An' they're hell-bent to go north with me, both of 'em. Neither of 'em 'll back out. Watrous is about half crazy with the grief they're givin' him, an' I've done everything but quit. I couldn't do that, could I?"

"No. . . ." Smith agreed. "You couldn't do that. But can't Watrous . . . ?"

"Watrous needs Carlisle's money or there won't be no herd," McBride interrupted bluntly. "Carlisle says that either him an' Shotridge go or he don't put up the cash. Watrous can't do nothin'. He tried to work on Shotridge. Shotridge had a job with Bud Sigloe, but he says if Carlisle goes with me he goes with me. Carlisle says he goes with me an' so does Shotridge or else there'll be no cattle. They both got pat hands an' they're sittin' there playin' 'em, an' I can't do a damned thing. An' neither can Watrous!"

A frown appeared on Slippery Smith's dark face.

"An'," McBride amplified, "if Shotridge goes along you an' me can't do what we'd planned. You know that. We'd never get by with it. I been checkin' up on Shotridge, an' he's a hand, from all I can hear, an' a pretty forked kind of fellow besides."

43

"How do you mean 'forked'?"

"He's the boy that sided that Ranger down at Arroyo Grande last year."

Smith's companion, slight, blue eyed and light haired, shifted in his chair. So far he had made no contribution to the talk. Now he asked a question. "What was that?"

"You was in the territory when it happened, Honey," Smith answered. "There was some fellows got tough around Arroyo Grande last fall an' took in the town. Austin sent a Ranger down to stop it. He got two or three of 'em arrested an' was takin' 'em out when the rest jumped him. They had him down an' hurt when another fello' come along. From what McBride says, it was Shotridge."

"It was Shotridge," McBride announced surlily. "He jumped in an' sided the Ranger, an' they just cleaned up. Both the Bascomb boys was killed, an' there was two-three more hurt pretty bad."

Smith said, "Ummmm," following McBride's statement, and the man called "Honey" surveyed the long fingers of his hand where they were spread on the table top.

"So Carlisle an' Shotridge are goin' along," McBride announced after a short pause. "It's all off, Slippery."

Again there was a long silence. "I'll be damned if I'm goin' to pass up seven or eight thousand dollars that easy!" Smith said savagely. "Damn this Shotridge. I . . ."

"It might be fixed so that he won't go." Honey Yates lifted his gaze from his fingers and stared mildly, first at McBride and then at Smith. "How much of a cut would I get if I fixed it for you, Slippery?"

Smith took a quick breath. "Shotridge is hangin' around with Sigloe an' Flanders," he warned. "They're friends of his."

Yates was nodding earnestly. "I've heard that," he agreed. "It makes it worth a little more money. How much, Slippery?"

Slippery Smith pulled his chair around so that he faced the table. Honey Yates also pulled his chair closer to the green felt. "It would be worth five hundred dollars," Smith announced. "Carlisle wouldn't bother you if Shotridge didn't go, would he, Scott?"

"I don't think so," McBride said uneasily. "No, I guess he wouldn't."

"Then it would be worth a little more if Shotridge didn't reach Dodge City," Smith said, looking at Honey Yates again.

Yates laughed mirthlessly. "It's worth a third," he announced coldly. "We'll cut it three ways instead of two. You know better than to fool with me, Slippery. Three ways?"

45

There was a moment of indecision, and then Slippery Smith nodded. "I'd ruther have some than none," he agreed. "Three ways if Shotridge don't reach Dodge, Honey."

Honey Yates gave a satisfied grunt. "That's settled then," he said. "How are you figurin' to work it, Slippery? I know you got some LM steers from last year an' I know that Watrous has bought all the LM steers left this year. How you goin' to put the two together?"

"Easy," Slippery Smith answered. "Just plumb easy, Honey. Scott an' me 'll fix that if you look after Shotridge. We got it all lined up. Got the boys hired an' everythin'."

McBride got up abruptly. "I'm goin' to pull out," he announced. "I come down to tell you that it was all off, Slippery, but if Honey cuts in an' takes care of Shotridge, I guess we'll go on. You tell Honey what it's all about. I'm goin'. It wouldn't look too good later if somebody remembered that you an' me had been together."

Wheeling from the card table, McBride went to the door, passed through it and so on out of the Tivoli Saloon. As he went up the street he passed the hotel. Rusty Shotridge was on the porch, and Marcia Carlisle, occupying a chair facing Rusty, was bent forward, talking earnestly. As McBride passed he scowled at the two on the porch. Rusty saw neither the passing trail boss nor his scowl.

It had been a bad day and night for Rusty. During practically all of that time he had been under fire. First Colonel Watrous had argued with him, ordering him to withdraw from the enterprise to which Rusty had been challenged. Watrous stormed and raged and threatened, and Rusty remained adamant. He could understand exactly how Watrous felt, but that did not change his own viewpoint. Nor had Scott McBride's arguments and threats altered his decision.

"You stay with this, an' I'll make hell look like a summer holiday to you," McBride promised. "I don't want you along an' I don't want Carlisle neither!"

Rusty stared balefully at the angry trail boss. Threats were not the proper weapons to use on Rusty Shotridge. "Go right ahead an' turn your wolf loose, McBride," Rusty invited. "But you want to remember one thing: There's two ends to the trail, an' I'll be at both of them. This end is yours, but the other one will be mine, an' don't you forget it." McBride, realizing the futility of his threat, snorted wrathfully and stamped away.

Then had come Ellen Watrous. Ellen almost made her point. She neither threatened nor argued. Her attacks were purely feminine, and under them Rusty weakened.

"You think a heap of Carlisle," he told the girl. "If he thinks as much of you as you do of him, he'll back out. It won't be any disgrace for him to back down, but I've got to live in this country. You talk to Carlisle, Ellen. If he backs down I'll step out too."

Ellen spread her hands in a helpless gesture of surrender. "I've talked to Leonard," she admitted. "He's determined to go through with it. You'll have to give in, Rusty. Please. For my sake."

For an instant Rusty was ready to agree, but Ellen, not content with what she had said, continued: "He's proud, Rusty, and he can't back out. It would hurt him."

Rusty bristled. "Mebbe you think I ain't a little proud!" he rasped. "No, Ellen. Carlisle made the bet, an' I called it. If he got out on a limb it's his fault. You go talk to him and not to me."

Of all those who talked to him, only Bud Sigloe and Tom Flanders agreed with Rusty, had understood at all or been on his side.

"You couldn't do nothin' else, kid," Flanders stated when Rusty presented his problem. "You had to do it."

Bud Sigloe seconded Flanders. "That's right," he agreed, and then, smiling at Rusty: "I hate to lose you off my crew, but you got to play your hand out. Tom an' me 'll meet you in Dodge City, an' we'll throw a whingding when you get there. Stay with it, kid."

That was the way that matters stood when Marcia Carlisle met Rusty on the porch of the Stockman Hotel and asked him to talk with her.

Rusty knew what was coming, but he could not well refuse the girl. As graciously as he was able, he accompanied her to where two chairs were placed side by side and, when Marcia was seated, took the other chair. Marcia proceeded at once to her attack.

"I want you to give up this foolish venture," she said. "Leonard is all I have, Mr. Shotridge. We were left orphans when we were children, and I've always looked after him. I'm a year older than my brother and I've always felt that responsibility. I can't let him go. Suppose that he was hurt? How would you feel if that happened? You'd be responsible."

Rusty considered the question and the girl. Marcia was beautiful as she sat there looking at him, and for an instant Rusty's mind wandered from the topic. A girl like Marcia Carlisle was . . .

"How would you feel?" Marcia demanded again.

"I reckon that would be bad," Rusty said gravely. "But there isn't much chance of his bein' hurt."

"But suppose he was?"

For some reason Rusty felt that he must explain his philosophy to his companion, justify himself in her eyes. He looked at Marcia very steadily. "A man," Rusty said, "has got to stand on his own two legs, Miss Carlisle. He's got to do that if he's goin' to be a man. You want your brother to be a man, don't you?"

Marcia could not answer that question other than in the affirmative. She took a new tack. "But what about me?" she asked. "Leonard's all that I have. I can't let him go. I don't think you understand."

"How old is your brother?" Rusty asked casually.

"Twenty-three," Marcia answered.

"I'm older than him," Rusty said. "Older than you too. I'm twenty-six. I've had experience. You've rode herd on your brother all his life, all yours too. You've spoiled him and pampered him and you've got him tied to your apron strings. It'll be good for both of you for him to get away. If he cuts loose he's got a fair chance of makin' a man of himself. Goin' up the trail will learn him some things he needs to know."

Anger darkened Marcia's eyes. Still she controlled her temper. "I'll pay you . . ." she began.

"*Pay* me?" Rusty snapped. "How could you pay me? If I backed down I'd be the laughin' stock of the country. I've got to live here; don't you understand that? No. I reckon you wouldn't. You don't know enough."

"But Leonard is all I have," the girl expostulated. "You . . ."

Rusty was thoroughly aroused. The offer of money had broken his restraint, and his own anger flared through. "Yeah," he drawled, "he's all you've got. An' he's a spoiled brat. Mebbe if he cuts loose from you he can turn into a man, an' mebbe if you cut him loose you'll have time to look around an' get you a man of your own!"

Marcia came up out of her chair. "Why, you . . ." she snapped, and her right hand, flashing out, spatted sharply against Rusty's cheek. "You . . . you . . ." She was gone then, flouncing along the porch, anger showing in every line of her lithe body. Rusty sat watching her go, rubbing his cheek gently, and amusement beginning to grow in his eyes.

"An' mebbe there was somethin' in what I said, at that," he murmured. "Well . . ."

He hoisted himself out of his chair and he, too, started down the porch. Before he reached the door Ellen Watrous appeared. Rusty stopped and waited for the girl to approach.

Ellen was dejected. She stopped beside Rusty, and Rusty, looking down at the girl, felt sudden compassion for her. "You talk to Carlisle, Sorrel-top?" he asked.

Ellen nodded her head.

"What did he say?"

"He's going. I talked to him but . . ." Ellen lifted her eyes to look at Rusty. "You know," she said, and there was a wondering note in her voice, "it isn't just because of you that Leonard's going. He's excited about it. He's . . . Why, he's happy, Rusty. As though he were getting away from something."

"Mebbe he is," Rusty said thoughtfully. "Yeah. I reckon he is gettin' away from somethin'. This trip isn't goin' to hurt that boy, Ellen. It's goin' to do him a lot of good."

"But suppose something happens to him?"

"Nothin's goin' to happen to him." Rusty

was very sure. Ellen placed her small hand on her companion's arm. She stared up into Rusty's eyes.

"Will you look after him, Rusty?" she asked, her voice small. "Will you take care of him for me?"

"He's big enough to take care of himself," Rusty answered, and sudden uneasiness welled up in his mind. Here was a turn of events he had not foreseen and did not like. "He's old enough to look after himself, Ellen." Rusty attempted to reassure himself as well as the girl.

"But he doesn't know," Ellen pleaded. "Promise me that you'll look after him, Rusty. Promise me."

Rusty could not refuse. Here was the little Sorrel-top that he had played with down along Arroyo Grande. "Yeah," Rusty said reluctantly. "All right, Ellen. I'll look after him for you."

Ellen rose on tiptoe. Impulsively her arms went around Rusty's neck and there, in full daylight, on the porch of the Stockman Hotel, she kissed Rusty Shotridge on the cheek.

Leonard Carlisle, coming from the door of the hotel in search of Ellen, was just in time to see that swift kiss. He stepped back hastily, so retiring that he did not see the end or hear the denouement. Rusty reached up and lifted Ellen's arms away. "Here," he ordered gruffly. "You made me enough trouble already. You save that for Carlisle."

For the remainder of the day Rusty was left alone. He did not seek companionship, and no one sought him. There was a good deal on Rusty's mind and none of it was pleasant. His promise to Ellen came constantly to remind him of the obligation he had undertaken, and his conversation with Marcia Carlisle arose to haunt him. Rusty could not keep his thoughts from the dark-haired girl. Wherever he turned her face confronted him. He was distrait and uneasy.

When evening came he joined Tom Flanders and Bud Sigloe for supper. After the meal, walking along the street side by side, Flanders asked Rusty a question.

"How'd you come out today, kid?"

"I had hell all day. They all worked on me."

"But yo're still goin' with Watrous?" Sigloe looked keenly at Rusty.

"Still goin'."

There was no disapproval in Flanders' silent nod or in Sigloe's grunt of agreement, but Rusty continued, voicing the thoughts that troubled him. "You know how it is. You ought to, anyhow. I've got to go through with it. I made my brags."

To the two men who flanked Rusty that was sufficient. Rusty had stated his position when he said that he had made his brags. Each of Rusty's companions had been in a similar predicament, and recently. Bud Sigloe, aching from inaction, had inflicted himself upon the town, and Flanders had been summoned to quiet him. As simple a thing as that had almost brought about tragedy. With no real reason for a quarrel, no cause other than their fierce pride, these two who walked beside Rusty had come to a point where, despite their friendship, they would have killed. And Rusty had saved them from that killing. Bud Sigloe took a long breath, and Tom Flanders spoke quietly:

"We know how it is, kid. But ain't you bein' as much a damned fool as Bud an' me were?"

Rusty shook his head. "That was different," he answered. "You an' Bud are friends an' you'd just got crossways with each other. Everybody knows that you ain't scared. You've proved it. If I backed out I'd get the horselaugh every place I went."

The statement was true and Flanders nodded. "Bud an' me are leavin' tomorrow," he said abruptly. "Marble wrote Bud that he's puttin' up a herd at Pinál, an' he wants Bud to come on. I'm goin' back to Dulcina, an' then on north."

Flanders hesitated, and Rusty looked keenly at the tall man. "We're right fond of you," Flanders continued after the instant's hesitation. "Damned if I know why." He grinned, belying his last words, and Rusty returned the grin.

"Go on an' tell him, Tom," Sigloe growled.

"I've got a friend or two in town," Flanders continued. "I hear things. So does Bud. Some of these friends we got ain't exactly what you'd call good citizens. I'd feel a heap easier if you was goin' with Bud."

Sigloe grunted affirmatively.

"Why don't you do that, kid?" Flanders asked persuasively. "Nobody'd think any less of you."

Rusty shook his head stubbornly. "I made my brags," he reminded. "I got to go through with 'em."

"I told you he'd say that, Tom," Sigloe announced.

"Yeah, you told me," Flanders agreed. "Well then, kid, keep yore eyes open."

Rusty looked sharply at Flanders, a question in the glance.

"I'd feel mighty bad if you didn't show up in Dodge to have that party with Bud an' me," Flanders said.

"So would I," Sigloe agreed. "It might be a good idea if we spread that word around, Tom."

"Not bad at all," Flanders agreed.

They were taking care of him, Rusty felt. His shoulders squared, and a spark came into his eyes. "You wouldn't feel half as bad about it as I would," he said quietly. "I'll make sure to be there."

"Uh-huh," Sigloe agreed.

A warning had been given, recognized and accepted. Flanders nodded. "We know you can take care of yorese'f, Rusty," he said apologetically. "We just thought . . . Here's the Bank. Let's step in awhile."

As night came on and darkness grew, the Bank Saloon filled. Bud Sigloe, Tom Flanders and Rusty stayed together. The morning would see their separation, and the thought was somehow depressing. In the short time they had been together a friendship had formed that bound them closely. They drank a little, talked a little, but for the most part were content simply to be together without talk or drink or other companionship. The few men who came to join them sensed their mood and did not stay.

About nine o'clock a boy, half grown,

came through the door of the Bank Saloon and spoke to the bartender. The barman nodded to the table that Rusty occupied with Sigloe and Flanders, and the boy came on back.

"Shotridge?" he asked, pausing beside the table.

"I'm Shotridge," Rusty said.

"There's a man wants to see you up at the hotel. He give me a quarter to tell you."

Rusty looked first at the boy and then at Flanders and Sigloe. "Watrous likely," he said. "He wants to take another round at me. I'll go see him, son."

The boy turned away, but Flanders halted him. "What does this man look like?" he questioned.

"He was on the porch when I come past an' he called to me," the boy said. "I didn't get to look at him good. It was dark."

Flanders nodded, and the boy went on his way. Rusty started to rise from his chair. Flanders and Sigloe had looked at each other, and now Sigloe reached out his hand to restrain Rusty's movement. "You can finish yore drink, can't you?" Sigloe demanded. "There ain't that much hurry, is there? After all, we're splittin' up tomorrow."

Rusty sat down again and picked up his half-emptied glass. Flanders arose. "I'll be back in a minute," he announced and abruptly left the table. Sigloe bent toward Rusty and spoke, and Rusty, who had been watching Flanders, turned back to his other companion.

Sigloe kept on talking, and perforce Rusty listened. His impatience grew. Bud was just making talk, and Flanders had not come back. When Sigloe paused Rusty spoke:

"Look, Bud. I'll go up an' see what Watrous wants. You wait an' tell Tom I'll be right back."

"All right," Sigloe agreed. "We'll leave word at the bar for him, an' I'll go with you."

There was no way for Rusty to refuse that suggestion, and so he arose, Sigloe also coming to his feet, and they started toward the door. At the door Bud Sigloe brushed past Rusty, stepping out into the street ahead of him.

San Marcial was dark. There were no street lights, and the only illumination came from the windows of the stores and saloons. Sigloe, taking the outside edge of the walk, started along toward the hotel, Rusty striding with him. There were few men on the street. They passed a man or two, and Rusty, looking past Sigloe, could see movement across the way. His thoughts intent on what was coming, he paid no attention to the movement. What argument would Watrous advance now? he wondered. What had happened that he should be sent for? Had Carlisle backed down? Had Marcia and Ellen and Watrous made their point?

"Mebbe I'll take that job with you after all, Bud," Rusty said. "Mebbe the colonel has worked things out an' sent for me to fire me. What would you think of that?"

"I'd think . . ." Sigloe began and stopped short. He thrust out his arm, sending Rusty staggering away. They were just at a corner, and Rusty reeled into the entryway of a darkened store. Across the street flame lanced out, and the roar of a shot filled the quiet.

Chapter IV

Instantly the lancing flame was answered. Across the street another gun spouted fire and lead and sound. Sigloe crouched at the edge of the sidewalk, and Rusty, recovering his balance, pulled his own heavy gun. Seemingly Sigloe was aware of the action, for his voice came short and hard. "Hold it, kid! That's Tom across the street!"

Rusty did not obey the order. Gun in hand, he came out of the doorway and charged. The street dust churned up about his boots as he ran, and behind him Sigloe growled a curse and followed. Rusty struck the opposite sidewalk, wheeled and ran along it. At the corner he checked. Tom Flanders appeared and came running toward him, and as Sigloe reached him he caught Rusty's arm. All along the street men, aroused by the shots, came pouring out of buildings.

"Missed him!" Flanders panted. "He run!"

Sigloe grunted and released Rusty's arm, and Flanders, his breath somewhat recovered, spoke again.

"See what I meant, kid? About yore not gettin' to Dodge?"

Rusty slipped his gun back into its scabbard. His voice was hard as he answered Flanders. "I see. Look, Tom. You, too, Bud. Don't say nothin' about this, will you? Say it was somebody after you."

"Why?" Sigloe snapped. "By God, I'll turn this town over. I treed it once. If they think they can do this to a friend of mine an' get away with it . . ."

"No, Bud!" Rusty's voice was urgent. "No."

"The kid's right, Bud," Flanders seconded.

"I'd like to know why!"

"Because," Rusty explained, "if they think I'm not lookin' they'll try again. I been a fool, but I got my eyes open now."

"But, damn it, I don't want 'em to try again." Sigloe still held his gun. He started to turn, and Rusty caught his arm and held him.

"An' I do want 'em to try again," Rusty rasped. "I want 'em to try when I'll be lookin' for 'em, an' I'll be lookin' for 'em from now on. I'll be watchin' everybody."

Sigloe grunted, and the tension of his body relaxed. Rusty freed the arm he held. The running men were almost upon the three.

"We might," Tom Flanders drawled, "go back to the Bank now. I don't reckon there was anybody really lookin' for you at the hotel, kid."

Rusty made no answer other than to turn and walk back along the street. Again Sigloe and Flanders fell into step on either side. So walking, they met the first of the inquisitive and stopped to answer the questions that were poured upon them. Even as he answered those questions Tom Flanders's eyes strayed from the questioners to Rusty Shotridge. Tom Flanders admired a man who killed his own snakes. He did indeed. And from now on Rusty would be on the alert and ready. It would be just too bad for anyone who took another crack at Rusty Shotridge.

When finally the street had quieted and San Marcial's marshal — the last of their questioners — had gone to prowl, searching for the man who he believed had taken a shot at Tom Flanders, Rusty spoke briefly to his friends. It was late and time to turn in, Rusty said. Promising that he would be on hand to see Tom and Bud leave in the morning, Rusty walked with his friends to the hotel where they left him.

The following morning, as he had agreed, Rusty saw the two depart. He had still some little time to spend in town, and with his two friends gone he felt at a loose end. There was no one left for companionship. Watrous was angry and short when Rusty spoke to him; McBride left Rusty strictly alone, and Ellen and Marcia shunned him.

During the remainder of his stay Rusty watched his step. Neither he nor his companions that night had commented freely about the shots fired in the street. Flanders, as Rusty had requested, intimated that it was some old enemy taking a pot shot at him and let it go at that. No mention was made of Rusty, save only that he was present. The marshal of San Marcial, investigating the disturbance, was content to let it drop when Flanders left town. Nothing untoward happened after Flanders and Sigloe left, and still it was with relief that Rusty rode out of San Marcial in company with the Watrous wagon and crew.

The crew was not a promising-looking lot. There were nine hard-faced men besides the foreman, Carlisle, the cook and the horse wrangler. Rusty met the men and sized them up. They were not prepossessing. Two of the bunch showed some possibilities, Rusty thought. There was a smooth-faced blond man named Yates that looked like a hand, and there was a youngster named Gil Travis who carried himself with a devil-may-care swagger and who sized up to be a rider. As for the rest, Rusty could not be impressed with their ability.

The wrangler, old Telesfor Maes would do. Spanish was a second tongue to Rusty, and he and Telesfor got right together. The cook, Joe Deems, was a sour old button, but a good cook who knew his business. Rusty found that out when he helped load the chuck wagon.

Their first stop was to pick up the remuda. Scott McBride had bought a hundred and ten head of horses and four head of mules to carry his men and pull his wagon north.

The Watrous crew and their foreman went out to a small pasture close to town where the remuda was penned. By the time McBride got through cutting Rusty's horses to him, Rusty knew that the trail boss had not been joking when he had promised to make hell look like a summer holiday to Rusty Shotridge. The foreman did his best to live up to the promise. McBride was a horseman. Rusty was certain of that when the mounts were cut. A man had to be a horseman to cut ten head of horses out of one hundred and ten and not pick a single good horse. Rusty's eyes were filled with awe when he looked at McBride, and the wonder grew when he turned to gaze at his string of horses. Hammerheads, broncs; there wasn't what a man would call a good horse in the bunch. Of course in buying a remuda for a trail herd there were apt to be some poor horses, but it seemed to Rusty that the distribution was just a little unfair.

"I'm goin' to have a sweet time with that bunch," he commented to young Gil Travis after the cutting was finished. "Look at 'em."

"You hired out for a tough hand, didn't you?" Travis drawled. "Looks like the old man took you up on it."

Rusty said no more. He was, he figured, a

hand. If that was the kind of horses he had to work on he'd do it. And he'd get the job done too!

With the horses, the trail crew moved north, the chuck wagon trailing along and everybody helping with the remuda. They made a night's camp at a creek, and the next night reached the Secáte ranch of the LM Cattle Company. There they threw the horses into the pasture, camped the wagon and set down. The following morning they were to receive cattle.

Morning came mighty early. The Watrous crew, fed and ready, saddled up and went out with McBride. Where two low hills formed an alleyway they stopped and waited. About nine o'clock two buggies came out from the ranch. Colonel Watrous and Ellen occupied one buggy and Leonard Carlisle and Marcia were in the other. Watrous and Carlisle went over to talk with McBride, and Ellen got out of her buggy and went over to join Marcia. Within half an hour after the arrival of Watrous and his partner the steers came, the crew of the LM pushing the long line of marching cattle. The Watrous hands tightened cinches and mounted, and McBride came trotting over to his riders. The LM manager came loping up and joined Watrous and Carlisle, and there was some discussion; then Watrous took a horse from one of his men and with the LM manager took station at the gap between the hills. McBride and the LM foreman took the other side, and with the Watrous hands helping, the cattle were marched through for a count.

Rusty was one of those told off to hold the counted cattle. In company with Travis and another he took station beyond the gap in the hills and held the steers up as they came through.

Watrous used pebbles to keep his count, but the other counters tied knots in their saddle ropes and let the knots slip through their fingers, one knot for every hundred steers. When the count was finished both crews held the herd while the counters forgathered. There was a small difference of opinion between the counters, Rusty could see. They argued back and forth, and then an agreement was reached. Rusty spoke casually to the LM hand who waited close beside him.

"You put in any beef for us to eat?"

"Eight head," the LM man responded. "Yearlin's. They done got together on the count. I guess you all will start trail brandin' now."

"Mebbe you'll help us," Rusty said cheerfully. "It's goin' to take some time to mark these steers. Twenty-five hundred head, isn't there?"

"That's right," the LM man agreed. "*Now* what do you reckon they're fussin' about?"

The argument was going again among the bosses. The LM foreman and manager seemed to take no part in it but sat by as spectators while McBride, Carlisle and Watrous talked. Seen from a distance, gesticulations indicated that Watrous was insisting on something and McBride was objecting. McBride turned to the LM manager and seemingly asked a question, for the LM man nodded. Carlisle spoke forcefully when McBride stopped talking, and to Rusty, looking on, it was apparent that Watrous was defeated. He shook his head, spread his hands apart and turned his horse to ride back toward the buggies. Carlisle, still talking, went with Watrous, and McBride came trotting up with the LM manager and foreman. McBride beckoned, and the Watrous trail hands assembled around him.

"We're goin' to earmark this herd," Mc-Bride announced when the last man had come up. "We bought all the LM steers an' we're not goin' to waste time brandin' 'em. We'll grub the right ear. I got a delivery date to make, an' trail brandin' would hang us

68

up too long."

It seemed to Rusty that McBride was making too long an explanation. Down on Arroyo Grande whenever Dan Shotridge reached a decision he stated it, and the men who worked for him took his word as final, accepted it without explanation. But McBride was explaining. He looked straight at Rusty as he talked, and Rusty returned the look. It might be funny business not to trail brand a herd — Rusty had never heard of its not being done — but he was certainly not going to say anything about it. That was up to Watrous and Carlisle. They owned the steers. If a grubbed ear for a trail brand suited them it suited Rusty. He shrugged his shoulders.

McBride was telling off ropers and men to hold the herd. Among these latter was Rusty. The orders given, men rode to their appointed places, and the men who were to rope took down their twines while the markers climbed down and, hobbling their horses, made ready. Rusty could see the man, whose horse Watrous had taken, coming up from between the hills. Presently the two buggies appeared, Carlisle and Watrous in one of them, Ellen driving the rig in which Marcia rode.

Earmarking was much more simple than

branding would have been. A roper selected an animal and draped his loop over horns or neck; and another, coming up behind, caught the steer's heels. Working together, the two men stretched out their catch, and then a knifeman, sometimes with the assistance of another man or two on foot, grubbed the right ear. The neck rope was freed then and the steer got up. The man who had his rope on the heels gave slack; the steer kicked out of the loop and, shaking his head — marked and ready for the trail — went trotting off. LM men and Watrous hands worked together, holding, roping and on the ground, but it was Watrous's men that did the actual marking. Sometimes, so swiftly did the men work, a steer would not be thrown at all but would be marked while still standing.

At noon the work ceased, and the cattle were held in loose herd by four men while the rest repaired to the wagon which was camped beyond the two hills. Rusty was one of those told off to hold the cattle. The buggies went in with the men, and the steers settled down and spread out, grazing.

When the crew returned, those who had been left to hold the herd went to camp where Deems had dinner waiting. McBride, before they left, had urged them to hurry back, and so, bolting their meal, they changed saddles to fresh horses and rode out again.

Rusty's horse was a half-broken bronco which fought all around the camp when Rusty tried to saddle him, arousing Deems's anxiety and squawling ire.

"Keep that damned horse out of the kitchen!" Deems yelled. "If you can't handle him git somebody that can."

Mad and sweating, Rusty hauled down on his rope and answered Deems: "If you're so damned good, saddle him yourself. He ain't exactly gentle."

Finally, by tying up a foot and with the help of an LM man, Rusty got the saddle on. The bronc stood, legs widespread and trembling, while Rusty twisted an ear and climbed up. When Rusty turned loose the ear the horse, exhausted by his exertions in fighting the saddle, bucked a few jumps and then trotted off, and Rusty, sitting deep and watchful, went out to the herd and fell into place, holding.

About three o'clock the buggies bearing Marcia and Ellen and Watrous and Carlisle came out to the herd once more. The two vehicles were halted some small distance from the cattle, and Carlisle and Watrous dismounted from their buggy and stood beside it, the girls remaining in the seat of the buggy they occupied. Carlisle had a saddled horse tied to the hames of the buggy horse, and after talking to Watrous for a time he got the horse and led him back. He stood there, holding the horse and talking to his partner. Rusty was looking toward the buggies when McBride came up.

"Go on an' rope awhile," McBride commanded.

Rusty stared unbelievingly at the foreman, not sure that he had understood the command. It was certain that his bronc had never been roped from, and it was even more certain that there would be doings the first time a rope was circled by a rider on the bronc's back. "Huh?" Rusty said.

"You heard me." McBride smiled tightly. "Yo're supposed to be a hand. Go on in an' rope. You can team up with Travis."

Rusty met McBride's eyes. The foreman did not look away, and his smile was malicious. Rusty reached for his rope string. If he was ordered to rope he would rope, but there was certainly going to be some excitement, and he was going to be right in the middle of it.

"You better tell the boys that are holdin' to look out for an earthquake," Rusty admonished mildly, freeing the rope and beginning to bend a figure-eight knot in the end. "When this bronc comes undone those steers aren't going to like it." With that he put the figure eight on his saddle horn, laid the coils of his rope across the horn and, bending gingerly, caught the front latigo and gave a heave, pulling the cinch tight.

"Afraid?" McBride taunted.

"Watch and see," Rusty retorted and turned toward the cattle.

The bronc moved along mincingly, ears laid back and head swinging. Just like Rusty, the bronc knew that something was coming. Carlisle, down beside the buggies, had mounted his home. He turned the animal and then paused for a final word with his partner. There was a clear space of perhaps a hundred yards between Rusty and the buggies. McBride, his order given, rode away, looking back over his shoulder.

Honey Yates and his partner had a steer down, a big roan that would weigh a thousand pounds. There had been trouble with the roan, but he was earmarked now. The men let the roan up and Yates gave slack. The roan kicked out of the rope and stood wide-legged and his head low, his attention riveted on the buggy. Rusty was picking out the steer he wanted, not watching roan or buggies or anything else except his steer and his horse. He had his rope ready and had shaken out an experimental loop just to see what his bronc would do. From the bronc's actions it was evident that he didn't like the rope.

"Here's for it," Rusty murmured, having selected his steer. "You an' me are even, horse: You haven't ever been roped from, an' I haven't ever roped from you, but I guess . . ." His statement to the bronc was interrupted by a scream. The roan steer had had enough indignities heaped upon him. He had been roped and thrown and his ear cut off. Now selecting the buggy that the girls occupied as the thing upon which to vent his wrath, he bellowed once and, with head lowered, charged. Marcia and Ellen saw him coming and voiced their fear.

Carlisle, riding toward the herd, was the man closest to the steer. Turning his head, Rusty saw what was happening and he did two things: He yelled, "Head him, Carlisle!" and he kicked with both spurred heels. Rusty's Pet Maker spurs took the bronc between the cinches, and the bronco, utterly surprised, jumped his full length.

Carlisle heard Rusty's yell and he saw the steer, but he was powerless to act. He was riding a good horse — one that Rusty would have given much to possess at the moment, one that could have done the thing Rusty commanded if Carlisle had known how to accomplish it. Carlisle, too, kicked with spurred heels, making his horse leap in a bound that almost unseated him.

Watrous ran toward the other buggy, his own equipage forgotten, and behind Rusty, McBride was shouting. Frightened out of her wits by the charging roan avalanche, Ellen lashed her buggy horse with the whip. The horse jumped, cramping the buggy wheels as he turned, and the buggy went over, spilling its occupants out on the ground in a cascade of skirts and petticoats and flying legs and screams. It would have been comical had not tragedy been so near.

Gil Travis was coming from the right but he was too far away, and it was up to Rusty and the bronc. Loop swinging, Rusty bore down upon the roan steer. Bending forward, he turned loose the rope, and that instant the bronc stopped running and vented all his fright and anger in a spasm of violent bucking. Bronco and steer hit the two ends of the rope when the horse was up in the air, and Rusty turned loose his stirrups and, with a prayer in his mind, quit the saddle. He had done what he could.

He hit the ground, rolled and came up. The horse, too, jerked down by the steer's weight, had hit the ground. Rusty flung himself on the bronco's head to hold him. The steer had been pulled around; Watrous had almost reached the girls where they had fallen; Travis was bent, ready for his throw. So much Rusty caught with the clarity of a photograph as he reached for the bronco's ears. Travis' rope settled as he heeled the roan. His horse, trained and wise, for all the excitement, set back on the rope and the steer went down. Rusty let his breath go then. It was all right. Everything was fine. From all directions men — some mounted, some on foot — converged on steer and girls and buggy. Under Rusty's restraining hands the bronco trembled.

The buggy was righted, and Ellen and Marcia were helped to their feet. Carlisle was beside Marcia, and Watrous was holding Ellen close. Three men were on the steer, one holding his head, one hauling his tail up between his extended hind legs and the third foolishly grasping Rusty's rope. There was a babble of comment and profanity, and above that babble Scott McBride made his voice heard.

"What the hell is this anyhow? Git to them cattle!" McBride, Rusty thought, might be a first-class so-and-such but he was a cowman, anyhow. That was the thing to do: get to the cattle. Rusty let the bronc up and the horse stood trembling.

"If you ain't goin' to use that rope," Rusty commented politely to the man who held his line, "you could turn it loose. I got this end tied so it can't get away."

The man who held the rope looked abashedly at Rusty and then flushed dull red and took the loop from the roan's neck. The men who held the roan turned the steer loose, and the roan lumbered to his feet, shook his head, kicked twice to free his hind feet and then trotted off to the herd. Rusty laid a gentle hand on the bronc's neck. "Easy now," he soothed. "It's all over. Yo're a good little horse. Plenty good. You're big enough. Yes sir!"

Travis, a grin on his young face, came up and stopped his horse. "Might make a rope horse out of him," he said, indicating the bronc. "That is, if you keep at it. He's got a kind of funny way of comin' up to a steer though. Don't know that I'd like it."

Rusty twisted out a stirrup and swung up on the bronc's back. The animal stood, sweat and dirt staining his golden-sorrel hide. "Don't you go runnin' down my horse," Rusty said severely. "Mebbe he's got queer ways, but he gets there. He suits me, Big Enough does."

"Ought to suit most anybody," Travis returned. "You goin' to rope some more off him?"

"I done it once," Rusty said. "Why not?"

Travis' glance was admiring. "Take their heads then an' I'll try to get their heels," he said.

Rusty nodded agreement and began to pull in and coil his rope. Big Enough watched the rope apprehensively. He didn't like that snaky line slithering across the ground toward him. Automatically Rusty soothed the horse. "Easy now. Just take it easy, Big Enough." Rusty's eyes were on the buggy where Leonard Carlisle stood, his arms lifted so that his hands were on the side of the seat. Marcia was leaning across Ellen, and each of the girls possessed one of Leonard Carlisle's hands.

Travis, too, must have been looking toward the buggy. His voice held no humor when he spoke. "He's goin' to be a big help, he is," Travis said shortly. "Quite a help. An' we'll have him all the way to Dodge City."

Rusty had his rope coiled. "Yeah," he drawled. And then: "What say we try it a whirl, Gil? I'll pick a little one for the first one."

The crew came in tired that night. McBride

assigned each man to a guard, and when he had finished he looked at Rusty, a malicious smile twitching at his lips.

"I clear forgot, Shotridge," McBride drawled. "Watrous wants to see you down at the headquarters. He said for me to send you down." The smile grew broader. "You'd better go now too," McBride completed. "You can eat yore supper down there while they're thankin' you for bein' a hero, an' I want you to get back in time to stand yore guard."

Rusty was about to reply and then thought better of it. He was tired and hungry, and it was suppertime. What Rusty wanted to do was stretch out and rest awhile after he had eaten. But orders were orders. He nodded to McBride and, wordlessly, walked over to where his night horse was staked. As he mounted and rode off McBride's parting sally came to his ears.

"A hell of a lookin' hero, if you ask me."

Rusty sent his horse along, the color gradually receding from his face and neck. Reaching the headquarters of the Secáte ranch he got down and tied his mount to a rail in front of the house. Then with a final glance at the horse he walked toward the porch. The light was dim, and the vine-covered porch was almost dark. Mounting the steps Rusty could not see who was on the porch. From its dim recesses Marcia Carlisle spoke softly, "Mr. Shotridge." Rusty turned toward the voice.

Marcia was seated in a hammock. Rusty paused before her. "Colonel Watrous sent for me," he said, wondering why whenever he appeared before this girl he felt awkward and uncouth. "I . . ."

"I asked Colonel Watrous to have you come," Marcia interrupted. "I wanted to thank you for what you did today."

Uncomfortably Rusty tried to answer. "I was just handy." He dismissed the thanks. "There wasn't anybody else close an' . . . Well, I had good luck."

"If that steer" — fright still colored Marcia's voice — "if you hadn't caught him, we might have been killed. Ellen says . . ."

"She's makin' somethin' big out of somethin' little," Rusty interrupted. "The steer was chargin' the buggy, not you. It was bad luck that the buggy spilled an' good luck that I happened to be handy. Any one of the other boys would have done the same thing an' likely done it better."

"You know that's not true!" Marcia rejected Rusty's statement. "Why won't you let me thank you, Rusty?" The name dropped naturally from her lips. "Why do you always make me feel . . . ?" She broke off. When she spoke again her voice was changed, slower, troubled, as though she found difficulty in what she said.

"Leonard was closer than you were. I saw him. He . . . he couldn't have done what you did. He . . ."

"He ain't had the chance to learn how," Rusty stated flatly.

The girl stirred in the hammock. Through the gloom Rusty could see the dim outline of her heart-shaped face. "You were right," she said. "I've given up. I've been selfish, and you were right. Leonard will . . . He must have his chance to be a man."

Deep in Rusty something stirred, some feeling, hidden and latent. "I'll look after him," Rusty said hoarsely. "I promised Ellen I would."

"Ellen?"

"She's in love with him. I promised her I'd take care of him. I'll do it. I'll bring him back."

There was no movement in the hammock. Marcia spoke no word. Wheeling, Colonel Watrous forgotten, Rusty walked toward the steps and down them. Why was it that when he saw Marcia Carlisle, when he spoke to her, when he thought of her, he felt so? Why was he always an awkward, tongue-tied

81

lout? Why?

"Rusty!"

Halfway to his horse Rusty stopped and turned back. Marcia stood on the porch, just above the steps. Her dress was mistily white in the night. Rusty took two steps toward her.

"When you come back . . ." Marcia said and paused.

"Yes?"

"You'll bring Leonard?"

"I promised you I would."

"You'll . . . Rusty?"

"Yes?"

"You'll be with him?"

"What difference does that make?" Deep in Rusty feeling broke in a rising surge. What difference could it make to the girl on the porch whether he, Rusty Shotridge, came back or not? Why?

"It makes a great deal of difference to me, Rusty," Marcia said softly, and then, with a rustle of skirts, she was gone.

Rusty Shotridge took another step toward the porch and stopped. For a long instant he stood there, looking at the steps and the deserted entrance above them. Then, turning, he went once more toward his horse and mechanically untied the animal and mounted.

Marcia Carlisle had said that it made a great deal of difference to her whether or not Rusty came back. A great deal of difference. A great deal . . .

He would come back. He'd come back to that girl. And when he did . . . Through the darkness Rusty rode on toward the camped wagon.

Chapter V

When the earmarking of the steers was finished the Watrous crew bade good-by to the Secáte ranch. Before they left Rusty had a word with Ellen Watrous, promising her again that he would look after the welfare of Leonard Carlisle. He did not talk with Marcia or Colonel Watrous.

Save for Carlisle, every man of the outfit knew his work. Accordingly, Carlisle could not go far wrong. He had only to imitate his companions, and he was smart enough to follow the procedure of the crew. Too, whenever anything threatened to go wrong at the place where Carlisle was posted, a competent, sun-tanned rider would opportunely appear and straighten out the difficulty. McBride was a good trail boss, a good hand with the cattle, and during the first few days men and steers shook down to trailing.

In the morning, before the sun came up, McBride would waken the cook and horse wrangler. Then while Deems cunningly rebuilt the fire Telesfor went out to the horses. Around the camp the night horses were staked, and presently the remuda came over the hill.

By this time the men were up, each rider breaking out of the canvas-covered cocoon that was his bed and, donning his hat, proceeded to pull on such clothing as he had discarded for the night. On the bed ground the steers came lumbering up, McBride and the two riders of the last guard on hand to care for them. The steers grazed, and in camp Deems wiped his doughy hands on the seat of his pants and called the crew to breakfast.

Their dishes in the wreck pan, wiping the last remnants of their meal from their lips, the trail hands went to the rope corral. Here, between two ropes stretched from the wheel and tongue of the wagon and the free ends held by men, the horses were penned. Telesfor roped out the horses that the men called for, and as the horses were roped riders let them out, bridled, and led the animals away.

Saddles in place and the night horses

freed, the trail hands let their mounts soak while beds were rolled and tossed up on the wagon. Then, mounting — some gingerly, some boldly — they betook themselves to the cattle. Sometimes a horse pitched and there was good-natured raillery and banter. Sometimes a bronc sulked and was coerced by spurs. Ahead of the crew the cattle drifted, and behind them Joe Deems washed and wiped the dishes, packed the wagon and extinguished the fire, while the remuda, under Telesfor's charge, went out on the best grass that could be found.

Reaching the steers, the riders bunched them and pushed them on, for Scott Mc-Bride drove off a bed ground. Other trail bosses might graze from a bed ground, but Scott McBride did not. Now the cattle marched, a line of them pointing to the north. Through the marching line the leaders worked their way until they were in front. Back in the ranks individual steers picked up their places, markers these, their presence telling the guardians who flanked the moving cattle that all were present. On either side, well out from the cattle, the point men rode, their duty to point the herd, to follow the trail and to drive off local cattle that might wish to join this marching army. Along the sides the swing riders held their posts, and in the rear the drag men rode in the dust while the steers walked steadily.

As the day gained age and the sun climbed up, the marching column slowed. When heat came the steers spread out, falling from column into wide dispersion until they grazed along, the riders falling back to rear and sides, allowing the cattle to have their will. Now the remuda and the wagon passed, pulling ahead of the cattle.

And then a steer lay down and then another until, save for a few, all were resting, chewing their cuds, taking their ease, while on flanks and rear the riders waited, alert as ever.

Up beyond the resting cattle the wagon camped and smoke trailed up and dust arose from the hoofs of the remuda.

Again the wagon and the remuda moved, and now the steers, rested, came to their feet. Sometimes they marched; sometimes they grazed, and always the ever-present trail hands watched them. Sometimes during the day, perhaps in the morning, perhaps during the evening hours when the sun sloped down, sometimes at noon, the herd came to water. Then, spreading along the bank of the stream or around the edges of the water holes, the cattle drank and the men, patient as any Job, sat their horses while their mounts drank also, and, the animals and men having satisfied themselves, all moved on again.

Scott McBride scouted ahead now and, coming to some grassy slope, some open spot where there was room, used a part of that instinct and knowledge that made him trail boss. More surely than a steer, McBride could pick a bed ground and, having picked it, he waited for his herd, sitting atop the rise, watching his cattle move slowly toward him.

Joe Deems made camp. The rope corral was erected; the herd, coming on leisurely, reached the selected spot, and riders, swinging across its front, checked it and held it up. As the sun sloped down into the west smoke from the cook's fire carried to the nostrils of the hungry men, and the remuda came in and was penned so that night horses might be caught. Now a steer lay down, now another and another, until, with the herd bedded, weary men made toward the camp, leaving two of their companions to ride about the cattle.

So they moved, following the grass, keeping to the trace pioneered for them by hardy predecessors. Peaceful and uneventful? Surely. But always with a potentiality of drastic, dramatic activity, prevented and staved off by bearded, bronzed riders. And as they moved the steers gained weight and the men became more lean, and the horses, despite the care and the good grass, became more and more gaunt and hard.

Rusty Shotridge rode on drag or flank. Others might rotate in position, shifting from drag to swing, from swing to point, from one side of the herd to the other. So in changing their position they were relieved from some monotony and from the dust, but Rusty rode always with the herd between him and the wind. In his ten head of horses there were but two that approximated cow horses. One of these, a big bay that bucked viciously each time he was saddled, Rusty chose for a night horse. The bay was honest: he bucked when he was saddled but after that was gentle enough, and he was clear footed and, even in his bucking, showed sense. Rusty called the bay Toughy and appreciated him. The other good horse was the bronco Big Enough upon which Rusty had roped the roan steer. The bronc was sorrel, high headed and high strung, but with brains. The bronc sweat and was nervous but learned readily. As for the other eight horses, they were either dead bellied or vicious. Other men might have a respite in the saddle, might doze and relax, but Rusty could not. To do so was to invite disaster, and so he kept continually on the alert. Each night he saddled Toughy and took the buck out of the bay before he staked him. Each morning he turned Toughy out with the remuda. Once in nine times he saddled Big Enough and enjoyed a little respite, a little relaxation, for it was a pleasure for Rusty Shotridge to teach a willing horse his trade.

As for the rest, his night guard was the middle watch so that his sleep was broken every night. His companions were taciturn, hard-faced men who eyed him questioningly whenever he spoke, who watched his actions and discussed him when he was not present. He had one friend, Telesfor Maes, with whom he talked in Spanish. Gil Travis sometimes joined him as they came in to camp or rode out to the cattle. Travis was younger than the rest and had a freakish sense of humor which came and went. Sometimes Travis was friendly, sometimes not. Joe Deems, the cook, made a companion of no one. Deems attended to his duties and ruled with an iron hand the little circle about the chuck wagon, from the end of the wagon tongue to the fire behind the wagon. Scott McBride kept his own counsel, talking only with Deems and with Leonard Carlisle, limiting his conversation with the rest of the crew to brief orders. Sometimes, seeing Carlisle at ease behind the wagon or in conversation with McBride, Rusty contrasted his own position with that of the dark man, for if Rusty Shotridge was the goat of the Watrous outfit, Leonard Carlisle was the pet.

Carlisle had the best string of horses in the remuda, saving only Scott McBride. His mount was gentle, and every horse was a cow horse. His guard was the first, so that, having finished his watch, he came to bed assured of unbroken rest for the remainder of the night. With the herd Carlisle rode in swing or point, always upwind of the cattle, always out of the dust. But, as with Rusty, the trail crew, saving only Honey Yates, eyed Carlisle and watched him and, among themselves, made comment, for they were jealous of the favors shown him and they knew that he was not a hand.

Carlisle did not notice the attitude of the riders or, if he did note it, accepted it as his due. For companionship he had McBride and Yates, and perhaps — unaccustomed as he was to Western usage — he considered the aloofness of the others as inferiority of position. After all, young Leonard Carlisle was one of the owners of the herd, a cut above the common men who handled the steers.

Gil Travis, riding in with Rusty from the herd, in one burst of frankness perhaps spoke the opinion of all. "That damned Carlisle!" Gil snapped. "He thinks he's a little tin god an' that he's too good for us."

The days dragged by, and the herd moved northward, sometimes eight, sometimes ten miles a day. Once when there was no water the crew drove steadily, and twenty miles were covered. The grass was green and plentiful; the little streams and water holes were full. There was no excitement, no trouble. The cattle handled as though some spell had been laid upon them.

They encountered but few men. Occasionally a rider for some outfit that ranged the country through which the herd passed dropped down on the camp, visited awhile and perhaps spent the night. From those occasional encounters they learned the news of the country, learned that there were two herds ahead of them, that there had been some trouble in the Nations, learned that a man had been killed in Tascosa by the marshal, heard that there was a Ranger company operating near the Palo Duro. No rider that they met was familiar or acquainted with any one of the crew, and yet, such was the fraternity of the country, each seemed to know the members of the Watrous outfit by reputation. Even Rusty's encounter with Flanders and Sigloe had been spread before him by the mysterious telepathy of the range.

So day followed peaceful day, and at length they came to the first stream of any size that had crossed their path: the Clear Fork.

There was a store and saloon at the crossing, a little building set into a hillside, half-dugout, half-log structure. This was the first sign of human habitation they had encountered, and they welcomed it. Too, at the Clear Fork crossing there was a bearded ranchman of the locality who came out with McBride and visited the camp. At McBride's invitation the ranchman went through the herd, looking for local cattle, and Rusty wondered why McBride had invited the inspection.

The local man, having weaved his pony in and out through the steers, rejoined the trail boss at the edge of the herd. They were close to Rusty, and he heard their conversation. "You got nothin' of ours in there," the rancher said to McBride. "Clean as a whistle. I notice you ain't trail branded."

"No need," McBride said. "We got all the steers the LM had. We earmarked in place of brandin'. It saved time."

"Yeh, but it's kind of dangerous," the ranchman commented.

"I don't figure it to be," McBride returned. "I got one of the owners with the outfit. Leonard Carlisle. He's goin' through with us. I'd like for you to meet him."

They rode away then, joining Carlisle, and Rusty could see the introduction and see Carlisle shake hands with the local man. Then McBride came back and the cattle were moved on to the ford and crossed. The Clear Fork was low, the deepest portion hardly reaching the hocks of the horses. On the other side the steers were thrown out to grass, and that night those men who did not have an early guard went back across the river to sample the entertainment afforded by the store. Rusty Shotridge did not go with them.

"You take first guard tonight, Shotridge," McBride ordered. "Carlisle ain't come back from the store yet." So Rusty accompanied Ben Nugget out on the first guard.

That was not all. Relieved by the second guard at ten o'clock, it seemed to Rusty that he had barely turned in his bed, hardly closed his eyes, before a man was shaking him. "Git up, kid," the rider ordered. "Time for yore guard."

"But I stood the first guard," Rusty expostulated. "I . . ."

"Carlisle ain't come back yet," the rider said. "McBride said to wake you up if they wasn't back at camp in time."

So Rusty Shotridge stood two guards that night, and Leonard Carlisle and Scott McBride, with others, played poker in the store.

They moved on from the Clear Fork, traveling slowly. The grass stayed good and the trail stretched out. Rains came, and men — their slickers forgotten in the wagon — rode soaking wet. Now the fly that Joe Deems spread from the wagon bows was a blessing, making one small spot where falling rain did not splash into plate or coffee cup. From one day to the next the beds were never dry, and Ben Nugget limped about, complaining of his rheumatism. In the rain, with all the country flooded, the Watrous herd reached the Brazos.

The stream was up, spread wide and running swift: swimming water. Along the banks the ground was soft and boggy. Here they waited, holding the herd until such a time as the river might subside. In two days the water level fell, and McBride decided to chance the crossing. McBride's horse was a black, the best water horse in the remuda. Riding him into the stream, McBride struck for the farther bank. Halfway across the black hit swimming water, and McBride turned him back and went upstream, prospecting for the ford. He found it and, working across the river, reached the farther bank. Though the Brazos was wide and high the water on the ford was not so deep as to preclude a crossing. McBride worked back and forth across the river, finding the limits of the shallow water, and eventually he returned to the south bank.

"We can make it," he announced. "There's swimmin' water above an' below the ford, but the wagon can get across all right. Think I'd better stake it for you, Joe?"

Joe Deems, his eyes narrow, looked at the river. "I guess not," he answered. "I've kind of got it picked out. I'll mebbe need some help."

"You'll get it," McBride promised. "There's some quicksand below that we'll have to watch. We'll cross the steers; that'll pack it some. All right, let's get at it."

Deems walked back to his wagons, and McBride, trotting off, circled his arm above his head and swept it down toward the crossing in a gesture that meant, "Bring the steers on."

Leonard Carlisle, in the peaceful days along the way, had, he believed, learned a good deal about handling cattle. He had ridden at point and at swing. He had pushed native cattle out of the way and he had turned errant steers back into the herd. He was, in his own opinion, a veteran of the trail, and now as the steers came up to the crossing he rode on the flank of the cattle and looked at the river, red and swollen, stretched across the way. If he had any doubts as to his ability to do his part in this coming task he kept them to himself and, as the cattle reached the bank and hesitated, he swung down to take a place below them.

The leaders, coming down to the stream's edge, snuffed nervously at the water and then, with pressure building up behind them, entered the river. Behind the herd the riders worked, urging laggards forward, shouting, jumping steers off the bank, forcing cattle into the water. The first steers splashed out into the shallows, went on along the pathway of the ford and, where the ford swung upstream, struck deeper water. Below the ford, as McBride had said, was swimming water, and the steers, reaching it, plunged in, heads lifted, long horns and noses protruding above the rolling river, only the top line of their backs showing behind their lifted heads. Naturally they went downstream with the current.

Leonard Carlisle had seen McBride explore the ford, and he had picked out the place for the steers to emerge. As they were swept downstream, swimming, he jumped his horse off into the river and set out to turn them back up toward the ford, not realizing that he was doing the wrong thing and mistaking the shouts that should have checked him for the yelling of men pushing cattle off the bank. Some of the steers were already scrambling up the farther bank when Carlisle reached the deeper portion of the river and his horse began to swim. There were only a few cattle across, and now as Carlisle appeared downstream and ahead of the rest, he caused a mill. He had headed the steers in the river, and they turned back. All about Leonard Carlisle there were the bobbing heads and low backs of swimming cattle, and his own horse was deep in the river and swimming. The cattle turned and started back, and the swimming horse followed. Carlisle tried desperately to check the turn but was helpless, more helpless than ever before in all his young life. He felt that helplessness and panic. His horse reached the edge of the shallows, sought for footing, was bumped by a steer and went down; and Carlisle, mouth open to shout, got a big drink of the Brazos that strangled him as he submerged. Floundering clear of the horse, he tried to swim, was struck by another lunging steer and went under again. Panic-stricken, he fought for the top. Then his shirt collar was seized in a powerful grip; he swung, bumping, into the side of a horse, swung clear again and, still almost submerged, was dragged along until his head came clear of the river.

Rusty Shotridge, fighting steers off the riverbank, had seen Carlisle pass the leaders and turn them back. Contempt filled him. Anybody, any fool who had ever seen a cow, would know better than to do what Carlisle had done. The steers were coming back, and there would be no stopping them. There was only one thing to do and that was pinch off the herd, let those that were in the river, come back and then jump them off again. Rusty plunged his horse into the streaming cattle to check their flow. Others, acting on the same idea, were working behind him and from the other side. The herd checked and turned back, and Rusty, lifting in his saddle, saw Carlisle's horse go down.

Instantly he swung his mount. The horse Rusty was riding was hammerheaded and vicious as a wolf, but that made no difference. Given a job, Rusty Shotridge could do it on any kind of horse, and he had a job now, saw his task clearly. He jumped his horse off the bank, forced the unwilling animal out into the stream and, reaching Carlisle, he leaned down, grasped Carlisle's collar with his right hand and brought his horse around. Fighting the horse, the river and the inert drag on his right arm, Rusty towed Leonard Carlisle out of the river a good deal as a man might pull along a sack. Reaching the bank, he released his hold and, dropping the man he held, went back to work again. There was plenty of work, plenty of yelling and plenty of fast riding on the slippery, muddy riverbank. Carlisle lay just where Rusty had dropped him and received no attention. The crew was busy.

Presently, assured that he was on land, that he was safe, that the river no longer possessed him, Carlisle sat up. By that time the cattle were stopped, had been straightened out and were being brought back to the river once more. Rusty Shotridge, leading Carlisle's horse, came up to where Carlisle sat, leaned down and tendered the reins with one short comment: "Here's yore horse."

In a daze Carlisle took the reins and Rusty

trotted off. Full of river water, sick with it, still frightened and feeling like hell, Leonard Carlisle sat there and held his horse, and the crew, once again masters of the cattle, made ready for the second attempt at the river.

After a time Carlisle got up. Water drained from his clothing. He was wet and shaken. No one paid any attention to him. The first crossing having been a failure, this second trial required the best efforts of every rider. Finally under much coercion the lead steers entered the river again and splashed out into it. Men applied pressure to the herd, shoving them in, jumping them off the bank. The leaders reached the channel, swam it, scrambled out and on the farther bank fell to grazing; and across the Brazos the Watrous trail herd streamed. Leonard Carlisle mounted his horse and, dubious and frightened, followed the last of the cattle into the river.

Carlisle's horse followed the ford. Gaining the other side, the cow pony almost automatically trotted off toward the grazing steers. Carlisle did not look back. He was sick and still weak with fright. He did not see the wagon cross the ford, aided by four men who, with ropes fastened to the axles, helped the straining mules. Leonard Carlisle had seen all he wanted of the Brazos. He never wanted to see it again. Humiliation as well as weakness filled him. He had made a fool of himself and, save for Rusty Shotridge, he might easily have drowned.

That night when camp was made, the river south of them but not forgotten, Carlisle approached Rusty, sitting close beside the fire that Joe Deems tended. Rusty's clothing, as was the clothing of every man present save only Deems, was damp. Rusty was tired with a bone weariness that was almost an ache. Capping all this, Joe Deems was late with supper. It was no time for a man to be condescending or even thankful. No time at all.

"You saved my life today, Shotridge," Carlisle said, and all about men turned to look at him. "I guess I've been mistaken about you. I guess you're all right after all." Tone and words were wrong. So might some medieval lordling have stooped to speak graciously to a slave who had held his stirrup. Rusty Shotridge remembered San Marcial; he remembered the string of bad horses; he remembered the dust that had followed him, day after day, the double guards he had stood at Clear Fork crossing.

"That's all right," Rusty said coolly, and his eyes encompassed Leonard Carlisle from

the top of his hat to the toes of his boots.
"You needn't thank me. It ain't hardly
worth mentionin'."

CHAPTER VI

It is natural that men thrown into close association select their companions and be-
come more friendly with some certain ones
than with others. Generally with a trail crew
the men who stand guards together form a
partnership. This was true of the Watrous
crew to a great extent, except in the instance
of Rusty Shotridge. His partner on the
middle guard was Gil Travis, and while Travis was more friendly toward him than the
rest, still there was no real bond between
them. As the herd went on toward the Red
River crossing Rusty noted that Travis'
periods of good humor became less and
less. He noted, too, that Honey Yates and
Leonard Carlisle, standing first guard together, became more and more friendly.
Carlisle broke over from his usual supercil-
ious air of patronage, admitting Yates to his
friendship, and Yates unobtrusively helped
Carlisle with those things he could not do
or did not understand.

Yates knew his business, Rusty could tell.
There was no better hand with the outfit

than Honey Yates. The man was built of rawhide and steel, was never weary, and was always pleasant and even tempered. Gil Travis was as good a man as Yates. Ben Nugget had once been a good hand, but age was slipping up on him. Nugget, Rusty guessed, was at least fifty years old and perhaps older. The rest were mediocre, just average. That was not surprising. Top hands were not common, even in Texas where any ranch-raised boy could ride and rope and handle cattle. Rusty knew himself to be a cut above them all. He bowed only to McBride. McBride was a trail boss and a good one. Yet as they moved along Rusty could sense, rather than see, that McBride was having trouble.

It seemed to Rusty — who was more or less on the outskirts, one of the crew and yet not of the crew — that there was a division in the camp. Telesfor Maes was an old Watrous hand, had been up the trail with a Watrous herd for four years or more. Joe Deems also was an old-timer, as was Ben Nugget. These men obeyed McBride willingly and cheerfully. Travis and Yates, too, did their work without question, but the rest were sluggish and seemingly a little resentful of authority. Somehow Rusty knew, without being able to put his finger on the trouble, that the Watrous crew was not a unit, not a smoothly working machine for the handling and moving of cattle. It worried him.

An insight into the existing difficulty came when the herd was two days below the Red River crossing. They had moved twenty miles during the day, the length of the march determined by the fact that McBride had wished to reach a definite locality before halting. McBride, thoroughly familiar with the trail, liked to bed the herd at certain spots. With a delivery date to make, McBride had arranged a sort of mental timetable and attempted to adhere to it insofar as possible. The cattle had been a little hard to handle, wishing to graze and reluctant to move on when the crew pushed them. Then, too, there had been more local cattle than usual to push out of the way. Carlisle, working one point, had not done an efficient job, and the swing men had been forced to do some riding. Coupled with all this, the day had been hot and the afternoon broken by a thunderstorm which drenched men and cattle. It was one of those days when things went wrong — not big things, but small ones — and there were some short tempers in camp.

As though to compensate for the trials of

the day Deems had cooked an extra-good supper. He had cut thin streaks from the quarter of a butchered yearling, dipped them in flour and fried them in a Dutch oven. There were plenty of steaks and gravy and Dutch-oven bread and molasses. It was a good feed, a regular spread. When the meal was almost over Travis and a heavy-set man, Pete Benbow, met at the Dutch oven that contained the steaks. There was one steak left.

Normally such a meeting would have caused some good-natured rivalry with the final result of the steak's being split between the two. Travis, reaching the oven half a step before Benbow, seized the long-handled fork and speared for the steak, missing it. Benbow, with his own fork, tried to get the steak, but Travis knocked his hand away and Benbow's wrist struck against the still-hot edge of the oven. Benbow, with a curse that carried no humor at all, threw his shoulder into Travis, sending the younger man reeling, and in place of reaching for the steak again, followed up his attack.

Travis had been, for a wonder, in one of his good moods. All day he had taken the minor difficulties with drawling equanimity and wit. Now as Benbow shoved against him, pitting his bull strength against the whipcord sinew and speed of the younger man, Travis shed his cheerfulness. He returned, snarling, to the attack, tripped Benbow and sprawled him on the ground. Of such minor matters is real trouble made. Benbow sprang up swearing and advanced on Travis, and Travis, equally angry as Benbow, retreated.

Neither man was armed. Each had laid aside the six-shooter that customarily rode at his hip. Travis, retreating, reached his bed and stretched down his hand for his weapon. Benbow wheeled and ran toward his own bed and weapon some fifteen feet away. McBride, sitting beside the wagon, his back against a wheel, sprang to his feet and called a sharp command:

"Stop that! Both of you. Stop it!"

Ordinarily Travis and Benbow would have heeded the wagon boss. His was the voice of authority. Angry as they were, they should have obeyed. Neither did. Travis had his belt, his gun still in its holster. Benbow snatched up his weapon, jerking it from the scabbard. Travis, too, drew his gun and dropped the belt. McBride ran forward, coming between the two men to stop the trouble, ordering them sharply to quit.

Neither Travis nor Benbow paid any attention to McBride. Travis, gun half raised, moved to the right. Benbow, equally ready, shifted to the left. McBride, between them, still trying vainly to stop the trouble, was in the line of fire.

"I told you to stop it!" he rasped. "I'll not have trouble on this crew. Travis, put that gun down!"

"Git out of the way, McBride," Travis snarled. "Move or you'll get hurt." He shifted again, trying to clear the wagon boss.

Carlisle was on his feet and seemed about ready to go to McBride's aid. Rusty, knowing that Carlisle would only endanger himself and accomplish nothing, reached up and caught Carlisle's arm, jerking the man down beside him and holding him there. Rusty had seen such things before. He knew that there could be no reasoning with either Travis or Benbow. Once in a branding camp he had seen a flanker snatch up an iron and strike his partner simply because that partner had made a habit of helping himself up by grasping a shoulder of the flanker. Rusty knew that tempers, once gone, cannot easily be recovered. The only hope here of averting tragedy was that McBride's authority would carry. And McBride, trying to exert that authority, was not getting the job done.

It was then that Honey Yates spoke from

close by the wagon. "Drop it! Benbow, put that gun down. Drop it, Travis!" Rusty Shotridge had never heard such cold menace in a man's voice. Involuntarily he glanced toward Yates.

Yates had not risen. He was sitting cross-legged on the ground, his plate in his lap, knife and fork laid on the plate. Yates wore his belt and weapon and, oddly, in Rusty's mind the thought occurred that he had never seen Yates put his gun aside. Yates was staring intently at the two angry men. Benbow hesitated, and Travis, who had been trying to dodge past McBride for a clear shot at Benbow, stopped where he stood.

"Drop it!" Yates commanded again. "Both of you!"

Sheepishly, like a small boy corrected by a stern teacher, Benbow lowered his gun and after a moment's hesitation turned toward his bed. Travis, too, hesitated and then, carrying his pistol, walked back to where his bed was unrolled. He sat down on the tarp, and Benbow, seeing Travis sitting down, dropped his Colt on his bedding. Yates picked up his knife and fork to resume eating, and McBride began to rage. This was his crew, McBride roared, and he'd have no such damned foolishness around his wagon. Another such stunt as this and somebody would have their time. He'd go on with a short crew. He wouldn't have it! McBride was working himself up. Yates, having deliberately cleaned his plate of the last morsel of food, got up, dropped plate and cup into the wreck pan and walked over to McBride. He spoke shortly, low voiced, and McBride suddenly broke off his tirade and returned to the wagon while Yates strolled over and seated himself beside Benbow.

Rusty realized for the first time that he was holding Leonard Carlisle's arm. So did Carlisle. Simultaneously they moved, Rusty releasing his hold, Carlisle wrenching his arm away. They looked at each other, and then Carlisle got up and started back to his deserted plate. For an instant, in the surprise of the swift trouble, they had forgotten their enmity.

Rusty, forgetting for the moment the trouble between Travis and Benbow, wondered at his own reaction. He had pulled Carlisle down and kept him out of danger. Now why was that? he wondered. And why had not Carlisle instantly resented it? He didn't like Carlisle, and Carlisle didn't like him. Why had they both reacted as they had?

But there were other things to think about. Rusty, his meal finished, put plate and cup in the wreck pan for Deems to wash and went to his rolled-out bed. He sat down on his tarp and fashioned a cigarette. McBride had failed. He had not been able to make Travis and Benbow drop their difficulty. All McBride's orders and actions had been unavailing, but short, curt words from Honey Yates had pierced the anger of the two combatants and caused them to put their trouble aside. Now why was that? Certainly it was odd that two hands should disobey and disregard their boss and then listen to an ordinary rider, listen to a man without authority. Rusty puffed slowly on his cigarette and thought about it. Other small facts appeared in his thoughts and memory, little items that before had carried no particular significance. He flipped his cigarette off into the dark and, reaching down, began to pull off his boots.

That night when he and Travis went out to relieve the guard on the herd Rusty was still thinking about the happenings at supper. The relieved guard went in to his bed and, riding in opposite directions, Rusty and Gil Travis slowly circled the cattle, staying well out from the dark mass of the bedded steers. An hour passed, and then as the two men met Travis spoke, low voiced. "Let's drop back an' take a smoke."

That was customary and all right. The two

retired away from the herd, rolled their cigarettes and, shielding the flames of their matches, lit the tobacco. Rusty shifted, preparatory to resuming his patrol. Travis spoke:

"I kind of went haywire at supper."

"Uh-huh," Rusty agreed.

"Benbow rubs me the wrong way." There was gritting hatred in Travis' voice. "Him an' me have had trouble before."

"Yeah?"

"Uh-huh."

A little silence. Then: "We come from the same country. I've knowed him a long time. Nothin' good about him neither."

If Gil Travis was in a mood for confidences Rusty was willing to let him talk. He drew on his cigarette and waited. Travis said no more. Rusty, after a long moment of silence, spoke: "Yates kind of horned in at supper. You fello's wasn't listenin' much to Mc-Bride."

"A man don't listen to a fello' that . . ." Travis stopped abruptly. "Guess we'd better go on," he said, his voice a different timbre, not carrying the savagery that it had before.

"Guess we'd better," Rusty agreed.

They resumed their patrol about the sleeping steers. As he rode Rusty pondered. What had Travis been about to say? "A man don't listen to a fello' that . . ." Travis had said and then stopped. To a fello' who does what? Rusty wondered.

Two days brought the Watrous herd to the crossing of Red River late in the afternoon. There were two houses and a store close by the crossing, and as the cattle came on, the wagon rolled past the herd and went to the store. McBride split off and joined the wagon, and Rusty knew that the foreman intended to restock his rolling commissary from the goods at the store. The cattle were moving on toward the crossing which was wide and shallow, the stage of water in the river being good. One or two others of the crew turned from the herd and went loping off toward the tiny settlement. The wagon had stopped at the store, and McBride and a stranger were riding down toward the herd. They wheeled in behind the cattle and rode along together, not fifteen feet from Rusty, who was working in the drag.

"I'd help you back with anythin' you cut," Rusty heard McBride say to his companion. "We ain't had water today, an' they'll be hard to hold for you to work."

The young man with the beard said: "All right, McBride. Shove 'em across an' I'll work your herd on the far side."

McBride rode away, and the trail cutter

fell in place beside Rusty as the cattle began to move.

The steers spread out along the river, watering, the lead steers knee-deep in the river. Rusty let his horse drink and came back from the stream, joining the trail cutter once more. They had introduced themselves. The trail cutter was Charlie Mitchell. He carried authority for most of the Texas brands and was hired by the recently formed association of Texas stockmen. At one time Mitchell had worked for Goodnight and, young as he was, he was well and favorably known, both to the drovers and to his employers.

There were four herds ahead of the Watrous outfit, Mitchell said, and there were any number behind. Sigloe, with Ad Marble's cattle, was more than a week's drive away. Mitchell had that word. Indeed Mitchell was informed as to the position of almost all the herds that were coming, at least of those within a week or two weeks' drive of the river.

"I've known McBride quite a while," Mitchell informed. "He's a good man. An' Watrous is all right."

Rusty nodded. The steers were still watering and Rusty kept his eye on them. When they lifted their heads and casually turned to come out of the stream, it would be time to go to work. Up ahead Rusty could see the men who had visited at the store, returning to the cattle.

"McBride's outfits are generally pretty clean," Mitchell said. "I don't have no trouble cuttin' 'em, anyhow. He's different from a lot."

"You have some trouble sometimes?" Rusty asked, not because he did not know that Mitchell had trouble, but just to keep the conversation going.

"Plenty," Mitchell answered curtly. "There's outfits come through here that pay their hands from the cattle they pick up along the drive. Never put out a cent of wages. A man that can't get eight or ten head of cows shoved into the herd ain't worth his keep, they figure."

Rusty said, "Uh-huh," thoughtfully. He had heard of outfits like that. They picked up local cattle as their herd moved and tried to get them past the trail cutter.

"Slippery Smith is comin' tomorrow," Mitchell commented.

Rusty wondered if the conversation had made Mitchell think of Smith. Apparently it had.

"He comes by his name honest," Mitchell stated. "That much about him is honest, anyhow."

"He's right behind us?" Rusty queried.

"Just a day behind you." Mitchell was looking at the cattle. "That's a funny way to trail brand a herd," he said, changing the subject abruptly. "Not too safe, I'd think."

"We got all the steers the LM gathered," Rusty explained. "McBride didn't want the delay of trail brandin' 'em so we brubbed an ear."

"I'd ruther burn a mark on 'em if it was me," Mitchell announced. "Well, looks like they're through drinkin'. You know how much water an old cow can drink?"

"Eight barrels, if you have to pump it," Rusty answered. "Well, here we go."

The cattle were through drinking now. In the center men were pushing steers on into the river. The Red was down. There was no swimming water. The steers splashed across. Along the wings and in the rear men threw cattle toward the center. Logy with water, the steers moved slowly but steadily toward the farther bank.

When the last of the cattle were across four men fell back to help ford the wagon, and the rest of the crew, throwing the steers together, held them for Mitchell.

Mitchell worked the herd expertly. Yates and Travis were with him, and when he saw an animal he wanted Mitchell designated it and either Yates or Travis cut it out. The herd was fairly clean. Mitchell did not cut more than a dozen animals, and some of these McBride himself showed him: known strays that had come into the herd along the trail. There was one steer with a grubbed ear that was cut out from the herd. That steer's brand was indistinct, but when the animal was thrown and the brand picked clean with a knife blade, the LM brand showed up.

Finished with the herd, Mitchell bade a business-like good-by to McBride and, with Rusty told off to help him, recrossed the animals he had cut out. The crew drifted the herd along toward the bed ground that McBride selected. The wagon and remuda being crossed, the whole outfit disappeared from sight in the folded hills north of the river.

Rusty helped Mitchell recross the cattle he had cut and, on the far bank of the Red River, stopped his horse. "You'll see Sigloe, won't you?" he asked needlessly.

"Sure," Mitchell agreed.

"Tell him I'll be lookin' for him in Dodge City," Rusty continued. "I'll get there first, an' Tom an' me will have the place all clean for him."

Mitchell grinned. "I heard about you an' Flanders an' Sigloe," he chuckled. "You're goin' to have a time of it in Dodge?"

"Figurin' on it."

"Wish I could be with you," Mitchell said. "I'll tell Sigloe. So long, Shotridge." He held out his hand and Rusty took it. Then for the third time that day he splashed his horse into the Red River.

When he reached camp, made below a little hill, he found that Telesfor had roped and staked Toughy, that the horses had gone out and that everything was in order. He found, too, that someone had taken time to go to the store at the crossing. There was whisky in camp, more than one bottle, and several men were smoking cigars. An air of expectation, almost of hilarity, pervaded the atmosphere about the wagon. Rusty could sense it but could not understand it. He ate his supper and saddled Toughy, mounted the horse briefly and, satisfied that Toughy had forsworn bucking for that evening at least, staked the horse. When he came back to carry his rolled bed from where it had been dumped, Benbow, surprisingly, came to give him a hand. Never, all through the long days of the trip north, had a man helped Rusty carry his bed, and now here was surly Benbow, the least likely of all, lending a hand.

"Thanks," Rusty said when they put the bed down on the spot he had chosen. "Everybody seems to be feelin' pretty good tonight."

"Why not?" Benbow retorted. "We're across the Red now. Why shouldn't we feel good?"

He walked off then, leaving Rusty standing there, following him with puzzled eyes. They were across the Red River all right, but why was that a matter for rejoicing? Rusty thrust his hat far back on his head and scratched his head in perplexity.

Chapter VII

As the herd moved on north above the Red River the good humor of the crew increased. To Rusty, watching, it became more and more apparent that McBride had little control over his men. There was first the matter of the whisky brought into camp at the Red River crossing. Ordinarily trail bosses, knowing that they were not dealing with cherubs and infants, did not attempt to curb the spirits of their men while in town. But on the trail it was different. On the trail the trail crew was an army, subject to discipline, for they were entrusted with a fortune in cattle. The Watrous herd, for example, would be worth seventy-five thousand dollars, delivered intact in Dodge City. Consequently drinking along the trail was discouraged. A man might have a good time in town, might listen to the wolf howl and hear the owl hoot, but he had to be ready to work the next morning if he wanted to hold his job. With the Watrous outfit supplied with whisky from the crossing store, it was different. Benbow was so drunk the night of the crossing that he could not stand his guard, and on the day following, another of the trail crew became so intoxicated that he could only ride in the bed wagon and sleep. Rusty waited for the explosion that he was sure would come from McBride. When it did not come he was surprised.

Gradually, with the loosening of spirits following the crossing, Rusty became certain of his knowledge. He and Carlisle, Nugget and Telesfor and Deems took their orders from McBride, but the others were only nominally under the supervision of the trail boss. It seemed to Rusty, an onlooker, that Honey Yates had more real authority than did McBride. McBride, Rusty believed, could not help but feel this as, he was certain, did Deems, Nugget and Telesfor. Of Carlisle Rusty could not be at all certain.

Carlisle and Yates were thick as thieves, always together around the camp, drawing their beds close together at night.

There was a change in Carlisle. He was not so arrogant, was a better fellow, not so standoffish. And, too, he was growing brown and lean as the days wore on.

The herd swung west after they had crossed the river. Why, McBride did not say, and no one asked. The trail followed the ridge between the Red River and the Canadian. East and north of them was the Comanche reservation and Camp Supply. Perhaps McBride's change in direction could be accounted for because of these. Perhaps he had heard at the crossing store that there was trouble on the reservation; or perhaps the trail boss, having seen the way his crew worked on the whisky purchased at the crossing, wished to eliminate any likelihood of a fresh supply of liquor being obtained at the army post. Well west of the regular trail they straightened out again and, as nearly as country, rivers and timber would permit, went north.

This was no man's land that the Watrous herd traversed. There was no law north of the Red River, no law at all save that casual law administered by the military, the few U.S. deputy marshals and the law a man carried on his hip or in a saddle scabbard. Outlaws, men who were "short" in Texas, whose names decorated the famous Ranger Black Book or who were wanted in Kansas or Nebraska or Colorado found sanctuary in the Nations. All his life Rusty Shotridge had heard of this country, and while the Big Bend and the country around Arroyo Grande were tough enough, he knew that it could not compare in sheer ferocity with the district through which they now traveled.

When camp was made two days north of the river the Watrous outfit had visitors. Four men, all young, all bearded, all heavily armed, came riding in and stopped their horses beyond the wagon. They did not dismount but sat their saddles, surveying the camp carefully. McBride walked out to them and spoke a greeting: "Howdy. Get down an' rest yorese'ves."

At that the tallest of the strangers answered: "Howdy," and came down from his horse. It was not until the tall man was on the ground that the others dismounted.

"Supper's about ready," McBride commented. "Come an' eat with us."

"Thank you kindly," the man who had first dismounted answered. "We'll do that. You got bacon for supper?"

"We have," McBride assured, and the tall man grinned. "Bacon, boys!" he said and then, turning to McBride: "We been out of bacon a long time. Coffee too."

"Make yorese'ves at home," McBride invited.

The four newcomers accepted the invitation, interpreting it literally. Rusty noted that they stayed together, that no man walked behind them and that they were always on the outside edge of the circle of men. He accepted these things as commonplace, for he knew what these strangers were. They were outlaws, living in the Nations because they could not dwell safely elsewhere. Apparently they had recently been engaged in some form of lawlessness or else they would have renewed their supplies. They were but just now coming from their hiding.

No one asked the newcomers their names, and no information in particular was given them. This was the Watrous trail crew, the strangers learned, and the steers were bound for Dodge City. In return the trail drivers learned that the tall man was Kansas, the smallest one Chico and that the other two were Gus and Red, all this by casual allusion and drawling talk. Kansas did the talking for the four, the other three remaining silent but watchful. The watchfulness, Rusty knew, was not because of outright suspicion but because of habit.

When supper was over Kansas paid for the meal with information.

"Yo're a right smart west of the trail," he observed. "Mebbe it's not such a good idea, neither. Ol' Eagle Claws is camped around ten miles west of you with a lot of young bucks. He had trouble with a herd or two last year. Made 'em give him some beef to go through his country."

McBride nodded. He knew that at times the Indians that inhabited the Nations demanded toll from passing herds. "I don't mind partin' with a beef or two," the trail boss answered. "I wanted to miss Camp Supply, an' the grass is better this way."

"Yeah," Kansas drawled. "It's dry over east, but there's plenty of grass here."

There was more talk. McBride urged his guests to spend the night. When they would not he saw that Deems gave them coffee and a chunk of bacon, forestalling any offer of payment that might have been made, and walked out with the four when they took their horses to depart. When Kansas and Red, Gus and Chico were gone there was an epidemic of story-telling about the fire. Each man on the Watrous crew, so it seemed, excepting only McBride, Carlisle, Rusty and Yates, had been in close contact with some famous outlaw. Each told his experiences. The talk went on into the night, the softly drawling voices of the raconteurs lulling Rusty to sleep after he had taken to his blankets.

In the morning the herd moved on through the well-watered, heavily grassed country, and as the day progressed clouds began to form in the east until a heavily lowering black line of them towered above the horizon, reaching down to it.

"Them fello's last night said that it was dry over east," Gil Travis commented to Rusty as they sat watching the steers graze. "It ain't dry there now. It's rainin' the bottom out."

"Rainin' straight down," Rusty agreed. "Looks like it's workin' this way an' we might get some of it."

"I ain't lived in this country long enough to prophesy the weather," Travis replied.

As the day drew to an end the lowering clouds closed down. There was an occasional low mutter of thunder, and when finally the herd was bedded and camp made, the trail hands were particularly watchful. They staked their horses with care, and Deems made down his bed under the wagon and not only hobbled but sidelined his mule teams. The cattle were restless, refusing to lie down as was their wont, and over all hung the clouds and the heavy, oppressive heat.

"If I was runnin' things," Travis announced, "I'd call a rain guard tonight. Mebbe the old man will do that."

But McBride gave no such order. The camp was silent, a tension on it, as though the little wind which had sprung up brought a foretaste of trouble. When Rusty Shotridge went to bed he simply took off his hat and turned in, boots and all. Rusty did not like the weather, the temper of the cattle or anything about the whole setup. He noted that neither Travis nor Nugget took off much clothing, and McBride was still up when Rusty went to bed.

At midnight, wakened for his guard, he went out to the cattle. The steers were standing, heads lifted, not a one of the twenty-five hundred lying down. With Gil Travis riding a circle against him, Rusty went around the herd. Over in the east, much nearer now, the lightning popped and crackled, and the constant, ominous growl of thunder hung almost constantly in the air.

Rusty sang. Not that singing would do

much good, but at least it told the steers that he was coming and so kept him from frightening them by sudden approach. *"La Noche Blanca," "Tres Años Hace,"* the old Spanish songs came not unmusically from Rusty's throat, and accompanying them was the constant diapason rumbling of the thunder. Gil Travis was singing, too, and before the guard was over McBride appeared for a brief inspection and circle.

Relieved of his guard, back in his blankets once more, Rusty tried to sleep but could not. He threw back the tarp, seeking coolness, and small drops of rain spattered upon him. Rusty pulled up the tarp again, covering his body but not his face. Staring up at the sky, overcast and gloomy, his thoughts drifted. He could almost see Marica in the cool dimness of the Secáte's porch, could almost hear her voice.

"It makes a great deal of difference to me. . . ."

How sweet her voice had been! Back at the Secáte on the honeysuckle-covered porch she had been close, and Rusty, like the fool he was, had walked on to his horse. He should have gone to her then. What if she had turned and fled? He should have followed her. But that was past and gone, and here he was, Rusty Shotridge, lying on

126

his soogans, letting the rain fall on his face and dreaming. If only he . . .

Rusty's head was close to the earth. Into his ears came now another rumbling sound, other than the roll of the thunder. He knew that low, sinister sound, the noise of many hoofs pounding on hard-packed ground. Somewhere, somewhere close by, there was a herd running. Rusty sprang up from his bed. As he came to his feet lightning flashed. The herd was a quarter of a mile away, west of the camp, and the blue flame flickering from the overhanging clouds gave an eerie picture that Rusty could not forget. There were the Watrous cattle, the black bulk of them, no individual discernible in the sudden flash of light, a milling sea of horns and lifted heads; and south of them, stretched out like a serpent, came a flowing river to join that sea, a tide of running cattle. Rusty's shrill shout brought men from their blankets. Rusty himself was already running toward his staked horse. As he reached Toughy and freed the stake rope another flash of lightning came and with it the crash of its accompanying thunder. That thunder crash was prolonged and echoed as the running cattle crashed into the Watrous steers, and the herd, as one, left the bed ground.

It was every man for himself and the

cattle. That was the rule. The cattle first, then the individual. Rusty went up on Toughy and started, and all about him Watrous riders hit their night horses and pulled out. For a little time there were shouts that rang in Rusty's ears. Then as Toughy really got down to work he split off. He knew the direction of the run, and his ears told him that he was closing in. Then through the night he could see the bulk of the cattle. But this was only for an instant, for as though some celestial hand had dumped a bucket, the rain came, torrents of it, closing down, shutting Rusty and his horse within a curtained space through which they moved at a mad run and which always accompanied them.

Ordinarily in a run the riders would bunch on one point of the cattle and make a concerted effort to turn them. By so doing they could cause a mill in the endless circle of which all the run would shortly be taken out of the steers. But with rain and invisibility this was impossible. Rusty, clinging to the flank of the herd, knew that it was splitting. They were in no recognized trail which the steers might blindly and instinctively follow. The idea was, as Rusty saw it, to stay with what he could. If the cattle split up then he would be with a bunch, could eventually turn and hold them when they grew tired and so keep at least a portion of the herd together.

As the rain came the lightning ceased. Generally lightning stays on the outskirts of a storm, at its front, along the sides, in the rear. The center, where heavy rain occurs, rarely carries electricity. It was pitch black; there were running cattle to his left, and Rusty thanked his fortune for Toughy, big and mean but honest and clear footed. Once the horse stumbled but recovered. Once they slid down a bank and scrambled up the other side. Rusty made no attempt at guidance. He had to trust his horse and he had to stay with him.

The pace slowed. The rain lessened. Presently the cattle were only trotting. It was then that Rusty made his move. With the thinning of the rain he could see a little and he put Toughy ahead, trying to reach the point of the steers. He gained that position and made his try. Yelling, shooting in front of the cattle, Rusty swung down on the leaders.

More than an hour had gone by since he had jumped from his blankets. The steers were tired, but they trotted steadily, apparently with no destination but only the fixed idea of getting away from the thing that had frightened them. The rain had thinned now so that it was no longer a curtain but rather a steady, methodical downpour. And, too, light was coming. Rusty had come off guard at two o'clock. He had spent nearly an hour in camp. He had been with the running cattle for more than an hour. It was nearing four o'clock and, save for the rain and overhanging clouds, daylight would have come. Now there was light enough to see. Rusty, surveying the steers, saw that he had a little bunch of about two hundred head. Where the others were he did not know and could not immediately ascertain. His own bunch was his immediate concern and so, as he crowded Toughy down on the leaders, as he popped the cartridges in his six-shooter, as he yelled and shouted, he did not worry about the rest of the cattle or the crew. The leaders, under Rusty's coercion, turned a trifle. He redoubled his efforts. The lead steers swung to the left, turned, swung further and presently came against the drags and followed them. Rusty had his mill made. Pulling Toughy back, he watched, alert to check any steer that might try to escape from the endless chain.

Gradually the pace of the cattle slowed and became a walk. Gradually the walk slowed. The mill shifted slightly, the ground sloping and the cattle following the slope. Then the movement ceased entirely, and Rusty pushed back his sopping hat and wiped water from his forehead and face. His bunch had stopped. He wondered about the rest now.

Seeking a vantage point for observation, Rusty left his charges and rode back toward the higher ground. As he rode he looked down. He could hardly see his horse's feet. He could not, after he had ridden two hundred yards, see the steers at all. The clouds hung lowering, reaching down to the earth. Fog was all about, blanketing the ground, cutting off vision. It was useless to try to spy out the country. Rusty could easily lose the cattle he had held. He turned and rode back, quick relief welling up in him as, coming down the slope, he came under the fog and could see the bulk of his steers looming through the mist. He rode around them. They were spread out slightly, grazing on the wet grass as peacefully as though they had never run, as though they had never been panic-stricken. The rain had ceased. Rusty stopped his horse. Toughy was weary, bone-tired. At the moment Rusty was mighty sorry for Toughy. Tired as the horse was, he could not rest. Rusty must hold the steers together or they would be lost in the fog. And so he stirred Toughy again and rode once more upon his slow circle. When the fog lifted, when the weather cleared, he would find the wagon and the outfit. He completed the circle, began on another and pulled Toughy to a halt. There was someone coming through the fog, a rider. Rusty called, and the dim figure came toward him. Rusty peered through the mist, staring to make certain. Then he spoke, calling a name:

"Carlisle. This way, Carlisle!"

The figure turned slightly from his course and came on. Wearily the horse stopped. Rusty looked at the rider, and Leonard Carlisle returned that look, his eyes blank and uncomprehending.

"Where's the rest of 'em, Carlisle?" Rusty demanded. "Do you know where the rest are? Where's the wagon?"

Still the blank stare from uncomprehending eyes. Leonard Carlisle spoke slowly, his voice thick with horror. "I was right beside him," he grated. "I heard him."

"Beside who?" Rusty snapped. "Who did you hear, Carlisle?"

"I was beside McBride," Carlisle replied, his words coming with an effort. "Right beside him. I could have touched him. I saw him go down and I heard him scream. I . . .

My God, I . . ." He covered his haggard face with his hands, and his horse — for companionship — took a step forward and stopped close by Toughy.

Rusty's own eyes were wide with reflected horror. He knew what Carlisle had heard, knew the thing he had seen, could picture it: the black bulk of fluidly running cattle, the rumble of their hoofs, the rattle of clashing horns and the steadying presence of a rider beside him, of a man who was along. And then the sudden drop, the blotting out of that man alongside and a rising scream that never reached a peak, that never finished but was lost in the thunder of pounding hoofs, cut short by them.

"Steady," Rusty commanded, his own voice a little shaken. "Steady, Carlisle. Maybe he isn't gone. Maybe you just lost him."

"I heard him scream and I saw him go down," Carlisle repeated shakenly. "I . . ." He stopped. There was a brief silence, and then Rusty Shotridge spoke the epitaph of the trail:

"That was the chance he took. Tough luck."

Somehow there was a bond between these two men at the moment. Rusty did not like Leonard Carlisle. He thought him a pompous, conceited young prig that could not hold his own on a man's job. Carlisle, for his part, hated Rusty Shotridge with all his heart. Rusty was just about everything that Carlisle would have liked to be and could not be: competent, ready, free of speech and action. And, too, Carlisle had seen Ellen Watrous kiss Rusty as they stood on the front porch of the Stockman Hotel in San Marcial. That recollection rankled, for Leonard Carlisle was in love with Ellen Watrous. And yet the tragedy that Carlisle had witnessed but a few hours before, the need for companionship that both riders felt, bound them momentarily.

"What will we do now?" Carlisle asked finally.

"Wait till the fog burns off an' find the outfit," Rusty answered. "The steers ran north. The wagon and remuda are someplace south of us."

"But they're scattered." Carlisle was awakening to the fact that his investment was in danger. "They . . ."

"There's men an' horses aplenty," Rusty interrupted curtly. "We'll gather cattle an' make a count. I wonder whose outfit it was that ran into us. They sure come a-hellin'."

"I don't know," Carlisle said. "The fog's thinning. I'll ride up and take a look around."

"All right," Rusty agreed and turned his horse to climb the slope.

As they rode side by side Carlisle spoke once more: "What will we do now?" he asked, more to himself than to his companion. "If McBride's dead what will we do?"

Rusty glanced at Carlisle from the corners of his eyes. For the first time in his life, Rusty judged, Leonard Carlisle was directly up against something, directly confronted with a question that he himself had to answer. Rusty presented that fact.

"That," he said, and there was grim satisfaction in his voice, "will be up to you, Carlisle. You're the owner of the steers. You an' Watrous."

CHAPTER VIII

When they reached the higher ground Rusty could see that the fog was moving, rolled by a wind and in the east whence the storm had come there was a breaking of the clouds. Looking back down the slope, Rusty could see the steers he had held, and not far to the west there was another little bunch of cattle. Rusty pointed to them.

"We've got to work back west," he said, forgetting that he had placed responsibility with Carlisle. "The wagon's someplace west an' south of us. We've got to have fresh horses an' work out all this country. We can throw our bunch with those other cattle."

Carlisle made no comment or suggestion but turned when Rusty turned and, with Rusty, rode back to the steers once more. Both the cattle and the horses were tired. It was a chore to gather the steers and string them out toward the west. This task was accomplished, and when the cattle finally moved the sun was shining through.

When the two riders finally reached the bunch of cattle that Rusty had seen they found the steers were not a part of the Watrous herd. There was more than one brand in the little bunch, but for the greater part they were trail branded with a hackamore mark run across the nose.

"These aren't our cattle," Carlisle said sharply as the two small herds joined. "We should have kept ours by themselves."

Rusty grunted. "These belong to the outfit that ran into us last night," he said. "It doesn't make any difference who they belong to. We'll have to throw everything we can gather into one bunch an' work the herd. The other outfit will be doin' the same thing."

Perforce Carlisle contented himself with

that. Rusty looked at the cattle. "I don't like to leave 'em," he stated. "We got anyhow three hundred head here. I don't like to ride off an' let 'em go, but we've got to find the wagon an' get fresh horses."

Carlisle looked at the cattle and then at his companion. "I'll stay here," he volunteered. "You go on. I . . ." Carlisle stopped. He had been about to admit that he could not find the wagon, that if he left the cattle he would be lost. Rusty sensed that. His courtesy made him give Carlisle an excuse.

"Mebbe that would be the best thing," Rusty agreed. "My horse is some fresher than yours."

It was not true. Toughy was on his last legs, using his last reservoir of strength, and Carlisle's horse, compared with Toughy, was fresh. Still Rusty gave Carlisle that graceful way out. "I'll be back as soon as I can get here," he said and, nodding to Carlisle, rode away toward the southwest.

Within three miles he found the wagon. Deems and Telesfor had moved it. With daybreak Deems and Telesfor, knowing that their presence was necessary, had loaded the wagon, brought up the remuda and come on. Deems had a fire built, and Telesfor had the remuda close by. Nugget and Benbow were at the wagon with Deems.

They hailed Rusty as he came up, demanding news.

Rusty had news only of Carlisle and McBride. He retailed his knowledge, telling the Watrous men what Carlisle had said of the wagon boss. Deems shook his head when he heard that word, and Nugget, his old face drawn and seamed with weariness, growled a curse. "We got to find him," Nugget announced.

To that Rusty agreed. Deems had coffee on the fire, and each of the men refreshed himself with a cup of the hot liquid.

"I've got to take a fresh horse out to Carlisle," Rusty announced, "an' pilot him to the wagon. We got about three hundred head together, some of ours an' some of the other outfit's. They're trail branded with a hackamore."

"Slippery Smith's outfit," Deems growled. "Damn him! His herd run right into ours an' started them. They was holdin' all right till that happened."

Rusty shrugged. Recriminations were of no use now. "I'll send Carlisle in," he announced. "I guess we'll all have to look for McBride, but I'll shove what cattle we got back this way."

Nugget nodded. "We . . ." he began and stopped. There was another rider coming toward the wagon, approaching from the south. "Here's Yates," Nugget said.

Honey Yates came on in, dismounted and let his weary horse stand. Walking up to the others, he looked at them, his smooth face impassive.

"What is it, Yates?" Nugget demanded.

"We found McBride," Yates answered slowly. "That was Slippery Smith's outfit that run into us last night. They're movin' along this way. McBride's in their wagon."

"Is he . . . ?" Deems began.

"Squashed to a pulp." Yates completed the unfinished question. "They all run over him, I guess. Where's Carlisle?"

"Out with a bunch of cattle," Rusty answered. "I'm goin' to take a fresh horse out to him now."

Yates nodded. "Get him in," he directed. "Benbow, you go with Shotridge an' help him shove what cattle he's got this way. We're goin' to have to bury McBride an' build a roundup."

Rusty, looking at Yates, wondered if the man was as calloused as he sounded. No matter. Yates had spoken the truth. Without reply Rusty moved toward his horse. He would change horses and take a fresh mount out to Carlisle.

"Take one of McBride's horses, Shotridge," Yates called after him. "That string of yore's is no good, an' McBride won't be usin' his."

Saddle changed over to his fresh horse, another horse in tow on a lead rope, Rusty started east again. Benbow, also freshly mounted, went with him. There was no conversation between the two men, no word spoken until they reached Carlisle. There Rusty reported briefly the knowledge that Yates had given him. He held the fresh horse while Carlisle changed his saddle, put the lead rope on Carlisle's weary mount and pointed.

"The wagon is down below that ridge," Rusty directed. "Just by a little motte of live oak. You can't miss it."

Carlisle nodded, swung up into his saddle and, leading his tired night horse, started ahead.

Rusty looked at Benbow and nodded toward the bunch of cattle. "Might as well start these in," he said.

The steers were reluctant to move. Rusty and Benbow worked at their task. They got their cattle started, kept them moving slowly and, coming to the ridge that Rusty had pointed out to Carlisle, saw that already a little congregation of cattle was collected below it. Some distance from the herd the

140

wagons were camped, two of them close together and with one fire. Evidently Slippery Smith's outfit had come up during Rusty's absence. With Benbow's help Rusty shoved his gather down the slope of the ridge and dropped them with the other cattle; then he and Benbow went to camp.

All the Watrous crew was in save only McBride. There were strangers, too, gathered about the fire, and Rusty saw Carlisle and Yates standing in conversation with the smoothly built, black-haired man who had talked out of turn in the Bank Saloon back in San Marcial. Rusty and Benbow dismounted and let their horses stand.

The talk about the fire was restrained. Tragedy hung over the camp. Ordinarily the riders would have been recounting their experiences during the run. Now they spoke briefly, their own past danger forgotten in the pall that hung about the wagons. Carlisle, Yates and Smith, who had stood a short distance away from the rest, approached the fire and stopped.

"You all know what happened," Slippery Smith said curtly. "We've got to bury Mac first an' then we've got to gather cattle."

No one moved or spoke. Carlisle advanced half a step. "Mr. Smith will give the orders," he announced, "for both crews while we're working cattle. Shotridge, you and Benbow take spades and dig a grave up there by the live oaks."

"You can borrow our spade, Benbow," Smith offered. "Get it for him, Sam."

One of the Smith riders walked off toward the wagon. Rusty got the spade from the Watrous wagon and stood waiting until Sam came back. Benbow wore a scowl on his face, but neither he nor Rusty made comment as they walked toward the motte of trees. Rusty had quarreled with Scott McBride, forced his presence on him, watched him and had seen his weakness, and now he was to help dig McBride's grave.

Up by the live-oak motte, out from it so that they would not dig through roots, the two fell to work cutting sod. They marked out an oblong, cut the sods from it and, sweating and in silence, delved into the rich earth beneath the grass. All along the trail there were graves such as this they made, graves unmarked and unadorned, graves that contained the bodies of men who had gone up the trail for the last time. Down into the earth they dug, Rusty and Benbow, their spades flashing in the sunlight that had come, sweat glistening on their foreheads, blisters forming on their hands from the unaccustomed labor.

Slippery Smith appeared above them and looked down. "Deep enough, I reckon," Smith announced.

Benbow and Rusty climbed out.

They stood leaning on their spades while the two trail crews came up the hill. Four men carried a tarpaulin-wrapped bundle on their shoulders and deposited it beside the newly turned earth. Saddle ropes came into play, and the bundle was lowered into the grave.

"Anybody know a prayer?" Smith demanded.

For a moment no one moved, then Deems stepped forward. "Ain't much of a prayer," he growled. "I know the Twenty-third Psalm."

Smith nodded. Battered hats were pulled from long, unkempt hair. Joe Deems's voice rasped in the quiet:

"The Lord is my Shepherd, I shall not want . . ."

A man stirred. Over in the live-oak motte a bird fluttered from one branch to another.

". . . And I shall dwell in the house of the Lord forever." Deems's rasping voice stopped. Somebody growled deep in his chest: "Amen." Telesfor crossed himself. The silence held for a moment, and then Slippery Smith said: "When you get through fillin' the grave come down to camp."

That was all. Shoveling loose earth back into the grave, Rusty let the damp clods slip from his shovel blade and considered events. Benbow had left his spade, and Gil Travis, assuming it without command, worked beside Rusty. It was Gil who broke the silence.

"I've saw worse funerals," Travis commented. "Several. . . . Who do you reckon would of thought that Deems could quote Bible talk?"

Rusty did not answer. He was rounding the mound, placing sods on it. The sods would root and the grass would grow, but Scott McBride would not ride again.

Slippery Smith, assuming command of the roundup, dispatched riders to the north and west. The storm had come from the east, and naturally most of the cattle, when the run was finished, would have drifted with the storm. Seemingly no one but Rusty had stayed with and held a bunch. Others spoke of having been with a bunch of cattle but, unable to hold them, the cattle were spilled. Apparently there were Hackamore cattle and LM cattle all over the country. Rusty and Gil Travis were sent north and east to see if there were any animals east of the ridge. They found none but, despite Rusty's expostulations, Travis kept going. Rusty was positive that no animals would have gone so far as he and Travis went on their circle. He lost his temper finally and told Travis that he was going back and that Travis could go on if he wanted to. Travis, instead of arguing, turned and went back with Rusty, but it was sundown before they reached camp. They saw, as they came in, that a sizable herd had been collected about the nucleus that Rusty and Benbow had thrown together in the morning. Rusty was tired, hungry and angry, and he had nothing to say when he reached camp. Travis made his report to Smith and Carlisle and sought the Dutch ovens for food, and Rusty joined him there.

The spirit of depression hung over the camp. There was no talking, no banter among the men. That night men from both outfits stood guards, and the single big herd was circled throughout the night by four riders. The following morning the gather was resumed. This time Rusty was sent southeast on a circle, accompanying a laconic rider from Smith's outfit. They worked out that southeastern country, finding no cattle or sign of cattle. Well south and east of the wagons Rusty did encounter sign of the passage of four horses. These had been ridden, for they went on a straight line, and, examining the tracks, Rusty believed that they had been made by the four visitors, Kansas and Chico, Gus and Red, who had dropped in on the Watrous wagons the day prior to the run. He had no definite reason for this idea; it was simply a possibility. When he and his companion came back to the camp once more it was almost as late as on the previous day. Once more Rusty was tired and angry. He had been sent on a fool's errand, or so it seemed.

The talk that night was more lively. The depression caused by McBride's death was wearing off. Coming in to camp, Rusty noted that someone had fashioned a cross from two live-oak trunks and had driven the cross at the head of McBride's grave.

He took no part in the conversation about the camp, but listened to it. The men of both outfits seemed to think that all the cattle had been gathered. Rusty saw Yates and Smith talking together at the endgate of Smith's wagon, and when that conversation broke up Yates sought out Carlisle and talked with him. That conversation, too, broke up. Carlisle went over to talk to Smith, and Yates came to the fire where the others were assembled. He squatted down beside it, rolled a cigarette and, singling out

Benbow as the person to whom he spoke, but in reality speaking to all, made an announcement.

"Carlisle's goin' to take McBride's place himself," Yates stated. "For a while he thought that he'd put me in charge, but I talked him out of it. They're his cattle, an' he ought to be the boss. I told him I'd help him out but that he ought to run the outfit." Yates paused and looked around at the other Watrous men. There was no comment from any of the crew. Carlisle, leaving Smith, came over to the group.

"I been tellin' the boys that you'd take the herd on, Mr. Carlisle," Yates said.

Carlisle nodded briskly. "That's right," he announced. "After all, they're my cattle, mine and Colonel Watrous's. Tomorrow we'll cut the herd and then trim up and make a count."

That was cowman talk. Rusty wondered who had put it in Carlisle's mouth. Rusty said no word. There was no comment that he could make.

"Honey will be my *segundo,*" Carlisle announced. "Has anyone any questions?"

There were no questions. Of course there were none. Rusty turned from his fellows and sought his bed. Sitting on his tarp still damp from the rain, he wondered who had

147

ribbed Carlisle up to assuming command. Carlisle had about as much business setting up for a trail boss as — Rusty tugged savagely at a boot — as . . . Hell! There just wasn't any simile for it. The boot came off with a jerk.

The following morning the two outfits cut cattle. Rusty did not work in the herd. He was on the north side of the bunch, holding. Smith, as was proper, cut to the south, so maintaining his respective position to the trail, and the Watrous outfit cut to the north. The men working the herd used a liberal rule. Whenever they found a number of cattle, most of which bore the Watrous brand, together at the edge of the herd, they sliced off that bunch and threw it to the cut. Both herds would be retrimmed anyhow, and there was no use in trying to work out one individual animal now. Cattle came out of the main bunch in streams and were thrown to the cuts. Gradually the cuts grew, and the mixed herd thinned down until finally there was no mixed herd left. Then Yates and Benbow and Carlisle trimmed the Hackamore herd while Smith and two of his riders performed a like service for the Watrous bunch. The few animals that did not belong where they were found were recut and put in their respective herds.

Rusty saw Smith shake hands with Carlisle and Yates and go back to his herd, and Carlisle trotted off toward the north while Yates came around the herd.

"We'll string 'em out for a count," he announced when he reached Rusty, "an' then move along a piece. Carlisle wants to get clear of Smith so they can't get together again."

Rusty made no comment. The herd needed water, he knew, and there should be a distance put between the two outfits, but he doubted Carlisle's ability to count.

The cattle were strung out. Yates had loped up and was sitting his horse opposite Carlisle. As the cattle began to file between the two men, Rusty — in the rear — noted that something was wrong. For a moment he was not sure, and then it came home to him that there were too few cattle. There was a bunch missing; Rusty could have sworn to it. Still he said nothing, but shoved cattle along toward the counters.

The last of the steers filed between Carlisle and Yates, and Yates rode over to his companion. Rusty, of course, was with the steers. He was examining them in earnest now, riding along the edge of the herd, picking out markers. Some he found, but several were missing. Rusty *knew* now that the herd was short. He wondered if Carlisle had caught the shortage in the count. Carlisle and Yates rode up, and Yates, with a sweep of his arm, signaled the men on the north side to let the steers go. Apparently they were going to string out on the trail. Rusty sat his horse and looked at Carlisle, at Yates and at the moving steers. Nugget, coming up beside him, spoke briefly:

"We're short some."

"I know it," Rusty answered.

Nugget swore. "Must have missed some when we gathered," he said. "I'm goin' to tell Carlisle."

"Carlisle counted 'em," Rusty pointed out.

"He couldn't count a pen of rabbits!" Nugget rasped. "Come on, Shotridge."

Automatically Rusty followed Nugget. They reached Carlisle and stopped. Carlisle looked at them questioningly.

"What's the matter?" he asked.

Nugget cleared his throat. "I been talkin' to Shotridge," he said apologetically. "I looked at the herd an' there's some markers missin'. How did they count out, Mr. Carlisle?"

Yates had come back and was stopped beside Carlisle. Benbow and two other men were coming over to join the group. Rusty waited for Carlisle's answer.

"I can count cattle," Carlisle said crisply. "The herd tallied out, Nugget. They're all there."

Old Ben Nugget looked at Rusty, a question in his eyes. Benbow and the other two joined the group, falling into place behind Yates. Yates was watching Rusty and Nugget narrowly.

"But . . ." Nugget began.

"Yates and I got the same count," Carlisle announced with asperity. "There isn't a steer missing. We're moving cattle, Nugget. You'd better get to your job."

Ben Nugget was an old man and he backed down. Wordlessly he turned his horse and started off. Rusty remained alone, confronting the others.

"How about you, Shotridge?" Yates demanded, staring at Rusty. "You think we missed our count?"

Rusty sized up the odds. There were three men besides Yates confronting him, three men that would obey Yates, that took orders from him. Carlisle had missed the count, and Yates had fooled him; Rusty knew that. He knew, too, that Carlisle would not believe anything that he might say, that the enmity that lay between them precluded any chance of Carlisle's believing him. He also knew that Yates and the three hard-eyed men who sat behind him were ready to go to war. There was no chance of being believed and no chance of coming out of trouble if it started. Rusty Shotridge was no fool. He grinned sardonically at Yates, and his voice was sweetly drawling when he spoke.

"You counted 'em, Yates. You ought to know how many there are. I just work here."

"Then why don't you get to work?" Yates snapped.

"Right now," Rusty agreed placidly. "I'm on my way." He wheeled his horse and loped off. Behind Yates, Benbow made a swift movement that was checked as Yates turned and shook his head. Reluctantly Benbow dropped his hand from the butt of his gun.

"Just a troublemaker, Mr. Carlisle," Yates said smoothly. "If there was any way of gettin' rid of him I'd do it."

Chapter IX

The herd did not move far during the short time that was left of the day. The steers were thrown on water, a little creek that, rain-swollen, cut through the country, flowing toward the Canadian; and when the cattle were watered they crossed the stream and bedded on high ground. After supper, with no word of explanation to anyone, Yates took a horse and rode back south. Rusty maintained his own counsel, watching the others with narrowed, questioning eyes. Ben Nugget talked to Joe Deems. Save for McBride's absence the appearance and conduct of the camp was as usual. But there was an undercurrent of unrest, an undefinable feeling of something amiss. Rusty sensed that there was a break coming. When it came he would be in the middle of it. He had stuck out his neck when he went to Carlisle and Yates with Nugget.

Roughly, Rusty estimated, there were five hundred head of cattle short from the herd. Somewhere back along the way those cattle were located. Rusty debated with himself. There was not much that he could do about it. His knowledge was a worthless thing. Carlisle, in his arrogance, would not listen to anything that Rusty Shotridge might have to say. And Yates had helped steal those cattle, else why had Yates made the short count come out true? Not only had Yates helped steal the cattle, but also he had the backing of every man with the bunch save only Rusty, Telesfor, Nugget and Deems. Carlisle did not count, and Gil Travis was doubtful. There had been trouble between Travis and Benbow, and maybe Gil was not on Yates's side.

Turning from general considerations, Rusty turned his thoughts to his own predicament. Certainly he was in a tight, between a rock and a hard spot. Yates was aware now that Rusty knew the herd was short. Just how long Rusty would be allowed to live and carry that dangerous knowledge was problematical. Certainly he and Ben Nugget could not be allowed to get to Dodge City. If he wanted to look after his own hide the thing for Rusty Shotridge to do was to pull out. He thought about that for a time, then he shook his head. He couldn't just get up and leave, and he knew it. He had promised Bud Sigloe that he would meet Bud in Dodge City. Suppose he turned up in Dodge after deserting his outfit? What would Bud say and think? What would Tom Flanders think? And, too, there was his promise to Ellen. He couldn't quit the herd and look after Carlisle too. He couldn't look after Carlisle anyhow; the young fool was too high-headed to be looked after. Rusty grimaced ruefully. There was no chance of looking out for a man if he wouldn't let a fellow do it. No, the only thing Rusty could do was to stick along for a while and see what happened. Likely what would happen would be a bullet in the back for Rusty Shotridge. He would have to look out for that. So deciding, Rusty pulled his bed over close to the chuck wagon and rolled it out. There were two men beside Nugget in the outfit that he could trust. Nugget was not much force, but Telesfor and Joe Deems might make full hands if trouble came. Joe Deems carried a shotgun in the wagon and was an old pup and full of poison. Rusty looked around to locate the cook. Deems had Carlisle off to one side, talking to the younger man, and now and then the old cook wagged his pipestem by way of emphasis. Deems was laying down the law. Maybe — Rusty shrugged — Carlisle would believe Deems. It was a cinch that Carlisle wouldn't believe Rusty Shotridge.

Deems finished his talking and came back to the wagon. He crawled under it, spread down his own bed and, without a word or glance at Rusty, turned in. Not until Deems was under his tarp did he speak, then his comment was terse. "We'll count again in the mornin'."

Rusty grunted. Trouble was postponed until morning anyhow. "Yeah?" he drawled, answering Deems.

Honey Yates, leaving the Watrous wagon, rode back along the trail, crossed the creek and within a mile or two found Slippery Smith's camp. He announced his advent by a call from the darkness and, when Smith stood up beside the fire, came riding in. Smith walked out to Yates as the latter dismounted, and when Yates was on the ground he spoke briefly.

"Why did you come back, Honey? Trouble in your bunch?"

"Shotridge an' Nugget," Yates answered succinctly. "They come up right after we'd finished countin'. They both know the herd's short."

"What did Carlisle do?"

"He took my count. Hell, he can't count cattle. He never missed the bunch we got. He hates Shotridge's guts an' he wouldn't listen to him."

Slippery Smith nodded. "Yo're goin' to have to get shed of Shotridge an' Nugget," he drawled. "Can't you handle that, Honey?"

There was a small, chiding reproach in Smith's tone, and Yates bristled. "I can handle him any time," he snarled. "The thing I come back for is this, Slippery: With McBride dead, why don't we just take the whole works? Why fool with five hundred head or so when we can have 'em all?"

Slippery Smith scratched his chin thoughtfully. "It might be a good idea at that," he drawled. "How would you work it, Honey?"

"We got to get rid of Shotridge anyhow; why not Carlisle too?" Yates demanded. "Hell! We're in the Nations. Most anything could happen to him."

"It would be damned hard to explain at Dodge City," Smith said.

"Take the cattle on north to Montana then," Yates answered. "Don't stop at Dodge. Go on with 'em."

"I'll think it over," Smith promised. "We're goin' to brand the Hackamore on what we got yesterday. That 'll take a while. You won't be goin' so fast that we won't catch up. Let me think a little, Honey. I think we can do it."

Honey Yates grunted. "Of course we can," he snapped. "We'd have to split with the boys, but what of it? We're goin' to have to pay them off anyhow. An' if things get out I ain't goin' to worry. Not when I'm runnin' my own place in Canada, I ain't."

"It might work," Smith said again. "I tell you, Honey: I'll come up tomorrow or the next day an' pay you a visit. How about that?"

"If you don't come in I'm goin' to take

'em myself," Yates warned. "I'll talk to the boys, an' they'll throw in with me. You better come along pretty quick, Slippery."

"Tomorrow or the next day," Smith promised again. "I think I'll go with you, Honey. I think I will."

Honey Yates grunted again. "Then break out yore bottle an' we'll have a drink on it," he said. "I'm dry as dust, ridin' herd on that bunch of kids an' bein' nice to Carlisle. Damn him, every time I speak to him it pretty near chokes me. The damned stuck-up brat!"

Slippery Smith laughed. "Come on an' I'll give you that drink," he ordered good-naturedly. "You need it."

Yates did not stay long after drinking. He talked a little further to Slippery and then, mounting his horse, rode back north. He had been unable to exact a promise from Smith and he did not much care. Honey Yates was becoming possessed of delusions of grandeur. If Slippery Smith did not want to throw in with him there were others that would. Back at the Watrous camp there were men who obeyed him and who would listen to his ideas. If Smith turned down the proposition Honey Yates was ready to carry it through alone. Two thousand big steers sold in Montana would bring a nice price, and from Montana it was just a step across the line into Canada. Yates's eyes narrowed, and the tip of his tongue touched his lips as he anticipated the wealth that was coming his way. When he reached the Watrous camp he staked his horse and went to bed. Tomorrow he would talk things over with the boys.

Rusty Shotridge heard Yates come in. There had been a reshuffling of the guard, due to Yates's absence and the fact that Carlisle, having promoted himself, no longer stood guard. Carlisle had changed the watches, but Rusty still held his old place with Travis: the midnight shift.

At midnight, wakened by the man he was to relieve, Rusty got up and rode out to the cattle. Toughy was played out, and Rusty had shifted over to Big Enough for a night horse. He rode the sorrel, Travis close beside him, until they reached the cattle, and then, relieving the man who had stayed with the steers, began his endless circling, singing softly as he rode. Rested now after their run, the steers might take another notion to jump the bed ground. Rusty did not think that they would, for they were well broken to the trail and had held well during the storm; in fact, they had held until Slippery Smith's cattle came down on them. Riding circle around the steers, Rusty fell to thinking about that stampede. McBride had taken his outfit off the regular trail. So, too, had Smith. Rusty wondered if there was any connection between the facts. Seemingly there was. Slippery Smith, Rusty thought, was the likely man to have those missing steers. He wondered what Smith hoped to do with them.

Slippery Smith! He didn't come by that name of Slippery through chance. Back at the Red River crossing the trail cutter had said that Slippery came by his name honestly. Likely Smith had already figured out some way of handling those steers. Rusty thought about that too. Grimly he smiled. It was almost a certainty that the success of Slippery's scheme would depend upon Rusty Shotridge's not reaching Dodge City. But he intended to reach Dodge. Out there in the darkness, alone save for the steers and Gil Travis over on the other side of the herd, Rusty nodded to himself. Yes sir! Regardless of Slippery Smith or Honey Yates or any of their followers, Rusty Shotridge was going to reach Dodge City. And when he got there he'd see the thing clear through. Not only on account of Colonel Watrous and Ellen, but just to show Leonard Carlisle and his sister that he was a man. He'd show them. Particularly Marcia Carlisle. He'd sure show *her!*

When he met Travis on the next round he suggested a smoke. They retired a little distance from their charges and, having rolled and lighted their cigarettes, sat for a short time in silent communion. Then Rusty spoke:

"Carlisle's goin' to count the herd again tomorrow mornin', Gil."

Travis was silent for half a dozen heartbeats. Then: "I wouldn't do it if I was him," he said quietly.

Rusty nodded. It was evident now that Travis was in with Yates and the rest. Rusty had suspected as much, and now the suspicion was confirmed.

"Mebbe," Rusty said softly, "a man 'll have a chance to show where he stands, Gil. That might happen tomorrow mornin'."

Travis made no reply. Rusty's voice was still soft. "What was it you was goin' to say about Scott McBride the other night? You said somethin' about not listenin' to a fello', an' then you stopped. Was it mebbe that you didn't think much of a fello' that had sold out his boss?"

Still Travis did not answer. Rusty carefully ground out his cigarette against the horn of his saddle. "You been takin' Colonel Watrous's wages for quite a while, Gil," he

161

drawled. "Well, I'm goin' round again." Rusty rode off, leaving Travis alone in the darkness, his location marked only by the tiny glow of his cigarette.

When finally the two were relieved Rusty rode into camp to find that Travis had not waited to drink a cup of coffee with him. Travis was in bed. Rusty sighed as he sat down and pulled off his boots. He had not got very far with Gil Travis.

When morning broke the men went about their accustomed tasks. The horses came in and were penned. Events went on as usual. Joe Deems called the crew to breakfast, and as the men selected their plates and cups and went to the fire for food, Rusty, last in line, stopped and looked to the east. There were riders silhouetted against the eastern light, four men that came on apace, and Rusty, stepping out for a clearer view, called the attention of the camp to their visitors.

"Company comin'," he announced.

The riders came on and stopped just away from the wagon. They were the same quartet that had once before visited the trail crew: Kansas, Red, Gus and Chico. Kansas grinned a laconic grin and swung down from his mount.

"Howdy," he drawled. "Me an' the boys got flooded out. We thought mebbe we could get a meal off you."

It was Carlisle who answered. "Get down," he invited. "Breakfast is just ready."

The outlaw's three companions dismounted and approached the wagon. When their plates were filled and they had formed a little group, backs against the wagon, Kansas spoke again.

"Where's McBride?"

"Killed," Carlisle answered briefly and continued, relating the events of the last few days.

"That's too damned bad," Kansas commented when Carlisle had finished. "I liked the old boy. I'd heard a lot about him. Who's runnin' the spread now?"

"I am," Carlisle answered.

The crew had finished breakfast, and, as though recalled to the duties of his position by Kansas's question, Carlisle turned toward his men. "We'll line out for a count as we go off the bed ground this morning," he announced, looking at Yates. "Nugget, you'll count with me."

The announcement was a bombshell to Honey Yates. He had not expected or anticipated it, but he reacted to it instantly and typically. "Ain't you satisfied with the count we got yesterday?" he demanded.

"No, I'm not," Carlisle answered bluntly.

He could not quite bring himself to say that he had lost track in the counting and had taken Yates's figures. Carlisle had not yet reached the point where he could confess his inadequacy. He continued to stare at Yates.

Yates scowled. "There's no need of it," he said. "I got a count yesterday. There's no need of the extra work."

Behind Yates those who were his men formed into a compact little group, Benbow and the rest. They, too, were scowling. Nugget and Deems were at the front of the wagon. Rusty shifted until he was behind Carlisle and a little to his left. Gil Travis was by the fire, and Kansas and his fellows remained beside the wagon, Kansas and Chico leaning their backs against the rear wheel.

"Is there any reason why we shouldn't count the cattle?" Carlisle demanded.

"There ain't no use of it," Yates answered. "We got 'em counted. It's just a fool idea of yores, Carlisle."

"By God!" Carlisle rasped. "I think Nugget was right. I think the count is short. I think you lied to me, Yates."

Dead silence followed the words. Rusty watched Yates narrowly. Carlisle wore a gun, but Rusty realized that the youth would be helpless if it came to using weapons. As far as Carlisle was concerned, that gun at his hip was just an invitation to death.

"We'll count them," Carlisle stated flatly.

Rusty shifted his eyes momentarily from Yates to Travis and then back again. This was a showdown, and he needed Travis.

"You been takin' wages a long time, Gil," he drawled smoothly. "It's time you made up your mind."

Travis moved. Very slowly he left the fire and advanced. Momentarily no one could be sure of the group he chose to join, of the leadership he would follow. Then he shifted his course, turning toward Carlisle and Rusty.

Rusty was watching Yates. He did not see Benbow's sudden action. Snatching his gun from his hip, Benbow half turned and fired, all in one fluid motion. Gil Travis, advancing, was struck by the heavy slug high in the breast. He took one more half step and pitchpolled down on his face. As Travis went down Benbow wheeled, leveling his gun toward Carlisle. Yates, surprised as any by Benbow's act, had his hand halfway to his own hip. Before he could draw Rusty had whipped two shots into Benbow's thick middle and crouched, confronting the others. Benbow dropped, limp as an empty

165

sack, his weapon — still hot and with smoke coming from it — falling before his body. Joe Deems had dragged his shotgun from under the wagon seat and with both hammers cocked leveled it at Yates and his followers. Nugget, now that the action was finished, pulled his weapon. Rusty's eyes were very narrow, and his voice was very thin as he asked his question:

"You want a little of this, Yates?"

For answer Honey Yates lowered his hand. He knew what Rusty meant and he was not a fool. Honey Yates would not buck certain death. Over by the wagon Joe Deems's crusty voice rasped a command. "Unbuckle them belts an' step out of 'em. There's buckshot in both barrels of this. Shed yore guns if you don't want the buckshot."

Again it was Yates who led the way. Surprise had given place to anger on his face. But he was not so angry that he would take chances. His left hand slowly came up to the buckle of his gun belt and released it. Gun and belt thudded down. Behind him the others also obeyed Deems's order. They were confronted by Rusty with a leveled Colt and flanked by Deems, the shotgun and Ben Nugget. Carlisle stood helpless, his hand resting on his gun butt. He had not drawn the weapon.

"That's right," Deems commended. "Now walk away from 'em."

Yates and his followers obeyed, taking short steps, like angry dogs whipped away from a victim.

"What you want 'em to do now, Shotridge?" Deems demanded.

"Keep on walkin'," Rusty rasped. "Just keep at it, Yates. You'll find your saddles an' beds here when you get back. Your friends are down below the creek. I guess they'll take care of you."

"You'd set a man afoot in this country?" Yates demanded. "Damn you, Shotridge. I'll get you for this. I'll . . ."

"You'll keep walkin' till you find your friend Smith," Rusty rasped. "He'll look after you, an' you know where he is. We'll leave your beds an' saddles right here. You can pick 'em up when you come along with Smith."

Yates took another step and stopped. "I'll . . ." he began.

Old Joe Deems gestured with the shotgun. "Vamoose!" he ordered.

Slowly, looking back, voicing their anger in threats and curses, Honey Yates and the men that followed him walked out of the camp. They tramped on down the slope below the wagons and the fire. They disappeared behind a clump of trees at the foot of the slope, and when they were gone Rusty Shotridge let his breath go in a long sigh and relaxed. He turned to face Carlisle, and Carlisle confronted Rusty.

"We're short of cattle," Rusty began, meeting Carlisle's eyes. "Yates was in on it. He counted . . ." Rusty stopped short. Over by the wagon a man laughed and, wheeling, Rusty faced toward the sound. Chico was grinning, and there were broad smiles on the faces of Gus and Red. Kansas was frankly venting his mirth.

"What's so damned funny?" Rusty snapped.

Kansas broke his laugh and fought his face to soberness. "Them fellers," he answered Rusty.

"An' what's funny about them?"

Kansas grinned, his eyes meeting Rusty's, friendliness filling them. "They was so damned surprised," he said. "They was all ready for you an' then they wasn't." He chuckled again. "An' they're goin' to be surprised when they look for Slippery Smith too," Kansas concluded.

"Why?" Rusty demanded.

"Because," Kansas began and then fell to laughing again.

"Let us in on it," Rusty rasped. "Why are

they goin' to be surprised when they look for Smith?"

"Because ol' Eagle Claws's bucks jumped Slippery last night an' run his cattle to hell an' gone west," Kansas answered, the sparkle in his eyes belying the gravity of his tone. "Me an' the boys come past Smith's camp this mornin' before we come here. Smith an' his whole outfit are out lookin' for their cattle, an' the cook is movin' camp west. Them boys you run out are goin' to have a damned long walk." Kansas broke once more into laughter. Chico's small face was seamed with his amusement, and Gus and Red joined in the merriment. Slowly the predicament of Honey Yates and his cohorts was borne home to Rusty Shot-ridge. A grin spread all across his own face.

"Well," he said slowly. "Well . . ."

Leaving Kansas and his men to their laughter, he turned again toward Carlisle. Carlisle had not, seemingly, recovered from the shock of the violent action about him. His face was white, and his eyes showed his fright. Rusty sobered. Beyond Carlisle he could see Benbow sprawled on the ground, and to Benbow's left Gil Travis lay very still and quiet. The sight of the bodies was like the shock of cold water thrown in Rusty's face. He walked past Carlisle and, stopping beside Travis, looked down at the man. Travis was dead; had died before he struck the ground.

"He picked his side," Rusty announced, looking up from the body. "He was goin' to come in with us."

"What will we do?" Carlisle's voice was unsteady. "What will we do now? We haven't any men. We've got the cattle to look after. What will we do?"

The man's words brought full realization of their plight to Rusty Shotridge. What *would* they do? He had driven Honey Yates and his fellows out of camp. Momentarily he and Carlisle, Deems and Nugget and Telesfor were safe. But what was there that they could do? There was a bunch of big steers to look after, steers that even now needed attendance. They were miles from their destination, miles from any place where help could be found. And down below them, scattered now but sure to come together, there were triple, no, quadruple, their number of enemies. Rusty met Carlisle's eyes, and his own were blank as he comprehended their predicament. For a long moment he stood so, then Rusty's lips closed firmly and a light lanced into his eyes. He turned toward Kansas.

"You say you were washed out by the

storm?" he demanded.

Kansas nodded. A glint of comprehension sprang into his eyes, but he remained silent. Chico and Gus and Red were looking questioningly at Rusty. Shotridge spoke again.

"Yo're out of grub. You've got no camp. We've got grub an' what goes with it, an' we're short of hands. How about it?"

Kansas appeared to chew mentally on the question. He looked at Rusty and then at Carlisle. He turned and questioned his fellows with his eyes. Then his gaze settled on Rusty once more.

"You the boss?" Kansas queried finally.

"I . . ." Rusty began and stopped. He turned a trifle so that he could see Carlisle. Carlisle was watching him narrowly, and it was apparent that the man was about to speak. Then and there Rusty Shotridge made his decision. Carlisle could not get in with the steers; he could not take this remnant of an outfit across the country. He would be hard pressed to take care of himself, let alone a herd of cattle and a crew of men. It was definitely up to Rusty.

"I'm the boss," Rusty rasped, and with his eyes he dared Carlisle to object. Over beside the wagon Joe Deems sighed with relief, and Kansas grinned slowly.

"I guess me an' the boys could go a ways with you then," he announced. "Yeah, I guess we could. We kind of like yore style."

Chapter X

When Rusty answered Kansas's query and assumed responsibility of the herd, the weight of the world settled on his young shoulders. To Deems and Telesfor and Nugget that announcement came as a relief. To Carlisle it was a challenge. Worse, it was a challenge that he dared not accept. Leonard Carlisle on one occasion had knocked Rusty down. Physically he was not afraid of the russet-haired, gray-eyed man, and yet he was afraid. He had seen Rusty in action, had seen the utter, devastating swiftness that had killed Benbow and cowed Honey Yates, had met the ruthless force that lay in Rusty. Carlisle could not argue against or overcome those things. He said no word.

Rusty, having assumed responsibility, gave commands. He knew the desperate necessity under which he operated. The fortuitous raid of the Comanches on Slippery Smith had given Rusty a little time, a breathing spell. But it was only a breathing spell. He was shorthanded and he had a miracle to accomplish. Rusty knew that he was no worker of miracles, but he would make a try. Nugget and Chico, under his orders, went out to the cattle. The others were immediately employed in camp.

The horses of the mutineers were unsaddled, and saddles and bedrolls were piled together. Fresh mounts were selected from these animals for the recent recruits, and the rest of the horses went to the remuda. The weapons taken from Yates and his followers were put in the wagon.

There was no time for proper burial of the dead men. Travis and Benbow were wrapped in tarps and hoisted high into crotches of the live-oak trees. An Indian burial was better than none at all, and while Rusty felt sorry about Travis, he knew that they must not linger any longer than necessary at the site. While Rusty's orders were being carried out he held a consultation with Kansas.

Kansas knew the country. He listened to Rusty's questions and answered them fully. The Canadian River was not far distant. Rusty wanted to put that water between him and Slippery Smith.

"We're goin' to curl our tails an' run," he said frankly. "You can't handle a herd of cattle an' fight. Someway you'll lose in a deal like that. Either we'd spill the steers or we'd lose the fight, an' we can't afford to do either."

Kansas knew that Rusty was right and that he was not afraid. There was a glint of admiration in the outlaw's eyes as he answered Rusty's questions.

The location of Slippery Smith and his men was of prime importance. Kansas was not definite as to that location. He knew and reported to Rusty something of what had happened to Smith. Eagle Claws's Comanches had sought beef and horses when they raided the Hackamore outfit. They had stampeded the cattle sometime after midnight. Just a little bunch of Indians, Kansas stated. Not more than eight or ten. In talking to Smith's cook he had learned that the Comanches had missed the Hackamore remuda but the cattle had run. Smith would gather cattle, and he had moved his wagon west to make a base for his roundup. One or two days would suffice for Smith to collect the cattle, Kansas thought, and Rusty agreed with him. Listening to Kansas, Rusty wished devoutly that Eagle Claws had been able to run off Smith's horses. He would have felt a great deal safer. When Honey Yates and his companions reached Smith they would do two things: arm themselves and get horses. Once that happened

Rusty's brief respite would be over. Yates would never pass up such an opportunity as the Watrous trail herd offered, and it was entirely possible that Smith and his whole crew would throw in with Yates. Indeed, as he thought of it, Rusty could see that such a combination was not only possible but very probable. It stood to reason that Yates and Smith were partners in this conspiracy.

To fight such a combination Rusty had three reliable men. Carlisle he discounted; Kansas and his fellows were an unknown quantity. At the moment they were with Rusty, but he could not say with certainty that they would stay with him when the going got tough. Probably they wouldn't. Kansas, seeming to sense Rusty's thoughts, came over and joined him.

"You made a mistake," Kansas stated without preamble.

"How was that?"

"You'll never have them fellers where you want 'em again. You should of let 'em have it."

Rusty met Kansas's eyes. "You'd have done that?" he drawled.

Kansas grinned. "No," he said equably. "I'd have done what you did. Just the same, you ought to of killed 'em. They'll make you plenty of grief."

"Where," Rusty demanded, "will you be when the grief hits us?"

Kansas grinned. "You got no way of knowin'," he drawled. "All you can do is wait an' find out. Right now we're with you an' we ought to be goin'."

That was true. Rusty gave Deems his orders, and the wagon pulled out. Telesfor left with the remuda, and Rusty Shotridge, with a crew of six men, started the cattle.

They moved steadily throughout the day. Deems camped the wagon off the line of march at noon, and as the herd came past, men detached themselves one at a time, rode to the wagon, ate, changed horses and returned to the herd. All through the day Rusty anticipated trouble. None came. That night he told off the guard, long guards now, and spoke to Kansas and the other newcomers of the characteristics of the horses, helping them select their night horses.

All through the night Rusty remained alert, dozing occasionally, getting up to ride out to the herd, spending most of his time with the cattle. In the morning, before sunrise, the camp was awake, and by full dawn the herd was moving.

At midmorning Rusty dispatched Kansas ahead to the river. He must know the stage of the water, and as Kansas knew the country, and the river crossings he was the logical pilot. Kansas came back at noon bearing bad news. The Canadian was up, bank full and raging.

"We can't cross 'em," he told Rusty. "We'll have to lay over an' wait for the water to go down."

Here was sheer tragedy. Rusty had counted on being able to put the river between himself and his enemies. Carlisle came up while Rusty and Kansas consulted.

Since Rusty's assumption of authority, Carlisle had kept to himself. He had not tried to talk to Rusty but had held a conference with Joe Deems. In that conference Deems had bluntly told Carlisle that he was lucky, that Rusty was the man to handle affairs and that Carlisle had better keep his nose out of business he did not understand and could not handle. That had rankled. As Carlisle stopped his horse Rusty turned to him.

"The Canadian's up," he informed. "We can't cross."

Carlisle shrugged. "There's no particular hurry, is there?" he asked. "Or are you trying to make a record now that you've set yourself up as trail boss?"

Rusty stared at the man, and a glint of anger came into his eyes. "I'm tryin' to save

177

your investment," he drawled. "I thought that would interest you." With no other word he turned back to Kansas, and Carlisle, feeling himself excluded, rode away after waiting a moment.

Kansas drawled a weary "How do you figure it, Shotridge?"

"I don't know how to figure it," Rusty answered frankly. "We're tied up and we're going to have trouble. There's no use of you boys stayin' if you don't want to."

Anger flitted across the outlaw's face. "Yo're hell on running men off," he drawled. "Don't you want us to stay?"

"You'd be mighty welcome."

"Then shut up about us not stayin'."

Rusty nodded his thanks and grinned. Kansas had told him, and that was Kansas' right. After an instant the outlaw also grinned. "It's a hell of a thing when a man's got to depend on horse thieves," he drawled.

"Good people to depend on sometimes," Rusty returned.

There was a brief silence. Then: "One thing's goin' to surprise 'em some," Kansas said. "They don't know we're with you."

A light broke over Rusty's face. "We might surprise 'em a little more," he said. "How far will you go with me, Kansas?"

"You'd be most scared to death if you

knew," Kansas answered.

Rusty started his horse ahead. The cattle had caught up and were filing past. Kansas fell into place beside Rusty. "Just how does the country lie ahead of us?" Rusty asked.

Kansas considered. "It's pretty flat," he answered. "There's some small hills an' some timber. The river comes down kind of southeast. It makes a bend, an' the ford is just south of that. Only there ain't no ford now."

"Kind of a tongue of land with the river on both sides?" Rusty asked quickly.

Kansas nodded.

The light in Rusty's eyes became a definite glint of satisfaction. "We'll throw the herd out on that tongue," he stated. "Make camp right below it. That way the river will hold the cattle, won't it?"

Kansas was nodding. "On three sides," he agreed. "Two men can stay below 'em an' hold 'em till hell gets wet."

"An' the only way they can get to us will be through the camp," Rusty announced with satisfaction. "That's what they'll want to do anyhow. Yates is goin' to make a try for me."

"That's right," Kansas agreed. "So . . . ?"

"So I'll be at the camp," Rusty said. "An' if you an' yore friends really want in on this you'll be off a piece, kind of hid out. An' when things start . . ."

"We'll get into it," Kansas completed. "An' somebody 'll really get surprised. Let's get on to the river if we can. God knows why they ain't jumped us before now."

Honey Yates and his followers were an angry, footsore crew when they reached the spot the Hackamore wagon had occupied. They had walked twelve miles, and every mile had been filled with curses and recriminations. Yates had been blamed for their predicament freely and frankly. If Yates had not hesitated, if he had gone to war when Benbow shot Travis, none of this would have happened. So claimed the limping, evil-tempered men who followed Yates south.

Yates paid no attention to curses or complaints. Anger seethed within him, a consuming fire that deafened him. That he, Honey Yates, gunman with a reputation that stretched from Kansas on down to Matamoras, had been outwitted and out-gamed by a youngster, particularly a youngster whose prowess he had discounted, was almost more than Yates could stand. He cursed himself and raged inwardly, going over in his mind all his mistakes. There in San Marcial he had taken a chance with

Rusty Shotridge and, because of Bud Sigloe and Tom Flanders, had failed. There were countless times along the trail when Yates could have killed Rusty. He had not taken advantage of the opportunities. Instead, satisfying his own catlike nature, he had played along, holding Rusty in contempt, certain that whenever he wanted to he could eliminate the other man. And now here he was, disarmed and set afoot by that same russet-haired boy. A burning desire to avenge the insult, to set things even, filled Yates. There was just one way that he could do that: kill Rusty Shotridge.

The footsore crew reached the site of Smith's camp and found it deserted. Before them they could read all the signs of recent occupancy, but there was no wagon and no men. Wheel tracks led west and that was all. Now the fury of the curses redoubled.

Yates faced his followers, his eyes blazing. Unarmed as he was, the men felt his fury. He was capable of killing, and before his anger their own shrank and became unimportant.

"We'll go on an' find Slippery," Yates snarled. "He's moved, but we'll find him. When we do we'll get horses an' then we'll get that redheaded sonofabitch that put us afoot. Come on!"

One follower had the temerity to object. "Honey . . ." he began and then stopped short as Yates turned on him.

"By God," Yates rasped, "you'll do what I say! All of you!"

There was no answer to that, and, turning again, Yates set out along the wagon tracks.

These men were horsemen. They were neither shod for nor trained for walking. They stumbled along in their boots, untrained muscles complaining, their feet tired and sore. Sometimes perforce they rested, and at those times Yates cursed with a virulence that they neither comprehended nor believed possible. Six long miles from the deserted camp site they found Slippery Smith and the Hackamore wagon.

It was growing dusk when they came in. Groaning men dropped where they stopped. Yates went on toward the wagon, and, rising from beside it, Slippery Smith came out to meet him. Smith's greeting was not such as soothed injured feelings.

"Good God, what happened to you, Honey?" Smith demanded.

"Never you mind what happened to me!" Yates snarled. "What happened to you, an' why in hell did you move the wagon?"

Smith sensed the temper of the man. Honey Yates was in a killing rage. Slippery's reply was soothing. "Come on an' have somethin' to eat. Come on up an' sit down. You look like you've had a hell of a time."

Yates sank down beside the fire. "I've had a hell of a time," he answered. "By God, I'll kill that Shotridge if it's the last thing I do."

Smith came from the wagon bearing a bottle. "Have a drink, Honey," he placated. "Have a drink an' tell me about it."

Yates took the bottle and drank deeply. "That damned Carlisle wasn't satisfied with the count," he rasped. "He wanted another count this mornin'. I stalled him. Travis, the bastard, went over to the other side an' Benbow shot him. Before I could move, by God, I tell you before I knew what had happened, Shotridge killed Benbow an' was shakin' his gun in my face, askin' if I wanted some of it. The damned cook dragged out a shotgun an' threw down on us. There wasn't a damned thing that we could do."

He drank again, finishing the bottle, and hurled it toward the fire. "They made us drop our guns an' set us afoot!" he raged. "We been walkin' all day, tryin' to find you. What in hell happened to you, Slippery?"

"I told you to get rid of Shotridge," Slippery Smith snapped. "I told you he was dangerous. You missed yore play at him in San Marcial an' then you just fooled along

183

with him. Why in hell didn't you kill him when you had the chance?"

"I'll tend to Shotridge," Yates snarled. "What I want to know is why you moved the wagon? You made us walk a million miles."

Smith grunted. Yates's snarl was not soothing to his own temper, never too good and very short at present. "We got jumped last night about midnight," he said. "Damned Comanches. There 'd been a couple of 'em in here wantin' beef, an' I run 'em off. They started the cattle an' went a-hellin'. I don't know how in hell they missed the remuda, but they did. We had everythin' fine, all my cattle gathered, an' we'd begun brandin' some of the LMs. It was just like clockwork. An' then this had to happen! The damned soldiers can't keep them Comanches corralled at all. Why in hell we pay taxes for an army I dunno! The only thing that saved our bacon was that the herd run into a creek an' turned the right way so we could mill 'em. We'd still be gatherin' cattle if it wasn't for that."

"You get 'em all?" Yates demanded.

"All but a few head."

The drink had strengthened and fortified Honey Yates. He glared at Slippery Smith. "We're goin' to get Shotridge," he rasped.

"Him an' Carlisle an' all the rest. Then we're goin' to take the rest of them steers. They're goin' to pay for all the walkin' we done. Yo're comin' in with me, Slippery!"

Slippery Smith did not answer at once. "I dunno," he said finally. "It's mighty risky, Honey."

"Hell!" Yates glared at his companion. "Are you gettin' cold feet? It's all you can do. If we don't stop Shotridge an' Carlisle now we're finished. They ain't fools. They know their herd's short an' they know who's got the cattle they're missin'. They know you got 'em. You got no chance of gettin' to Dodge City an' sellin' your herd. Not if Shotridge an' Carlisle get there."

Smith shook his head dubiously. "Shotridge is shorthanded," he commented. "He ain't goin' to get to Dodge in any hurry. An', anyhow, I ain't goin' to Dodge. You give me an idea, Honey. I'm goin' west from here. I'll strike the old Goodnight trail an' go over into Colorado, maybe clear over into Utah. I can sell there just as good as I can at Dodge City."

Yates looked disgustedly at Slippery Smith. "I never thought that you was yellow," he snarled.

Smith flushed. "I ain't yellow," he refuted. "But I got a herd on my hands an' I got all

185

them cattle we took to brand. I don't see the sense of riskin' what I got on the chance of gettin' some more. Not when there's another way out."

"Then I'll go it alone," Yates stated. "I'll take what boys are with me an' get them cattle. I'll get Shotridge an' the rest too. By God, I will! Yo're goin' to stake us to horses an' guns, Slippery. You're goin' to do that."

Slippery Smith was canny. As he had said, he could see no use for his taking further risks, particularly when he had an instrument at hand to take the risks for him. In a tight place Slippery Smith would stand and fight like a cornered rat, but this was not a tight place. Not yet.

"How many men has Shotridge got?" he questioned.

"There's him an' Carlisle an' Nugget," Yates answered. "Then there's the horse wrangler an' the cook. That's all. I don't need yore help, Slippery. All I need from you is horses an' guns."

Pursing his lips, Slippery Smith nodded. "I'll let you have 'em," he said. "There's some spare guns, I guess. I got a extra Colt myse'f. But see here, Honey. If I give you horses an' guns I got to have a cut of what you get."

Honey Yates tipped back and glared. "By

God, the nerve of you!" he rasped. "You want a cut an' don't do a damned thing to get it!"

"I lend the horses an' the guns," Smith stated quietly. "You can't get no place without 'em."

It was true and Yates knew it. Nevertheless, he continued to glare at his companion. The other footsore members of Yates's party were limping into the camp now. The cook was busy and Smith's riders were clustered about the newcomers. There was a good deal of talk, a good many angry curses.

"All right," Yates snarled. "You'll get a cut. But I want them horses an' guns."

Slippery Smith nodded his satisfaction. Honey Yates would try to double-cross him, he knew. He must make plans and provisions to prevent that. "Let's eat," he suggested. "We can talk some more then an' scheme things out. You can't do nothin' till tomorrow anyhow, Honey."

For answer Honey got up and took two limping steps toward the fire.

"Mebbe not," he rasped. "But tomorrow evenin', just about sundown, I'm goin' to do plenty. I'm goin' to take that outfit, an' I'm goin' to get Shotridge alive."

He sauntered back from the fire and stopped, his eyes boring down into Slippery

Smith's upturned face. Slippery Smith was hard himself, but momentarily he recoiled from the blazing-eyed man who stared down at him. He knew Yates's reputation, did Slippery Smith, knew the cold-blooded fierceness of the man, knew him for what he was: a ruthless, merciless killer.

"What 'll you do, Honey?" Smith's voice was so low as to be almost a whisper.

Yates laughed, one short, harsh bark of sound that had no mirth in it. "Do?" he rasped. "What do you think I'll do? You ever seen a man after the Comanches had finished with him? You ever see a man that had been staked out on an anthill an' his eyelids cut off so that he had to look at the sun? You ever see a man try to walk when his skin had been ripped off him an' his guts was draggin' on the ground? I'll get Shotridge alive, an' before I finish with him he'll cuss his mother for havin' him. You stick around. You'll see what I'll do!"

Slippery Smith could not take his eyes from Yates. The terrible ferocity of the man charmed him as a snake charms a bird. "You can't do that, Honey," he said, his voice barely a murmur. "My God, you ain't human. You . . ."

Smith's voice trailed off. He did not finish the sentence he had begun. He knew, sitting there looking up at the man who towered above him, that Honey Yates meant every word he said. He knew that Honey Yates would carry out the vengeance he had planned, carry it out to the bitter end. He could not stop Yates. Nothing could stop him. No one. Slippery's smooth shoulders shuddered involuntarily, and he lowered his eyes.

"You wait an' see," rasped Honey Yates. "Just wait, Slippery. An' don't you try to stop me!"

CHAPTER XI

Rusty Shotridge and his crew moved the herd on toward the Canadian. When Kansas, leaving Rusty, loped ahead to point the way toward the river, Rusty fell into place in the drag. Carlisle was already there and Rusty rode beside him. The herd moved with the precision of an infantry regiment, and Rusty cheerfully commented on the fact. "These boys know how to handle cattle. Guess they'd ought to; they've likely stolen plenty."

Carlisle, mistaking Rusty's cheerfulness for an apology, chose the moment to unload the things he had been holding in his mind.

"Thieves!" he said bitterly. "They ought

to be run out of camp."

"We'd be in poor shape without 'em," Rusty retorted sharply. "I already run one bunch of thieves out of camp. Ain't that enough for you?"

"You had no proof that they were thieves," Carlisle flared. "I don't . . ."

"No proof?" Rusty demanded incredulously. "An' Honey Yates ready to kill you if you kept on pressin' him to take a count? Are you crazy, Carlisle?"

Carlisle did not answer. His position was not tenable and he knew it. Still his anger, his animosity and his jealousy of Rusty Shotridge would not let him stop. "You've taken a whole lot on yourself," he snapped. "You declared yourself. You set yourself up to boss this herd. Anything that happens is your responsibility, Shotridge! I still think that all this is useless and that the trouble could have been avoided. I think those men were killed because of you. Their death is on your hands."

"Mine?" Rusty stared at Carlisle.

"Yours."

For a moment Rusty was silent. Then his voice came slowly. "I was havin' a little hope for you, Carlisle," he said. "I thought maybe you'd learn, but I guess you can't." The slow voice was weary now. "All right, it's my responsibility an' I'll take it. I'll see this thing through."

"You'll have to," Carlisle snapped. "And I'll have nothing to do with it. When we get to Dodge City I'll report your actions to Colonel Watrous and the proper authorities. I think all this trouble is of your making."

The accusation was so unreasonable, so untrue, that Rusty gasped. Carlisle was staring at him, his frown making harsh lines in his young face.

Rusty recovered and returned Carlisle's stare. "You do that," he drawled. "You run an' tell your story an' I'll tell mine. But along about tonight, Carlisle, when the trouble starts, don't come runnin' to me for help."

Carlisle flushed. "I don't intend to," he snapped. "And I don't intend to help. You've set yourself up as trail boss. You've hired a crew. It's up to you. From now on I'll have nothing to do with it. I'll not work under your orders and I'll not . . . ."

Leonard Carlisle stopped. Rusty had pushed his horse close and, reaching out, caught Carlisle's bridle reins. He bent forward until his face almost touched Carlisle's.

"You'll take orders an' you'll work," he rasped. "You've been tryin' to ride me; now

I'll ride you awhile. The minute you don't do what I tell you I'll set you afoot an' let you walk to Dodge City, an' if you try to use that gun you sport on me I'll make you eat it. You'd better believe me, Carlisle."

Carlisle stared into gray-green eyes. Some of his anger drained away and was supplanted by a cold fear. Rusty had declared himself and there was no disbelieving him.

"An' now you push the steers along," Rusty concluded, releasing the reins he held. "I promised to look after you, Carlisle, but I didn't know it was goin' to be such a chore. I didn't know how much of a fool you are!" With that he wheeled his horse and loped toward the steers, and after a moment Leonard Carlisle followed.

Kansas took the herd straight on. Within an hour they saw the trees that marked the river, and now the thin stream of cattle was bent toward the west. The country lay, as Kansas had said, with its flatness broken by low knolls and little clumps of timber. The wagon was rolling along up the river toward the herd, and the dust of the remuda showed ahead of the wagon. Rusty watched Telesfor and the horses come out from behind a knoll and precede the cattle. He saw Kansas leave the point and lope across to the wagon. He saw Deems turn, drive a little farther and stop. The point men had fallen off now and the cattle drifted, their momentum not quite lost. Rusty left Carlisle to bring up the drag and loped ahead to join Kansas. As he rode he noted that Deems had stopped the wagon close beside a motte of cottonwoods. Rusty nodded approvingly. Joe Deems had used good judgment in selecting a place for a camp.

When he reached Kansas he could better see the conformation of river and land that lay ahead. Just as Kansas had said, there was a great tongue of land covering several hundred acres, circled by the river. Rusty grunted his satisfaction. There was a fence of water to hold the herd, and two riders on the neck of the tongue could prevent any drifting. Too, the grass was good and there were places where the steers could go down to water. It was a natural pasture and, better, a natural fort, a strong defensive position.

Kansas jerked his thumb toward the trees. "Good place for me an' the boys," he commented. "They'll see you an' come ridin' down. Maybe the shooting will run some steers into the river, but we dropped 'em far enough back so they'll have quite a ways to run. An' me an' the boys can come out about the right time an' sort of mix in from the side. That is, when they come."

Rusty nodded. The plan of battle was set. "There's not any use bein' halfway about things," he said. "This 'll be the only time they'll be surprised, an' we might as well make it a good one."

"Uh-huh." Kansas had the idea. Rusty wanted the battle carried through clear to the end. "Mebbe," the lanky man continued, "we can learn 'em enough this once so as they won't come to school again. That the way you want it?"

"That's the way I want it," Rusty agreed. "You'd better get gone now. Maybe some of 'em are watchin' us now from the timber. If they are our surprise isn't goin' to be worth a damn."

Telesfor had brought in the horses, and, seeing that the remuda was penned and that the cattle were grazing, every man of the Watrous crew headed for camp. There was very little talk as they changed horses. Rusty helped Telesfor hobble a few animals in the remuda and then gave him orders to take the horses on, through the herd and well up into the tongue of land. He wanted the horses beyond the cattle. Horses were important.

Telesfor left on his errand while Nugget and Carlisle stayed in camp. Rusty rode out toward the west, stationing himself below the cattle. When he reached a vantage point and looked back he could see only Carlisle, Deems and Nugget at the camp. The others had gone. Rusty's thoughts turned at once to Carlisle. He had to take care of Carlisle. The best and safest place for Carlisle would be in camp, he judged. When Nugget came out to join him, Rusty sent the old man loping back with orders to tell Carlisle that he was to stay with Deems.

All about the countryside the last sloping sunlight was dying. Shadows came crawling across the neck of land. The steers were grazing, heads lowered, jaws steadily cropping grass. Rusty looked at the steers. They were in better shape than when they had been received, heavier, in better flesh. The horse he rode lifted his head and, turning, stared intently toward a clump of timber some two hundred yards below the narrow neck where Rusty held position. Rusty followed the horse's interest, staring at the timber. For an instant he studied the clump of trees and then he reached back for his gun. A horse came charging out of the timber, the rider bent low because of overhanging limbs. Other horses followed. The first rider straightened. Rusty, gun out, lifted it and fired a shot in the air, a warning signal. Three men were coming straight toward him, their horses running full out. Three others were headed toward the camp. Rusty reined his horse around, his action automatic, until his right side was toward the approaching horsemen. Between Rusty and the three riders the interval closed rapidly. There was a crackle of gunfire, shrill yelling, the pound of running horses. Here was the attack!

Accurate fire from a running horse is difficult, almost impossible. Honey Yates and the two men who followed him in his charge found that to be true. They scored no hits as they came on, albeit the lead from their guns smacked harshly through the air all about the man who waited for them. Their strategy was at fault. Yates realized that suddenly. Himself a horseman, he had thought to attack on horseback. He would have done better if he had waited for darkness and come on afoot.

Rusty, too, was loath to sacrifice mobility for accuracy. But he was a more rapid thinker than Yates. As the distance closed he dismounted, his horse a barricade between himself and the onrushing riders. His strategy also was at fault. He had not thought that any attacking party would split. The spilt spoiled the surprise, made his hidden force less effective. There had been an error on both sides. Rusty's horse, frightened, pulled back, jerked, and the rein Rusty held was gone. He crouched, leveled his gun and pulled trigger. The shot had no result. One of the charging men swung wide and stopped his horse. Rusty saw him working at his weapon. Eagerness had made that man unload his pistol outside effective range.

Again Rusty aimed and fired. A horse, hit, swung wide and, stung by the slug, cold-jawed and bolted straight toward camp. There was no time for Rusty to see more, for Yates was upon him. Horse and man came on, intent to run Rusty down, to over-ride him. Rusty dodged left, fired again, hurried his next shot and missed. One more shell in the Colt. Yates turned his mount short, cutting back, bringing the horse around on its hind legs. Mighty good man with a horse, Rusty thought. Mighty good horse. His Colt, with one shell left, came up and bounced back as he pulled the trigger. He had misestimated. His target, moving, had not come into line. Yates was standing in his stirrups, chopping down with the Colt in his hand. Here it came, Rusty thought coolly. This was it, the end of Rusty Shot-ridge. But no flame spewed from the gun as it fell level. Rusty had a glimpse of Yates's face, a snarling mask of hate. Yates, too, had unloaded his gun. That last shot just wasn't there. Then Yates and his horse were gone and another rider took his place. Kansas, hat lost in the battle, body lying almost flat along his horse's neck, arm outthrust and tipped with steel, came charging past. Rusty flipped open the loading gate of his weapon, began to jack out spent shells. For a fleeting instant he had time to survey the battle.

But there was no battle. A riderless horse stood some small distance from the wagons. Another trotted in an aimless circle down below the neck of land. There was a crashing in the timber below the neck that told of flight and pursuit. Beyond the camp a rifle chanted two harsh notes, paused in its song and spoke again. Rusty shoved shells into the cylinder of his gun and looked around. His horse was twenty feet away, head up, anchored by a foot planted on a trailing rein. Rusty walked toward his horse.

"Whoa," he ordered. "Whoa, now!"

The horse surveyed his approach anxiously and tried to move. The rein came free and the horse walked off, trailing the reins. Rusty said, "Whoa," and, holding out his hand, tried to catch the reins. He did not see Ben Nugget until the latter appeared beside the loose horse and, reaching down, caught the reins that Rusty wanted.

"Here's yore horse," Nugget said as though this were an everyday occurrence. Rusty took the tendered reins, holstered his Colt and mounted. In the saddle he turned toward the south again. Men were coming back from below the neck, converging upon him. Kansas came up and stopped. Chico joined Kansas, and Gus and Red joined Chico.

"You get hurt?" Rusty asked sharply.

"The damned trees like to beat me to death," Kansas answered. "I wasn't hurt. How about it, Chico?"

"No," Chico said.

"Yo're bleedin'," Red announced. "They hit you, Shotridge."

Rusty looked down at his left hand in surprise. There was blood flowing from his finger tips, and his arm felt curiously numb. "I guess I am," he said slowly.

"They split on us an' that made it tough," Kansas drawled. "We taken care of the bunch that jumped the camp an' then come on. It made us a little slow. They was surprised all right. You better come along an' get that looked after, Shotridge."

"I'll do that," Rusty agreed.

Kansas rode beside him as they went to

the camp. Nugget and Chico, Gus and Red rode together. They were just like a six-horse outfit, trailing to the camp, only there was no wagon behind them. Deems, his shotgun across his arm, met them at the wagon, and Carlisle, carrying a rifle, came walking down the slope toward the fire. Carlisle's face was white and strained in the firelight.

"Shotridge is hit," Kansas said, dismounting, and stepping over beside Rusty. "Get out yore rags, Deems."

Chico climbed down from his horse and the others, too, dismounted. Carlisle had stopped beside the fire.

"I meant to tell you," Chico said to Carlisle, "that gun shoots a little high."

"I hit a man," Carlisle said, his voice curiously flat. "He's out there someplace." He gestured toward the south. The dusk was closing in, night filling it.

"Let's look at that arm," Deems rasped.

Rusty, his shirt off and white torso exposed, looked curiously at his arm. There was a deep cut in the inner side of the biceps where a bullet had torn through. Deems doctored the cut with turpentine that burned like fire, and rags torn from a clean flour sack. Kansas was fooling around the back of the wagon. He joined Rusty and the group about him, carrying Deems's lantern.

"I'm goin' out an' take a look," he announced.

Chico and Red went with Kansas. Gus discovered that he had a bullet burn just above the knee on his left leg, and Deems transferred his attentions to him.

Carlisle stood staring at Rusty. "I hit a man," he insisted. "He was riding off, I hit him." Carlisle's voice was rising in pitch and his eyes were wild. Rusty looked at him sharply, saw the hysteria in the youth's eyes and took steps to prevent it.

"Maybe you did!" he rasped. "What of it? They come askin' for it. You an' Nugget get out an' watch the herd. Go on, now!"

The harshness of Rusty's voice, his gruffness, the hard command, lifted Carlisle from his depression. He glared angrily at Rusty, seemed about to refuse the order and then turned abruptly toward his horse. Rusty spoke, low toned, to Ben Nugget. "Don't leave him alone. If he gets to talkin' snap him out of it. I'll be out in a minute."

Down below the camp the lantern was bobbing along. The firefly speck of light stopped, was hidden by a man's interposed body and then appeared again, motionless.

"Come on, Carlisle," Nugget directed.

"Let's go."

Carlisle mounted, and he and Nugget rode away. Gus, his leg bandaged, pulled up his overalls. Close by the wagon there was a sudden cracking sound and the men wheeled toward it. Gus took three steps and then stopped.

"Well, I'll be damned," he said, his voice incredulous. "My horse just fell over. He was standin' there an' he just fell."

Going to the horse, Gus made a hurried examination and straightened. "Must of been the slug that grazed my leg," he said. "It hit the horse an' he bled to death inside. First time a thing like that's happened to me."

"Lucky for you it was the horse," Deems rasped.

The lantern was coming on, bobbing along from the south. Kansas and Red and Chico came up to the fire. Kansas set the lantern carefully on the ground.

"Two of 'em," he said soberly, reaching into his shirt pocket for tobacco and papers. "They're both dead. Carlisle was right, Shotridge. He hit one of 'em. I can tell the kind of hole a .38–.55 makes."

"He can't," Rusty said significantly. "No use tellin' him. He's upset enough the way it is."

Kansas nodded. "Want to go see who they are?" he asked.

"I'll go in a minute," Rusty answered. "We'll have to do somethin' with 'em tonight. Tomorrow we can . . ." His voice trailed off. Kansas nodded. Tomorrow they could bury the bodies.

"Tomorrow," Chico announced abruptly, "I'm goin' to take a little *pasear* down south. Kind of look the country over. Mebbe I can . . ."

"You bloodthirsty little devil!" Kansas's voice was very matter-of-fact. "Tomorrow you'll stand a day herd on the steers, that's what you'll do."

Chico lapsed into sultry silence, and Deems's voice rasped. "You git yore saddle off that dead horse, Gus. Some of the rest of you put ropes on him an' drag him off. He's damned near in my kitchen. Think anybody can sleep with a dead horse in the kitchen?"

"Think anybody can sleep?" Red rasped. "*All* right, Gus. I'll help you get yore saddle."

There was no sleep in the camp that night. Deems kept a pot of coffee on the fire. Carlisle and Nugget were relieved by Telesfor and Red. In turn Rusty and Kansas took a guard, riding slowly, side by side, back and forth across the neck of land that led to the tongue. Morning broke, blue and crimson, gold and gray, beautiful, unaffected by the evil of men. In the morning men stirred to activity.

There was much to be done. A day herd must be kept on the steers, but one man could attend to that detail. There was work for the others. Carlisle, Rusty put on day herd, seeking to spare the young man's feelings. He had no compunctions concerning the others. Salted and seasoned as they were, imbued with the philosophy that death and danger were a part of living, he used them as he would. Graves were dug, and blanket-wrapped bodies lowered into them. There were no other services, and Kansas remarked grimly that if a town ever was situated here at the river crossing it would have the advantage of a boot hill already started. Gus's horse was dragged farther from the camp, and the buzzards, scenting it, circled out of nowhere and settled down. And when these things were done, always with alert eyes scanning the southern country, Rusty and Kansas and Chico took fresh horses and rode.

For a time they had a trail to follow. Then that trail grew thinner, and presently Rusty stopped.

"No use goin' any further," he said. "We

could mebbe run into 'em an' I don't want that. I think they'll let us alone awhile."

Kansas agreed. "They got a jolt," he said. "Likely it learned 'em. For now, anyhow. What's the program, Shotridge?"

"Stay where we are an' cross the river as soon as it goes down some," Rusty answered. "Let's go back now."

And that was the program. For the remainder of the day the men relieved each other on day herd, those that were free loafing around the camp, always with a watch kept toward the south. Nothing happened, nothing occurred to break the peace. That night the guard rode back and forth across the narrow neck of land. In the morning the day herding was resumed. By afternoon of the second day Rusty, testing the stage of the water, rode Toughy into the ford and found it passable for horses and cattle. The wagon was another matter. He returned to camp, and for an hour or two the ringing of an ax resounded and men pulled cottonwood logs down to the river at the end of their saddle ropes. With the logs floated other ropes were brought into play, and the timbers were lashed together. Again saddle ropes were used, and men pushed and tugged at wheels while the wagon was maneuvered into the water. Then when it stood axle-deep the raft logs were brought and fastened to the axles. Three men swam their horses across, the saddle ropes, fastened together, making guy lines. The floating wagon was pushed from the bank and, secured by the guy lines, caught by the current, swept downstream in a long arc and grounded in the shallows on the northern bank.

There was more work then, cutting down the bank with ax and spade to form a road for the wagon to follow to the top. Men sweated and strained and swore, and finally their purpose was accomplished. Wet through with river water and sweat, Rusty surveyed their accomplishment.

"Now we got to cross the cattle," he said. "Let's get at it."

So again the crew entered the river, only Joe Deems remaining on the northern bank. Once more horses were changed, and then the riders pushed the cattle down from the tongue of land and, marching them along, swung in a great semicircle toward the ford. The steers were logy and unwilling, but the men were their masters. The lead steers entered the river, splashed through the shallows and, reaching swimming water, forgot their loginess and headed for the opposite bank. This time there was no mill to turn them back. This time the crew, working with precision and dispatch, was each an efficient unit of the whole. Downstream on the further bank, the cattle grounded and splashed out and fell to grazing until the whole herd was across.

It was not a difficult matter to cross the remuda, and when that was done every man felt relief. The Canadian was between them and danger.

"I feel," Kansas said, riding beside Rusty, "kind of like sayin', 'Thank God.' We're pretty near in Dodge City now."

Rusty looked at the river and nodded.

"Pretty near," he agreed. "Pretty near to Dodge."

"An' you'll be glad when you get there," Kansas commented, looking at his companion.

"Yeah," Rusty drawled. "I'll be glad. I'll be half finished when we get there."

Kansas's eyes were very sharp but he said nothing more. Rusty Shotridge would be half done with his job when the steers reached Dodge City. Kansas had an idea as to the other half of the work that Rusty had laid out for himself. Over by the wagons Joe Deems called:

"Come an' get it, you water dogs. Eat or I'll throw it out."

Chapter XII

Bud Sigloe, with a delivery date in Kansas that was not pressing, moved along toward the north by stops and starts, like a thermometer on a hot day. The Wichita held him for two days; the Clear Fork, running bank full, delayed him once more, and the quicksand added to the delay. Ad Marble had bought stock cattle, and Sigloe had a herd of two- and three-year-old heifers bound to stock some range in the North. The heifers would not travel like steers. Being feminine and therefore notionate, they required careful handling. Bud's temper grew shorter by the moment, but he applied the old trailman's axiom: "He was hard on the men and horses and easy on the cattle."

The heifers ran once between the Wichita and the Clear Fork, once between the Clear Fork and the Red, and by the time the herd came trailing down toward this latter river Bud Sigloe was referring to his charges, and not at all affectionately, as "them little bitches."

The Red River was up. There was no crossing and there were two herds already water-bound. Bud Sigloe threw off the trail, kept the heifers on good grass, bought his men a box of cigars and a quart of whisky when he restocked his wagon at the crossing store and waited with what patience he possessed.

Time played its part and the water went down. One ambitious trail boss, mistaking valor for judgment, tried to cross before the stage of the water was right and had a poor time, losing some cattle by drowning and a few head in the quicksand. Bud waited two days more and then, taking his turn, moved up the river. Mitchell cut his herd and after the few strays had been weeded out gave Sigloe a warning.

"You'd better hang on the trail," the trail cutter advised. "Cut down as close to Camp Supply as you can. Ol' Eagle Claws an' his bucks are cuttin' trail west of Supply, an' from what I hear they're raisin' hell."

"How do you mean 'hell'?" Sigloe inquired, staring down the length of his short and pugnacious nose at the trail cutter.

"They're takin' beef." Mitchell amplified his original statement. "There's been a troop out from the fort tryin' to round him up, but so far they ain't had much luck. He dodges 'em. The gov'ament is behind on the beef ration, an' Eagle Claws is doin' what he can to make up for it. Word's come back that he's makin' the herds pay him off before he lets 'em through. That's what he's doin'. He's takin' a few beeves from every herd."

"He'll play hell takin' any from me," Sigloe snorted. "What does he think I'm runnin'? A granger outfit?"

Mitchell took a chew, proffered the plug to Bud who refused it, got his tobacco under control and spat judgmatically. "It's better," Mitchell said, "to give him a few head of cattle than to have him hangin' on clear across to the North Fork, raisin' hell and stampedin' the herd. You know that, Sigloe."

Bud Sigloe did know that. A few runs would knock more tallow off a herd than any other thing. He simply could not afford to have his cattle choused, and so he would pay blackmail to the Comanche chief. He grunted, shook hands with Mitchell and said, "Thanks."

"An' I got a message for you," Mitchell said. "There was a fello' with the Watrous outfit that went through here over a week ago. Fello' named Shotridge. He said he'd be lookin' for you in Dodge an' that him an Flanders would have the place all swept out an' peaceful for you when you got there." Mitchell grinned, and Sigloe's bearded face cracked in appreciation and anticipation.

"He'll do it too," the trail boss announced.

"All swept out an' clean, he said?"

"That's right."

"Then," Bud Sigloe drawled, "I'd better be gettin' on before somebody gets it dirty again. So long."

Mitchell grinned and said, "So long," and Bud Sigloe loped off after his traveling cattle.

Veteran that he was, Sigloe took some precautions following Mitchell's warning. Cale Minnitree and Pat Moran, relics of many a drive to the North, were detached from active duty with the heifers and dispatched ahead to scout the country. Two days north of the river they returned to the herd with information. They had seen Eagle Claws's wickiups on a creek perhaps ten miles to the north, and they were sure that Eagle Claws would be on deck when the herd came up. Bud Sigloe put a man to night-wrangling horses, had a few more hobbled when the remuda was turned out that evening and announced a new division of the guards, putting on an extra man and stretching the hours of watching.

Nothing happened during the night, and the following morning the herd moved on. They were not molested during the day. Not until the cattle were going to the bed ground Bud had chosen did Eagle Claws appear. Then ten Indians — most of them fat; all of them dirty and unkempt — came riding down toward the cattle. Sigloe, reinforced by Minnitree and Moran, went to meet them.

Most Comanches talked Spanish. Their raids into Mexico were not far in the past, and the younger bucks learned Spanish as they learned their own language, at their mothers' breasts. Both parties stopped, and one of the Indians, detaching himself from his companions, came forward. Bud Sigloe also left his men and rode to meet the brave.

There was grease upon Eagle Claws's braids, his face, his fat body and the scanty buckskin that covered it. He rode a pinto decked with a lion skin as a saddle, and across his thighs he carried a Winchester of the latest model. Bud discounted the Winchester. He knew that it was fouled, had never been cleaned after use and was about as accurate as a slingshot. The two men met, stopped, surveyed each other, and Eagle Claws said: "How?"

"¿Como está?" Bud replied.

That established a common ground. Eagle Claws waved a plump and greasy hand toward the heifers and bluntly stated his errand. This was his country, he announced. The cattle were using his grass. He demanded payment. Ten head of heifers.

Bud, with difficulty, restrained his anger. He would part with no ten head of heifers to any Indian. Bud did not tell Eagle Claws that. Instead he gestured toward the wagon, camped now below the cattle, and smoothly invited Eagle Claws to come to camp. Eagle Claws beckoned to his waiting warriors and they came up. Minnitree and Moran joined the caucus. Was there, Eagle Claws wished to know, whisky in the camp?

There was no whisky.

Then why go? The savage diplomat shook his head. He would settle for ten head of heifers and not visit with his friend. Some men who drove cattle through his country had encountered much bad luck. He hoped that it would not dog the heels of this, his friend.

Bud Sigloe tapped his chest. "Yo soy 'Bud Tejano,' " he announced.

Eagle Claws's face remained blank, but his eyes shifted nervously. Bud had given the name that the Comanches called him. Several Indians, attempting to run a blazer on Sigloe-bossed herds, had encountered much difficulty. "Bud Tejano" was something of a conjure word along the trail. Eagle Claws turned and spoke to his followers, employing Comanche for the dialogue. The nine greasy bucks trailed off, and Eagle Claws politely said that he would visit "Bud Tejano" in his camp.

When they reached camp Eagle Claws, as was his right, chose to sit down. For this purpose he selected Cale Minnitree's un-rolled bed. Sigloe's cook made coffee and the Comanche drank three cups, each heavily sweetened with molasses. He dis-coursed solemnly with Bud for a time and then, mounting his pinto, took departure.

"You hold the remuda between the camp an' the herd tonight," Bud instructed his horse wrangler. "Hobble 'em like last night, an' we'll take the same guards. What you doin', Cale?"

"Huntin' an anthill," Minnitree growled. He held his blankets gingerly in his hands, and his eyes searched the ground about the camp. "That damned Injun set on 'em. I ain't goin' to take any chances on gettin' lousy. I'm goin' to stake these blankets over a anthill an' let the ants have the lice."

"An' sleep with me, I reckon," Moran said. "Well, damn it, if you do you got to stay quiet an' not turn like a pinwheel. That's what you done the last time."

Again the guard on the herd was doubled, and the remuda, held between camp and herd, had a night wrangler to care for it.

Apparently the precautions were not necessary for the night was peaceful. In the morning Eagle Claws turned up at the camp, again accompanied by his braves. Eagle Claws wanted to trade.

It was a matter of face-saving, Bud knew. The Comanche did not want to let a herd go through without payment of toll. But he did not want to tangle with "Bud Tejano." Accordingly he had taken this route out of his difficulty. The buck that Eagle Claws beckoned came up and dumped two hides on the ground. These were fairly fresh and had not yet attained the flintlike hardness characteristic of hides. Eagle Claws entered into a monologue. He would trade the hides for two heifers. They were good hides.

"Cale," Bud Sigloe called. "You an' Pat cut that crippled YH heifer out an' drive her over here." The order given, he turned to Eagle Claws again. Reputation and actions had won Bud through. He could trade the crippled heifer for the hides, and everyone would be satisfied. *"Una vaca,"* Bud said, holding up one finger.

When Minnitree and Moran came back with the heifer the trade was made. Eagle Claws, his dignity satisfied and his reputation secure, gestured to his braves and the heifer was driven away. Cale Minnitree, curious as to who had lost the cattle from which the hides had been taken, opened the rolls and looked for the brands. Sigloe came over to join him.

"LM," Minnitree said. "Didn't Watrous have the LM steers?"

"Yeah," Bud Sigloe growled. "Looks like McBride has run into some trouble."

"I didn't know that Watrous trail branded a hackamore," Minnitree commented. "Look here. They skinned out the heads when they took the hides, an' there's a hackamore across the nose of this one."

Sigloe bent down and examined the mark, then straightened without examining the other hide. "Roll 'em up an' throw 'em in the possum belly on the wagon," he ordered. "We got to get goin'. That damned Eagle Claws has killed half a day for us."

Minnitree rolled the hides, and Sigloe, mounting, trotted out toward his herd. He hoped that when the Watrous outfit had lost those cattle they hadn't lost anything else: say, a rusty-haired, gray-eyed young man.

"I bet you," Bud Sigloe muttered as he rode, "that if the kid had been bossin' that outfit they wouldn't of lost no cattle at all. I'll bet on that."

Minnitree loped up beside his boss. "Funny," Minnitree said, "there wasn't no hackamore trail brand on that other hide. I looked for it, an' it wasn't there."

Bud Sigloe paid no attention to his man. Up ahead the cattle were moving. Bud lifted in his stirrups and swung his hat around his head to attract attention. He wanted the cattle pointed a little more east.

Some twenty-five miles north and west of Bud Sigloe's heifers there were other men discussing hides and stolen cattle. Honey Yates and Slippery Smith stood beside the wagon and glared at each other. Yates had made a demand and Slippery Smith was in the process of refusing it.

"I tell you," Yates snarled, "I didn't know them fellows was with Shotridge. If I'd known we'd done it different. We've helped you brand the steers you got; now I want horses. I'm goin' to take another try at him."

"Not with my men or my horses," he said decisively. "He's too many for you, Honey. Look what happened. You went up there with five men. You jumped him. He was fixed an' waitin' for you. You got two men killed an' another shot all to hell. I ain't goin' to loan you no more horses an' I need my boys to handle my cattle. Besides, they're across the Canadian by now, an' you couldn't do nothin' with 'em. Hell, they ought to be pretty near in Kansas by now."

Honey Yates made a sudden, violent gesture. All the things that Slippery Smith said were true and he knew it. That knowledge did not soothe his injured feelings. He took a step toward Slippery, and as he moved his hand rose swiftly. From the tail gate of the wagon a man spoke sharply:

"Hold it!"

Honey Yates stopped. Under Slippery Smith's mustache his lips curled contemptuously. "You think I'd take a chance on you, Honey?" Slippery drawled. "Hell, no! Sam's been watchin' you ever since you braced me. Yo're all done, Honey. Yo're washed up. You get funny an' Sam 'll kill you right here."

The anger drained out of Yates, leaving him deflated. He dropped his hand from his weapon and his eyes lowered. Smith's voice went on, coldly disdainful: "That's my gun yo're wearin'. You can shuck it off. Sam 'll take it."

Mechanically Yates's hand lifted to his belt buckle. The gun and belt thudded down around his feet. Slippery Smith, master of the situation, spoke again.

"You set up to be a gunman," he drawled, contempt in his voice. "You wouldn't make a pimple on a gunman's nose. You want to jump Shotridge again. Hell, I'm savin' yore life. You wouldn't even have a saddle an' bed if he hadn't felt sorry for you an' left 'em stacked when he pulled out."

Honey Yates continued to stare at the ground. Smith, having waited a moment, continued: "If you don't like it here you can pull out. I'll stake you to a horse. I'll do that for you."

Still Yates said nothing. Smith grunted, one short, harsh bark. "Nothin' like losin' yore nerve," he sneered. "If you don't want to pull out you can go on north with me. I'll cut you in like the rest of the boys; I'm that generous. You helped run a hackamore on them LM steers we got when we stampeded. Yo're entitled to somethin'. What do you say, Honey?"

Slowly Yates nodded. He did not lift his eyes. Smith grinned sardonically. "An' we won't go to Dodge City," he amplified. "I'll save yore life again. If we went to Dodge an' you run into Shotridge he'd kill you. So we'll turn west an' go over to the Goodnight trail. We'll hit Trinchera Pass an' go into Colorado. We'll sell out up there someplace, an' you can go on to Canada. You ought to be safe up there."

Abruptly Slippery Smith turned and strode away. Sam came from his position at the wagon end, stooped and gathered up the fallen belt and weapon. "You won't be needin' these, Honey," Sam drawled. "I'll take care of 'em for you."

Sam, too, strode away. It was not until Sam was gone that Honey Yates lifted his head. His eyes, blue and inflamed, red rimmed, glared at Slippery Smith's broad back.

"I'll go with you," Honey Yates muttered deep in his throat, so low that the words did not carry, "all the way to Colorado. I'll go all the way to hell with you, Slippery. An' sometime I'll get a gun an' the deck won't be stacked. Then we'll see."

Slippery Smith turned. He looked at Honey, and Yates lowered his eyes again. "If yo're goin' on with us," Smith drawled, "you'd better go get a horse from the remuda. It's time you started makin' a hand an' earnin' yore keep, Honey."

Chapter XIII

There is a difference between handling cattle when the crew is divided and when it acts as a unit. Leonard Carlisle sensed that difference as day followed peaceful day. Of all the men who accompanied the Watrous herd, only he himself was out of step. The others were compact, tightly knit, a force driven by one directing influence. Rusty Shotridge was that influence, and Kansas and Red, Chico and Gus, Ben Nugget and Telesfor, even Joe Deems, were simply adjuncts to the trail boss. As the weeks grew older Carlisle came to wish that he, too, were of the group, but he could not bring himself to join it. It is doubtful that the others would have allowed him to join had he tried.

There was in Rusty that combination of iron nerve, self-respect and friendliness which, coupled with ability, makes the born leader of men. The crew, from Telesfor on to Kansas, the top hand, liked Rusty, were his friends, and yet they respected him. Not that his actions held him aloof from the rest; it was simply that he was the boss and they the hands. Carlisle was not given to self-analysis. Had he been he might have seen his errors and departed from them. Sensing Rusty's leadership, jealous of it, resentful of it and yet perforce bowing to it, Leonard Carlisle was not happy.

His own inadequacy was borne home to him now, came keenly to his notice. Where before Honey Yates had been a buffer, had by word and deed inflated Carlisle's ego, now the men who were his daily associates took it for granted that he could not do those things that they did as a matter of course. He was not a full hand. His associates knew it and acted accordingly. And in this they, as well as Rusty, were unfair.

It might have been that under happier circumstances Rusty would have acted differently. Under other conditions Rusty would have helped Carlisle, given him quiet, unobtrusive instructions and brought him along. But this was not possible. Carlisle had flared up, challenged Rusty's leadership, made unfair accusations, and Rusty could not forget that. On the other hand Carlisle remembered Rusty's threat, felt that he had been neglected, that his position as part owner of the steers had been slighted; and, too, he remembered the scene on the porch of the Stockman Hotel when Ellen Watrous had kissed Rusty. The memory rankled. The trip, begun in anger, inspired by a desire to free himself from his sister's dominance, now came to be a grim journey, a task that must be finished. Left to himself, without companionship other than the casual words which were spoken to him by the trail hands, Leonard Carlisle brooded. He forgot his own part, forgot that it was his own desire, his own jealousy, his own anger that had placed him where he was.

Spoiled all his life, a leader in his own group at school, dominated by his sister since his infancy, Leonard Carlisle was not equipped to solve his present problems. It was natural that his unhappiness, his jealousy and his hatred should center on one man. Rusty Shotridge became the focus of all these things, the evil genius that had brought Carlisle to a realization of his own short-comings.

And there was nothing that he could do. His brooding, resolving into hatred, could find no outlet. There was no one to whom he could talk and so rid his mind of his troubles. There was no chance for action that would free his pent-up emotions. Had Carlisle rebelled against the trail boss, had he sought to vent his hatred upon Rusty, the men who moved the cattle would have killed him. Carlisle sensed it, felt it, knew it.

Yet beneath all his resentment and hate there was in Carlisle an innate fairness. He told himself that his present predicament was all Rusty's fault; that the shortage of the herd, the fact that there were now two thousand in place of twenty-five hundred steers, was because of Rusty; that the reason they were shorthanded, that the necessity for constant watchfulness, was due to Rusty. These things he thought and forced himself to believe, and yet he knew they were not true. As the herd moved on north of the Canadian, the Kansas line growing closer as each day ended, Leonard Carlisle was heated in the fire that dwelt within himself, forged on the anvil of circumstances by the hammer of his own nature. From that furnace and by that forging something must be made. Carlisle did not realize and could not know what type of man would emerge at the end of the trail.

Rusty was too occupied to give a great deal of thought to Carlisle. The daily problems that confronted him took all his attention. There was at first the constant fear of attack to worry Rusty. Then as that dimmed, other problems took its place. Rusty, too, was finding himself. For the first time in his life all the responsibility was his own. Daily there was the problem of the cattle, daily the problems of route, of water, of bed ground, the thousand and one things that confronted a trail boss. And Rusty had never before been solely responsible, had always, until now, been able to fall back upon more mature judgment. He, too, was being forged by the trail, and gradually his patience grew and his temper became less and more amenable to control. Rusty Shotridge, just as Leonard Carlisle, was growing into a man.

So the miles went by and the camps were made and deserted, and the bed grounds one by one were left behind. And now, striking the trail again, finding daily the evidences of other herds that had preceded them, they came at last to the Kansas line and the last stage of their journey. And two days' drive above that line they encountered the last difficulty, the last barrier erected against them.

They camped that second day above the line beside a creek that ran toward the east. The cattle were bedded on a slope above the creek and the remuda, between the herd and the wagon, grazed in the lush grass of the creek bottom. There was peace all about them, and Rusty was beginning to feel the let-down of tension that comes to any man as the completion of a task draws near. He was squatted beside the wagon, his plate balanced on his knees, when Kansas spoke.

"Visitors comin'," Kansas said.

Rusty looked up. Kansas and his three companions were gathering close beside the wagon, and down the slope, coming past the cattle, there were two men tiding toward the camp. Rusty hastily took the last bite from his plate, swallowed the last gulp of coffee from his cup and stood up. As the riders came closer to the camped wagon Rusty walked out to meet them.

The newcomers were bearded men and curiously unlike. One wore bib overalls, a black hat, and his feet were covered by heavy shoes. The other plainly was a cowman. Lee Farrel was the cowman's name, and he introduced his companion as Joel Peters. They dismounted at Rusty's invitation and walked over to the wagon. Rusty gestured toward the coffeepot and suggested that supper was just finished but that there was plenty left.

"We've ate," Farrel announced. "Thanks."

The silence was awkward. Kansas, Red, Chico and Gus were not in evidence. Rusty could see them riding out toward the herd to relieve Nugget and Carlisle. Save for Deems and his visitors, he was alone in the camp. It was never Rusty's way to be backward. "You got somethin' on yore minds?" he asked.

Farrel and Peters exchanged glances and Peters, clearing his throat, spoke. "Yo're bound through to Dodge City?"

"That's a fact," Rusty said.

Peters cleared his throat again. "There's crops planted north of here," he announced.

"They're fenced. You can't go through that way."

Rusty studied Peters's face. "Well," he said reasonably, "there's got to be some way through. All the country isn't fenced, is it?"

It was Farrel who now took up the tale. "Peters is representin' the farmers," he said shortly. "They've had some trouble with herds this season. There's been some fence pulled down an' some wheat stomped out."

"I'm not interested in pullin' down fence," Rusty assured. "My steers do well enough on grass, so I don't pasture 'em on wheat. I won't bother your fence line, Mr. Peters. You tell me a route that 'll take me by you an' I won't come anyplace near."

Peters nodded but Farrel's face was sober. "That's where I come in, Shotridge," he announced. "I got range west of the farms, an' me an' the rest that are usin' that country have set up a quarantine."

"A quarantine?" Rusty asked incredulously. "But look here, there's been herds through here before this one. How'd they get by?"

"That's what I'm tryin' to tell you," Farrel explained patiently. "Along about a month ago a Texas herd come through that was loaded with ticks. They dropped off the Texas cattle an' started tick fever on our range. Natchully it was bad, so we set up this quarantine. We had some trouble, an' the next cattle that come up the trail was stopped. They turned east an' broke through the farmers' fences an' tromped out their wheat an' went on. Now the stockmen an' the farmers got together. We're goin' to hold any Texas cattle that come up below Kaw Creek here until frost comes. We can't have tick fever spread, an' we ain't goin' to have the fences tore down."

Rusty looked at his visitors. There was utter sincerity on their faces. He had to believe them and he had to believe that they were honest. This was no holdup, engineered by men who would exploit the trail drivers. This was the real thing.

"We're hopin' that we won't have trouble," Farrel said slowly. "That's why Peters an' me come down here. But if we do have trouble we're fixed to take care of it."

"But I've got a delivery date to make at Dodge," Rusty protested. "There's herds behind me that have delivery dates too. What about them?"

"We ain't goin' to have tick fever on our ranges," Farrel persisted doggedly.

"An' we ain't goin' to have no more cattle go through our fields." Peters's voice was iron hard.

"There's no ticks on these cattle," Rusty said triumphantly. "This herd don't come from the tick country. They're clean. They aren't . . ."

"We're sorry for you, but that's the way it stands: All Texas cattle stay below the line," Farrel interrupted.

"How far west does this quarantine run?" Rusty asked.

"It goes pretty near to the Colorado line," Farrel answered.

Rusty shook his head. "You can't make it stick," he announced. "You're goin' to have to let trail cattle through. Why . . ."

"There's about five hundred men that are ready to make it stick," Farrel snapped.

"But isn't there some way?"

"There might of been a week ago." Farrel's bearded face was hard. "There ain't now. We wanted to make a lane for the first herd that come through. The trail boss wouldn't listen to us. He said that the country had always been open, an' he was goin' to keep it that way. We wasn't organized. My son-in-law was killed. There ain't no way open now, an' there won't be till after frost."

Carlisle, relieved at the herd by Kansas and the others, had ridden up and dismounted. He had overheard the last portion of the talk. Now he entered it.

"These are my cattle," he announced. "We've got a delivery date to keep in Dodge City. We've got to go through."

Farrel looked at the speaker and shrugged. "You ain't goin' through," he said flatly. "I've told you. Come on, Joel."

Peters looked unhappily at Rusty, glanced at Carlisle and, turning, followed his companion to where their horses stood. Wordlessly both men mounted and rode away. They did not look back. Rusty stood watching them and, when they were out of sight, turned to look at Leonard Carlisle. Carlisle was smiling.

"Can you get around that, Shotridge?" he challenged. "Can you?"

As always, Rusty met Carlisle's antagonism with rising anger. Carefully he held himself in check. "Do you think you could go through, Carlisle?" he demanded.

Here was a counterchallenge. Carlisle felt it, and suddenly an idea came into his mind. Here was a thing that Rusty could not break, could not handle. But Carlisle could handle it. He was sure that he could. Now he would prove his superiority. Now he would show this gray-eyed man who stared at him so coolly that he, Leonard Carlisle, was capable.

"I'll wait until you fall down," Carlisle said complacently. "Then I'll get the herd through."

Rusty bristled. His temper was gone, lost before Carlisle's cool effrontery. "You won't have to take 'em through!" Rusty snapped. "I'll get along without yore help."

"By killing another man or two, I suppose?" Carlisle drawled. "I don't think you can do it, Shotridge. Not this time. There are too many of them, and there is law in Kansas."

Rusty opened his mouth to retort, thought better of it and, wheeling, strode to his horse. Untying the animal, he mounted and trotted out toward the cattle.

Kansas and his three friends were bunched beside the cattle. Rusty stopped and, as always, looked at the herd. They were spread out, each big steer with a little space about him. Some were lying down, peacefully chewing their cuds. Others were still on their feet, grazing. Rusty turned from the cattle to the men. Briefly he recounted the conversation that had just taken place back by the wagon. When he had finished Kansas asked a question:

"Yo're goin' through?"

"I got to," Rusty said simply.

"How?"

Rusty pushed back his hat. "It must be open range that Farrel an' his bunch are usin'," he answered. "We'll move west. Then along about dark we'll start the steers. They'll run, an' before they stop they'll be through the line an' there won't be any quarantine left. We'll gather 'em an' go on to Dodge. I don't want to start from here because there's fences north of us, an' I don't want cattle piled up against wire an' cut to pieces. I think . . ." He stopped. There was something in Kansas' face that made him check.

"Don't you think that would work?" Rusty demanded. "Hell, I'm not goin' to hurt their range. There aren't any ticks on these cattle."

"It would work all right," Kansas agreed. "You wouldn't do 'em no damage neither, an' I guess it would be the right thing to do. But there's somethin' else botherin' me an' the boys, Rusty."

"What?"

Kansas looked at his companions and then back to the trail boss. "We can't go no further with you," he said apologetically. "We . . . Well, we're kind of wanted in this country. I been meanin' to tell you that we was goin' to have to quit pretty quick. Now with this business of bein' held up here an' what with fellers that 'll come out visitin' the herd an' all, we think mebbe we'd better pull our freight back where we come from." He looked anxiously into Rusty's eyes.

Rusty could not help but grin. Bad as the news was, bad as was the position in which he would be left when these men were gone, still he could not help but feel the grim humor of the situation.

Kansas, seeing the whisper of a smile twitch Rusty's lips, let his own grin spread over his homely face. "It's just a matter of a few horses that was missin' up here," he confided. "It ain't nothin' serious, but you cain't never tell how these grangers are goin' to take a thing. An' they know we done it too. That feller that was talkin' to you owned some of the horses."

Rusty laughed. "I don't blame you boys a bit," he said when his laughter was done. "You stuck out yore necks when you came this far with me. I'm sure obliged to you. The thing is I'm goin' to have trouble payin' you off. I haven't any money an' no letter of credit. I don't know exactly how to handle it, an' from what you say you don't want to stick around."

"We talked about that too," Kansas said. "We figured that mebbe you could spare us

233

a few horses."

"Why, I can do that," Rusty agreed.

"An' we ain't goin' to leave you up a tree," Kansas continued. "We'll hang around awhile until you can get some men to help handle the steers. It's just that we dasn't go any further. You know how it is, don't you?"

Rusty nodded. "I know," he answered. "An' like I say, I'm obliged to you boys a whole lot."

"Guess we can go back to camp now," Chico said. "Seems like they're gone."

Rusty laughed again and, with Kansas and Chico beside him, started back toward the wagon.

As he rode he considered briefly the change in his circumstances. He had had not twenty minutes ago a crew that would follow him and obey him, and in his mind had been a plan that would take him through the quarantine line. Now he had neither crew nor plan. He could not — as he had told them — blame Kansas and his fellows a bit for quitting. They had risked themselves coming so far with the herd. Rusty felt a thrill of pride and satisfaction because he knew that the risk had been taken on his account. But the fact remained that because of their own safety the men would go no further.

And that spoiled Rusty's plan. Any man that he might employ, always provided that he could get men, would be from the locality. Their loyalty would not be to the herd or to the trail boss, but to the dollar that hired them. Men like that would not take chances. They would not stampede a herd of steers through a quarantine line and then abide by the consequences. The scheme that Rusty had outlined to Kansas and his fellows was out. And if it was out, how could Rusty take the Watrous herd through to Dodge City? How could he meet the delivery date which was not more than a week away? Rusty did not know.

He was silent when he reached the wagon and, dismounting, tied his horse. He walked to his unrolled bed and, sitting down on it, rolled a cigarette. Over and over in his mind he turned possibilities and could find no solution to his problem. There was no way out. And now a grim struggle began in Rusty. Carlisle had a scheme. Carlisle thought that he could take the cattle through the quarantine. Maybe Carlisle could do it. Rusty's pride rebelled against the idea, against the fact that Carlisle might succeed where he, Rusty Shotridge, had failed. But there was the herd to consider, and Colonel Watrous waiting in Dodge City. Rusty remembered how he had talked to Gil Travis away back there below the Canadian. Rusty had told Travis that he had taken Colonel Watrous's wages a long time. He had been appealing to Travis's loyalty, and because of that appeal Travis had started to join in when the trouble began. Gil Travis was dead. Was a man's pride any more than a man's life? Was Gil Travis a better man than Rusty Shotridge?

Rusty got up from his bed and walked over to where Carlisle sat. He stood looking down at Carlisle, and the dark-eyed youth stared up at him.

"I'm stumped, Carlisle," Rusty said levelly. "I don't know how to get through this quarantine. You said you could do it. If you can I'll take your orders."

Chapter XIV

At first Carlisle, looking up at Rusty, thought that this was some trick, some trap that was being set for him. Then he realized that his suspicion had no foundation. Rusty Shotridge was surrendering. He was stepping out and putting Carlisle in charge. The knowledge flooded the younger man, filling him with sudden, savage satisfaction. He continued to stare at Rusty.

"So you can't get through?" Carlisle drawled. "You've found something you can't do. Well, I can do it, Shotridge, and you'll go with me while I do it."

"I've said I'd take your orders, Carlisle," Rusty answered steadily. "Have you got any?"

"Not now," Carlisle answered. "But tomorrow morning you'll go with me."

Rusty nodded and, turning, walked back to his bed. He seated himself, and after a little time Carlisle could see the intermittent glowing of Rusty's cigarette.

Leonard Carlisle lay back upon his bed, locked his hands behind his head and stared at the stars. Why Rusty had surrendered Carlisle did not know. He only knew that the surrender had come and that the fact was sweet.

In the morning, when the camp was wakened and the usual morning chores were done, Carlisle nodded to Rusty. "We'll go now," he said and smiled maliciously.

Rusty made no comment. He turned to Nugget who stood close by and spoke briefly: "We'll hold the steers right where we are. Just day herd 'em."

Nugget nodded, and Kansas, coming up from saddling a horse, spoke: "What about . . . ?"

"I'd be obliged if you boys could wait around for a while," Rusty said, answering the unfinished question. "It's too big a job for Ben to handle alone, an' Telesfor can't help him much till I get back. Will that suit you?"

Kansas stood silent a moment before answering. "We'll stay as long as we can," he agreed. "But somethin' might come up that would make us go. We'll do the best we can for you, Rusty."

"That's all any man could ask," Rusty said.

Carlisle spoke impatiently. "Come on, Shotridge."

"Comin'," Rusty answered.

The two rode away side by side, Kansas and Nugget following their broad backs with questioning eyes. Two hundred yards from the wagon Carlisle spoke to his companion. "I want to find the men who came to camp yesterday: Peters and Farrel. Do you know where we can find them?"

"Farrel has a place over west," Rusty answered. "I don't know where we can locate Peters."

"You should have asked." Carlisle's voice chastised Rusty. "Well, no matter. I want to find them."

"Then the best thing to do is to strike

west," Rusty said. "There 'll be somebody watchin' along the creek, an' we can find out about Farrel from him."

Not a mile from the wagon Rusty's prophecy was fulfilled. As they crossed the little stream that Farrel had called Kaw Creek a man came riding down toward them from a knoll. He carried a rifle across his arm, and his gray beard was stained with tobacco juice. "Goin' someplace?" he asked casually.

"We're looking for Mr. Farrel," Carlisle answered.

The guard thought for a moment, studying the two cowmen as he rolled his tobacco back and forth in his mouth. Then he nodded.

"No harm in that, I guess," he drawled. "Farrel's place is about eight miles west an' north of here. You can't miss it. Jest foller the creek."

Carlisle turned his horse and started on, and Rusty, smiling at the guard, drawled: "Thanks."

As the two rode along the creek heavy grass lay all about them, rustling against their stirrups as they rode. This was a paradise for cattle, this flat, plains country. The creek grew smaller and finally became a series of potholes, the grass growing so heavy that it overhung the water.

"I don't see . . ." Carlisle began petulantly.

"It's over there," Rusty said and pointed. Following the direction of the pointing arm, Carlisle could see a clump of trees. There were horses in the trees, and close by the timber a little mound.

"Soddy," Rusty explained. "Likely Farrel lives in it. There's a sod barn behind the house."

Carlisle could see another, bigger, knoll now as they turned to ride toward the timber.

Details presented themselves as the two approached. The horses in the timber were saddled and tied. There were a dozen of them. A tin chimney stuck through the roof of the sod house; a corral, hidden because of the trees, showed behind the length of the sod barn. Men loafed in the shade of the barn, and as Carlisle and Rusty came up Farrel himself climbed the steps from the soddy and stood there, waiting. Carlisle stopped and dismounted, and Rusty, swinging down, took the reins of both horses and held them while Carlisle advanced.

"I've come over to talk to you, Mr. Farrel," Carlisle said.

Farrel made a gesture toward the door of the sod house. "Come in," he invited. "We're havin' a sort of committee meetin'.

Come in."

Carlisle, at the top step, looked back at his companion. "Tie the horses and come on," he commanded curtly.

Rusty tied his own reins to the horn of Carlisle's saddle, Carlisle's reins to the horn of his own. Head to tail the horses stood, swishing at flies in the early-morning sunlight. The horses fastened, Rusty followed Carlisle down the steps.

There was light from the door and from a glazed window in the sod house. Not much light, for the window was dirty and the door gave only enough space for sunlight to form an oblong pool upon the earthen floor. Carlisle was sitting on a bench close to the door, and opposite him, along the wall and beside a table, men sat, grave faced, silent, as though met in judgment. There were six of them. Rusty paused beside Carlisle, leaning his back against the wall and standing utterly relaxed. Carlisle had waited for Rusty to come before he began. He wanted Rusty to see his triumph, wanted Rusty to witness his success in the task that Rusty had failed and relinquished.

"I've come over to see you this morning," Carlisle announced, some condescension in his tone. "I wanted to get together with you about this quarantine."

No one answered for a moment. Rusty could see Joel Peters shifting nervously. The others sat still as stones. When answer came it was Farrel who made it.

"Yes?"

Carlisle nodded. "I've got a delivery date to make in Dodge City," he announced. "I've got my cattle sold and I've got to get them there."

Rusty could see the tightening in the still faces that confronted him. Carlisle was not getting very far, Rusty thought.

"There's no sense in this quarantine," Carlisle continued. "We can get together about it."

"*We* already got together." A gray-haired, gray-bearded man close beside Farrel spoke. "We made a quarantine line an' it ain't goin' to be broke."

Carlisle looked at the speaker and then turned again to Farrel. "We aren't going to try to break it," he said.

Relief came into the room, definitely, entering almost as a man might come down the steps. "But I'm going to get my cattle to Dodge City," Carlisle continued. The relief was gone, as definitely as it had come.

Farrel shook his head. "You can't," he said bluntly.

"Yes, I can," Carlisle said confidently.

"Trail cattle mean too much to Kansas for you men to hold us out. The merchants in Dodge City and the cattle buyers won't let you keep up this farce."

Quiet followed that announcement, and into the silence Farrel threw words. "The Dodge City people ain't got fences to be cut or cattle that can get tick fever. It ain't them that's set a quarantine. It's us."

Along the wall men nodded their heads. Carlisle spoke quickly: "That's why I came to see you. I thought . . ."

Farrel interrupted. "Arguin' won't get you anyplace. We made a bargain with each other an' we're goin' to keep it. You can't get through."

"But wait until you hear what I've got to say," Carlisle protested. "I want to do the fair thing for you. Now I'll tell you what I'll do: I'll buy a passage through your quarantine for my cattle. How is that?"

Here was his idea. Here was the thing that he had thought of, the plan that would show his superiority over Rusty Shotridge, the scheme that would get the herd through to Dodge City. In that little room, with dirt walls all about, it fell flat.

"What 'll you buy it with?" Farrel asked after a moment. "How you goin' to pay for spreadin' ticks on our range? Or how you goin' to pay for wheat that's tramped out? You ain't got enough money."

"But I'll pay . . ." Carlisle began.

"You might buy one wheat field," Farrel interrupted, "but you couldn't buy 'em all. There's more behind the first one. An' you can't buy passage through my country. My son-in-law . . ."

"He was my boy," Peters rasped. "You damned wild Texas cowmen killed him."

"But . . ." Carlisle began.

"You can't do it," Farrel rasped. "There ain't enough money to buy a lane through this country."

Dead silence followed that announcement. In the quiet came a little creaking sound as Rusty Shotridge shifted his weight against the door. For a moment more the tension held, and then Rusty asked calmly: "Yo're the men that set up the quarantine, aren't you? Yo're the bosses?"

All eyes left Carlisle's face and settled on Rusty's own. Farrel nodded very slowly. Rusty's voice drawled on casually, a commonplace voice, and yet carrying a depth and force that prevented interruption.

"We're goin' to take the cattle through. We got to."

In the dim corner of the room a man moved. Rusty shifted again, just a fraction, his left shoulder against the doorcasing, right arm and hand hanging free.

"Wait!" he ordered. The man in the corner checked his movement, and Rusty's voice went on: "Let me talk a minute."

"Talk then!" Farrel snapped. "But if you think . . ."

"A man's got a kind of pride," Rusty drawled as Farrel paused. "You've got pride an' I've got it. I've come from Texas with these cattle. I've got to get 'em to Dodge City. We've had a poor time on the trail. We've had some steers stolen an' we've lost some men. The trail boss that started with the herd was killed in a stampede. I saw a man that would of made a friend killed, an' I killed the man that shot him. We've had a poor time but we've come so far. Now we're goin' on."

He paused a moment, glancing around the room, demanding the attention of his listeners with his eyes. "You've set up this quarantine, an' it's yore pride to hold it," he said softly. "I've brought the herd so far, an' it's my pride to take it on. This is a showdown. You can do one of two things: Either you can let my herd through or you can take to shootin'."

Rusty let his shoulders slump. Other than that he made no movement, and in the silence that followed his words a man cleared his throat nervously. Farrel's eyes were sharp and bright as he looked at the young rider, and Rusty met Farrel's gaze squarely. There was a glint of admiration in Farrel's eyes. This man at the door, this medium-sized, commonplace fellow with the torn clothing and the dust and dirt of the trail upon him, had made his declaration and was willing to abide by it. Farrel knew that Rusty could be killed. He knew, too, that Rusty did not care. The man at the door was right. Pride, and pride alone, stood between the opponents. Carlisle was of no account. It was with Rusty Shotridge that the rangemen had to deal.

"Mebbe there's another way," Farrel said softly. "You got any more ideas, Shotridge?"

The tension broke. Over in the corner the man who had drawn his gun returned it carefully to its scabbard. A man let go his pent-up breath in a sigh. A gleam came into Rusty's eyes. He had won!

"I think there is," he answered Farrel. "Mr. Carlisle's offered to buy a lane through for the cattle," he continued. "It's a good idea. But money won't buy it. I know that. It's got to be somethin' else. You've had trouble an' yo're mad. I don't blame you. But you aren't thinkin' about what's goin'

246

to come. There 'll be herds piled up below your line. More an' more of 'em. There 'll be men that are pretty desperate, an' they'll try to break through. You'll kill some of them an' they'll kill some of you. It ain't worth it. Not when it comes to killin'. You've already decided that."

"So . . . ?" Farrel rasped into the stillness that followed Rusty's statement.

"So," Rusty drawled, "let's not have it. Let's get together now."

"How?"

"Give us a lane through. Put riders with my steers to see that they don't break out of the lane. Make it a way that all the herds that are comin' can follow. Do that an' I'll go to every drover in Dodge City an' speak to 'em. I'll make 'em promise to meet their herds an' hold 'em in the lane. Give us a lane through or let's settle it right here."

He waited. On the bench Joel Peters stirred. "It was my boy that was killed," Peters said. "I . . . Hell! Give him his road, Farrel."

Farrel looked around at the others. Heads were slowly nodding, and Farrel turned back to Rusty. "You give us yore word that you'll do that?" he demanded. "You'll talk to the drovers? You'll have 'em meet their herds an' hold 'em in the lane we set?"

Rusty nodded. It was enough. The tension that had gripped the sod house relaxed. "I'll want you to put riders with my cattle," Rusty said. "I'll want them to pilot us through."

"We'll do that," Farrel assured. "Now . . ." He turned to the others. Rusty remained relaxed against the doorcasing while the talk went on between Farrel and his companions, while they decided upon the route they would open through their quarantine line. Somehow Rusty felt drained, all the strength gone out of him.

"You can go back to yore camp, Shotridge," Farrel announced at length. "We'll send some men down. I'll come with 'em." He laughed shortly. "Yo're a powerful persuasive orator." he concluded. "Half an hour ago I'd of said there was as much chance of us makin' a lane through for you as there is for a snowball lastin' in hell. We'll be along shortly."

"I'm obliged to you," Rusty said. He looked down at Carlisle. Answering the look, Carlisle arose and followed Rusty out of the sod house.

The two men did not talk as they rode back to the wagon. They followed along the creek, through the good grass, and presently came within sight of the grazing herd. There were two men with the cattle, Ben Nugget and Telesfor Maes. At the wagon Joe Deems came out and waited for Rusty to dismount.

"You lost yore crew," Deems announced when Rusty was off his horse. "They pulled out half an hour after you left. They've taken twelve horses. Said that you told 'em they could have 'em."

Rusty nodded.

"A long-whiskered granger come in after you left," Deems continued. "Seemed like Kansas an' them knew him. They didn't waste no time leavin' after he pulled out."

Rusty felt a sudden pang of loneliness. He had liked Kansas and Chico and Gus and Red. They were gone, gone back into that country below the Canadian. Likely he would never see them again. Deems seemed to sense Rusty's thought.

"Kansas said to tell you 'so long' before he left," the cook announced. "An' he said to tell you that he'd likely see you sometime."

"I hope so." Rusty stood looking at the cook. "Well, they're gone. You'd better get dinner for a crowd today, Joe. I don't know how many 'll be here, but cook for a big crew. We'll move cattle this afternoon."

"But . . ." Deems said.

"We got a lane to go through," Rusty

explained. "Cook a big dinner, Joe, an' make it a good one."

There was a question in the cook's eyes, but Rusty did not answer it. He turned to Carlisle, standing silently beside him. "I think I'll go out an' spell the boys for a while," he said. "They've been standin' day herd ever since we left."

Carlisle turned toward his waiting horse. "I'll go with you," he announced shortly.

Just before noon a group of riders came down from the northwest. There were ten of them, and in the lead was the gray-bearded man who had been beside Farrel in the sod house. Rusty came into camp and was there to meet the strangers. Nugget and Telesfor he dispatched to the herd so that only he and Deems were in camp when the men arrived.

Invited to refresh themselves, the Kansas men made free with the plates and cups, the knives and forks and the good dinner that Deems had prepared, and while they ate the gray-haired man talked to Rusty. The lane had been made, its boundaries outlined by the committee in Farrel's sod house. The herd was to move west along the creek and then turn north after about two miles. They would follow definite landmarks. The gray-bearded Kansan spoke familiarly of these.

"You'll be with us," Rusty said. "I couldn't keep all that country straight in my head anyhow. Why don't you boys just handle the steers? You could pilot us that way."

Graybeard agreed to the suggestion and when the meal was finished called his men together, and they rode out to the loosely grazing herd, Rusty accompanying them.

He found occasion to speak briefly to Nugget, and old Ben loped off to carry Rusty's word to Telesfor and Carlisle. The Kansas men bunched the cattle, and the steers, well broken as they were to the trail, made no trouble but strung out in marching order. Nugget, Carlisle and Telesfor loped back to the wagon to eat and change horses, and Rusty, freshly mounted, remained with the cattle.

The gray-bearded man rode on a point, and Rusty took the other. Behind those two came the steers, riders flanking swing and drag. Rising in his stirrups, Rusty looked back. There was activity at the camp. Deems was already packing the wagon, and before he settled in his saddle again Rusty could see Telesfor bunching the horses.

An hour after the herd had begun to move Farrel came riding in from the west. He spoke briefly to Rusty, swung across to speak to Graybeard and then rode back along the herd. When he returned to Rusty, riding on the point, he asked a question:

"Where's yore crew, Shotridge?"

"You've seen 'em," Rusty said briefly. "I'm a little shy on men."

Farrel, riding beside the trail boss, was silent as he considered that. Then, swift as sunlight coming through a cloud, a grin broke across his bearded face. "There's three of you an' a horse wrangler an' a cook," he said.

"That's right," Rusty agreed gravely.

"An' you got about two thousand head of steers in this bunch?"

"That's right."

Farrel began to laugh. "You talked us into lettin' you through," he said when his laughter died. "Then on top of that you got us to furnish a crew to move you. You'd get by with murder in a church, Shotridge."

"I don't ever aim to try it," Rusty answered soberly. "But sometimes a man's got to do something, ain't he?"

Farrel laughed unrestrained and heartily. "I'm damned glad to get you through my country," he announced finally. "It 'll be a relief when yo're gone. By golly, if we hadn't let you through when we did you'd of talked us into loanin' you some horses too."

"The boys are all ridin' their own horses the way it is," Rusty said thoughtfully, a twinkle in his eyes. "They make pretty good trail hands."

Farrel laughed again, and after a moment Rusty joined him. When Farrel sobered Rusty spoke: "You think I could hire any of these boys to take us on to Dodge? After we're through quarantine, I mean? I'd talk nice to 'em an' feed 'em good an' pay 'em wages."

Farrel grinned. "There 'll be some go with you," he said. "I'm goin' to pull out now an' head for home. If I stay here with you you'll have *me* talked into helpin' you into Dodge City with yore steers, an' I can't go. I got work to do. So long, Shotridge. You won't forget yore promise, will you?"

"No," Rusty said, "you can depend on it; I won't."

Farrel stopped his horse. Rusty also halted. Farrel's broad hand shot out and Rusty took it. "I know I can depend on you," Farrel said. "Good-by an' good luck. I'll be seein' you."

Chapter XV

They camped that night ten miles above Kaw Creek. After supper Rusty made casual conversation with the new men. These, as had Farrel, knew his weakness and enjoyed the deception that he had put upon them. It pleased them to be deceived. The russet-haired trail boss was smart; he had put one over, for not only had he talked a way for himself through the quarantine, but he had also talked the makers of the quarantine into giving him a crew to move the cattle. There were some young men in the crew, farmers' sons who were part cow-puncher and part farmer. Rusty, sounding out his companions, knew that he could hire a few to go on with the steers when finally they were through the quarantine line.

The fire was low, a glowing thing made from cow chips, and the voices about the wagon were as low as the fire when the steady sound of a horse trotting up from the south caused a check in the talk. The horse came on, stopped, and out in the dusk a voice spoke: "Rusty? You there?"

Rusty knew that voice. He had risen when the horse stopped and now, taking a step toward the voice, he answered it: "I'm here. Come on in to the fire, Bud."

Again there was the sound of the moving horse, and then Bud Sigloe appeared, rode close and, stopping, dismounted. He walked casually up to the fire, stopped in front of

Rusty and, after a moment's survey, thrust out his hand. Almost three months ago these men had parted in San Marcial. Now, as though the parting had been but yesterday, they shook hands briefly and dropped their palms apart.

"How are you?" Sigloe asked.

"Pretty good. An' you?"

"All right. I'm camped down below the quarantine line. Got a herd of stock cattle. A fello' down there told me you'd come through, so I rode up to see you."

"I'm mighty glad you did." Sigloe turned abruptly, walked toward the wagon and, reaching it, sat down, leaning his back against the wagon tongue. Rusty sat down beside Sigloe.

"They told me they'd made a lane through for you," Sigloe announced, producing pipe and tobacco. "How was that?"

"I talked to Farrel an' some others," Rusty said. "You know Farrel?"

"He told me you were here." Bud Sigloe filled his pipe.

"I made 'em a promise," Rusty said. "I told them that I'd go to every drover in Dodge City an' talk to 'em. It looked like trouble for a while."

"Farrel told me that too." In the dusk Sigloe's match showed his face, strong and bearded, as he lit his pipe. "I'm goin' to follow the lane, Rusty. They're givin' me a pilot in the mornin'."

Rusty felt relief. He had made a bargain without being sure that he could fulfill it. But if Bud Sigloe was satisfied, if he was going to follow the lane through the quarantine, then things would work out. Bud Sigloe could set a precedent for other trail bosses to follow.

"That's good, Bud," Rusty said thankfully.

Sigloe peered curiously at his companion. "You changed some, kid," he drawled. "Yo're older. How does it happen yo're runnin' this outfit? What happened?"

"McBride got killed in a stampede down below the Canadian," Rusty answered. "We had some trouble. It kind of looked like I had to run things."

Sigloe tamped his pipe with a calloused finger. "Tell me about it," he commanded briefly.

Rusty tipped back against the wagon tongue, pulled up one knee and, locking his fingers about it, began to talk. His voice drawled on, flatly monotonous, as he recounted the events of the trail. Once or twice he paused, collecting his thoughts, putting events in proper sequence. Sigloe listened, the pipe in his hand growing cold.

"So," Rusty concluded, "we got stopped by the quarantine. I couldn't figure a way through, but Carlisle thought he had one, an' we went over to talk to Farrel and the rest. Carlisle figured that we could buy a way through. They wouldn't listen to money, so we had to figure somethin' else. I made a proposition an' they took me up on it. You think that the drovers will listen to me, Bud? Do you think they'll meet their herds an' hold them in the lane?"

"I'll go with you an' talk to 'em," Sigloe said shortly. "I think they'll listen. Tom will go along, too, you know."

Rusty nodded. With Bud Sigloe and Tom Flanders behind him he knew that the drovers, awaiting their herds in Dodge City, would listen and eventually agree.

"How's Carlisle doin'?" Sigloe asked.

"He's makin' a hand," Rusty answered.

Sigloe did not speak again for a minute. He was revolving in his mind all the things that Rusty had told him. "You think that Slippery Smith got them cattle you lost?" he asked.

"I know it," Rusty said positively.

Sigloe thought a moment before he spoke. "You've had yore share of grief," he commented, drawing on his pipe. "Anyhow, yore share. I come through the Nations right after you. I had a little run-in with Eagle Claws myse'f. He didn't help me near as much as he helped you. I traded him a crippled heifer for two hides. Both the hides I got was branded LM. Did you trail brand yore cattle after you left?"

"We grubbed an ear," Rusty answered. "We never put an iron on 'em. I've never had a full enough crew nor time enough to really mark 'em."

"Both the hides I've got was skinned by Comanches," Sigloe said, apparently apropos of nothing. "A Comanche don't waste any hide. He takes all of it, even the head."

"Yeah?" Rusty looked through the gloom at his companion.

"Yeah." Sigloe's voice was flat. "Both hides are shy an ear, an' one of 'em has got a hackamore burned across the nose."

Rusty stared thoughtfully at the dying fire. "That was how he figured it then," he said slowly. "Slippery Smith must of had some LM steers cached someplace. He could throw what he stole from us in with what he already had, brand 'em an' come on. That was the way he could get 'em by. Do you think that's it, Bud?"

"That's the only way it could be," Sigloe answered.

Now both men were silent, both thinking.

It was plain enough now that Bud Sigloe had spoken of the hides. Slippery Smith, with some LM steers that he lawfully owned, had planned to increase his herd. The steers lost by the Watrous outfit in the stampede had been collected by Smith's riders and held, hidden, when the two herds were gathered and separated. Then when the Watrous trail herd had gone on, Smith could run his hackamore road brand on the stolen cattle, doctor his bill of sale and continue up the trail. No one could prove that the freshly branded cattle were not his. Arriving at a market, he could sell them. It was a foolproof scheme, but to work it needed the connivance and knowledge of Scott McBride and the men who drove the Watrous cattle.

"Scott McBride . . ." Sigloe began.

"Is dead," Rusty completed.

Bud Sigloe said no more. It was true. Scott McBride was dead, and there was no use of recriminations, of accusing a dead man of treachery to his employer.

"I don't like to show up with a short count," Rusty drawled. "I don't like that."

"Slippery will never head for Dodge now," Sigloe announced. "He knows he can't get by with his steal. He'll head for someplace else."

"Uh-huh." Rusty nodded.

Once more Bud Sigloe lit his pipe and drew on it thoughtfully. "Slippery Smith an' Honey Yates," he mused. "It must of been one of them that tried for you in San Marcial."

"That's right," Rusty agreed.

"I wonder why Honey let you go as long as he did," Sigloe mused. "There must of been a dozen times he could have killed you comin' up the trail. I reckon God had his arm around yore neck, Rusty."

"I guess that's right."

"Well" — Bud Sigloe puffed twice on his pipe — "I'll stay the night if you can stake me to a bed."

"You can have mine," Rusty proffered. "I've got a bunch of new men an' I'll be up most of the night. A blanket will do me for what sleep I'll get."

"Let's drink a cup of coffee," Sigloe suggested. "I'll be ridin' early tomorrow. I want to get back an' pick up my pilot an' start my cattle through this lane you made."

Rusty hoisted himself to his feet. "Let's drink a cup of coffee then," he said.

They drank their coffee, and Rusty showed Sigloe his bed. Sigloe sat down on the tarp, and Rusty, before he turned away, spoke once more. "I was mighty glad to hear you

260

call tonight," he said.

"You wasn't no gladder than I was when I heard you answer," Sigloe said gruffly. "Well, good night, kid. Ain't many times a trail boss can sleep a night through, an' I'm goin' to take advantage of the chance I got."

"Good night," Rusty said and, turning, walked out to where his night horse was staked.

The stars seemed very close to Rusty as he rode out to the bedded steers. The sky pressed down and the air was clear, cool after the heat of the day. It would not be long now. Not long before he could relinquish the responsibility he had shouldered, not long before he would be free again. The thought was good. At the herd a man sang softly and Rusty, well away from the cattle, drew his horse to a halt and waited, listening and watchful. The singing died away into a murmur, and another voice drew close.

"Carlisle?" Rusty said.

The voice stopped. A mounted man, black against the sky, came from the dark blotch that was the herd and stopped.

"I wanted to tell you," Rusty said. "It was your idea that got us through. I'd never thought of buyin' a way. It was your idea."

Silence fell between the two men for a

long moment, then Carlisle spoke, his voice choked. "It was you that got us through, Shotridge."

Again the silence. Once more the choked voice broke it. "I've been wrong all along, Rusty. I've been a damned fool."

"No you ain't," sharply.

"I have."

"Look," Rusty said, "why don't you just forget it? You . . ."

"I can't forget it. Everything I've done has made trouble. I was sore at you. I . . . I've been a damned fool."

"We're goin' to be in Dodge City pretty soon," Rusty said. "The trail is all behind us. As far as I'm concerned it's goin' to stay that way."

Carlisle gulped. Rusty shifted in his saddle. Through the darkness Carlisle spoke again. "Ellen will be in Dodge City," he said. "I . . . I hope you'll be very happy, Rusty."

"I'll be damned happy to get shut of this job," Rusty said frankly.

"And I hope that the two of you . . ." Carlisle broke off miserably. Apparently he had not heard Rusty's words.

"The two of us?" Rusty's voice was incredulous. "What do you mean, Carlisle?"

"I saw you on the porch of the hotel,"

Carlisle said. "You and Ellen. She kissed you. I . . ."

Rusty stared at the man who faced him, trying to find Carlisle's eyes. "She kissed me?" Rusty said.

"Yes, she . . ."

"Look here, Carlisle, are you in love with Ellen?"

For an instant Leonard Carlisle did not answer. Then: "Yes, I'm in love with her!" His voice was defiant.

"An' you saw her kiss me an' you thought . . . ?" Rusty broke off. The laugh that followed the words was light, filled with amusement and nothing more. "Good gosh," Rusty exclaimed after the laugh. "You thought we were in love with each other? Is that it?"

"What else could I think?" Carlisle spoke stiffly.

Rusty chuckled. "I don't mean no more to Ellen Watrous than that pony yo're ridin'," he said. "Not a thing more. An' I'm not in love with her either."

The silence was filled with blank surprise. Then: "Why did she kiss you?" Carlisle demanded.

Again Rusty chuckled. "She grew up followin' me around," he said. "We've always been friends. Out there on the porch she

263

was workin' on me. I was sore at you, an' you were sore at me. She made me promise to look after you, an' when I promised she reached out an' kissed me. Hell, man! Ellen Watrous is in love with you. That's who she's in love with!"

"But . . ." Carlisle began.

"You said you were a damned fool, an' maybe yo're right," Rusty interrupted. "All this time you been worried about that. That's why you didn't like me, isn't it?"

"That's why," Carlisle said frankly. "And I was jealous. I . . . Well, that was it."

Once more Rusty laughed. "You *are* a damned fool," he declared. "Here's Ellen waitin' for you in Dodge an' worryin' about you, an' you been jealous of *me.* I wish you'd told me, Carlisle."

"I wish I had," Carlisle assented. "Rusty, you're more of a man than I am. You . . ."

"I ain't no more man nor a better one. I went along as high-headed as you, an' just as stubborn. Well . . . that's over now, isn't it?"

"It's over," Carlisle agreed. "I . . . Rusty, I don't know how to thank you."

For an instant Rusty hesitated. The air was clear between him and Carlisle now, clear as far as Carlisle was concerned, but how about Rusty? Should he speak out now?

Should he tell Carlisle that as surely as he, Leonard Carlisle, loved Ellen Watrous, it was certain that Rusty was in love with Marcia? Should he? Rusty shook his head. It would not do, not yet. When the end of the trail was reached, when the cattle — all the cattle — were in Dodge City, then he could speak. Until that time he must hold his peace.

"Forget it!" There in the darkness Rusty's shoulders squared. Once more he was the trail boss, the man in charge. "It's time for your relief," he announced. "Better ride in an' wake 'em up. I'll make a circle around the herd."

Turning his horse, he rode away, leaving Carlisle alone there in the starlit darkness.

When morning came Bud Sigloe rode back toward the south, and the Watrous cattle went on north. That day they covered fifteen miles, and that night Rusty Shotridge hired six men from the Kansas riders who had come to take him through the quarantine. He talked to Carlisle before he hired the new crew, suggesting that as partial owner of the steers Carlisle should have a voice in the matter. Carlisle shook his head.

"You're the trail boss," he answered Rusty's suggestion. "It's up to you." So

Rusty hired the men.

The next day they moved and the next, and on the third day, approaching sundown, a buggy came toward them from the north. Colonel John Watrous was in the buggy.

Carlisle was riding point with Rusty. When the buggy stopped close by the line of march, he left his place and loped over to the vehicle. Rusty did not go. Now that Watrous had come, now that the end of the journey was at hand, he was frightened. He had done what he believed necessary, but how would Watrous look at it? Somehow Rusty was uneasy in his mind. He saw Carlisle reach the buggy and dismount. Saw him shake hands with Colonel Watrous. Then Ben Nugget moved up to take Carlisle's place on point, and the cattle were between Rusty, the buggy and its occupants.

Leonard Carlisle, reaching the buggy, found that Watrous was alone. Some word of what had happened, some word that all was not well with his cattle, had reached the colonel. He greeted Carlisle anxiously. When the two men had shaken hands Watrous bade Carlisle climb in beside him, and after tying his horse to the backstrap of the buggy horse, Carlisle complied. The colonel watched the steers file by, the long line of steadily moving animals strung out across the prairie. A familiar sight and yet always a fascinating one, the colonel waited until the herd had passed before speaking.

"We're short of cattle," he said when the drags had passed. "They aren't all there."

"We're short about five hundred head," Carlisle said steadily. "They were stolen, Colonel."

Watrous turned toward his partner. Normally a ruddy, full-faced man, the colonel looked old now, and tired. "We can't deliver our contract then," he said slowly. "This will just about break me, Leonard."

Carlisle shook his head. "No, it won't, Colonel," he objected.

"How did it happen?"

"I'll tell you," Carlisle answered. "Part of it was my fault. I'll tell you how it happened." He began his story then. He spoke of the first days of the drive, of the progress north toward the Red River, of crossing that stream. He recounted the tale of the stampede, speaking briefly of the death of Scott McBride and of his burial.

"Scott had driven for me for years," Watrous interrupted at that point. "I'm sorry to lose him. I . . ."

"Wait," Carlisle commanded. "Wait until you hear the rest of it."

He went on then, telling his companion of

the roundup that followed the stampede, of how he had counted cattle with Honey Yates, how he had taken Yates's count, knowing his own to be unreliable.

"I know better now," he said. "I think I could count a herd now, but I couldn't then. Nugget and Shotridge came to me and told me that the count was short, but I wouldn't listen to them. It wasn't until Deems talked to me that I consented to a recount. And there was trouble over that."

Watrous listened to Carlisle's story of what had happened in the camp that morning, following his declaration that the cattle would be recounted. When Carlisle told of Rusty's swift reaction, of the death of Gil Travis and Benbow, the colonel's color returned and his eyes were bright.

"We went on then," Carlisle said. "I made a fool of myself and Shotridge took charge. Someone had to. I didn't know enough and he knew it, so he took over. He hired four outlaws that had come into camp to take the place of the men that were gone, and we came on to the Canadian."

Carlisle paused. Watrous looked at him curiously. "We had trouble at the Canadian," Carlisle continued. "Yates and the men that had gone with him jumped us there."

Now came the story of the fight, swift and abrupt and savage. Carlisle's voice sank a tone and his eyes would not meet Watrous's. "I hit a man in that fight," Carlisle said. "I'd borrowed a rifle from Chico, one of the men Shotridge had hired. I think I killed the man I hit."

There was a long silence following that statement, and Watrous, reaching over, placed his hand on Carlisle's knee. With a start Carlisle came from his introspection and continued his story. The Canadian crossing, the march on north, he passed over briefly. Then came the denouement of his tale, the story of the quarantine and of how Rusty had won a way through it.

"We heard in Dodge City that there had been a quarantine line set up," Watrous said. "That's one reason I came out. I thought . . . Well, no matter."

Carlisle nodded. "You see, it was Mc-Bride." he said. "It must have been Mc-Bride. He must have made some agreement with Smith to steal cattle from us, Colonel. That's what it must have been."

For a time Watrous was silent. Then he said: "I trusted Scott, Leonard. I think . . ."

"You've got a man that you can trust now," Carlisle said harshly. "We lost some cattle, Colonel, but the only reason we've got any left at all is because of Rusty Shot-ridge."

Colonel John Watrous looked curiously at his companion. Carlisle was staring straight ahead, looking over the back of the buggy horse.

"You and Shotridge didn't hit it off," the colonel ventured. "You didn't like him, Leonard. I've been worried. . . ."

"It makes no difference to Shotridge who likes him and who doesn't," Carlisle said shortly. "He's man enough to get along."

There was a silence in the buggy while the horse trotted along, then Watrous spoke: "I'm sorry, Leonard. I'm sorry about all the trouble and about the loss. I talked you into this deal. When we sell the steers I'll take the loss out of my share."

"You'll do no such thing," Carlisle flared. "It was my fault, and I'll take the loss."

Watrous looked at the young man who rode beside him. Carlisle's jaw was square and outthrust, and his eyes met Watrous's gaze steadily. John Watrous shrugged. "But . . ." he began.

"We're partners," Carlisle stated. "We can talk about that later on. If you'll stop the buggy, Colonel, I'll take my horse and go out to the herd. We'll be throwing off the trail shortly and I'm needed."

Again the colonel looked sharply at his companion, then he pulled on the lines and said, "Whoa!" The horse stopped. Carlisle dismounted from the buggy, and Colonel Watrous leaned across the seat. "You haven't asked about your sister," he said. "She's in Dodge City with Ellen, waiting for us."

Carlisle untied his horse. "Is Ellen all right?" he asked.

A little glint of amusement came into John Watrous's eyes. "From your question," he answered enigmatically, "I'd judge that Ellen is all right. Go on out to your cattle now, Leonard. I'll see you at the wagon."

CHAPTER XVI

Colonel Watrous stayed at the wagon that night. He talked briefly to Rusty, checking on the story that Carlisle had told him. He left the herd next morning and returned to Dodge City, and when camp was made that evening there remained but half a day's drive. Rusty was anxious to go into the town, anxious because of his promise to Farrel, but Watrous had promised to talk to his drover friends who were awaiting the arrival of their herds, and Rusty felt that he should stay with his own outfit. Watrous could do more to make good Rusty's promise to Farrel than Rusty could himself.

They moved on the next day and by noon were within five miles of the town where, as he had been instructed, Rusty held up his herd. Shortly after their arrival Watrous drove up in his buggy, accompanied by two cattle buyers. Carlisle joined the men, and there was a conference in which Rusty played no part; then the group broke up and Watrous gave Rusty orders to string out for a count. This was done; there was some further consultation, then Watrous drove back toward town.

Carlisle, joining Rusty, made a casual announcement: "We'll deliver tomorrow. They're going to take the steers even though we are short."

"You lose much money?" Rusty demanded.

"Some," Carlisle said briefly. "Do you want to go to town tonight?"

"I'd kind of like to," Rusty admitted, "but if we're goin' to deliver tomorrow I'd better stay here. Why don't you go in?"

"I'll stay here too," Carlisle announced.

Since their talk in the night Carlisle had been close to Rusty. The enmity that each had fostered through the long days of the trail was gone now, burned away like morning haze by a bright sun. Rusty grinned companionably.

"You'd better go to town," he urged. "I'm goin' to let Ben an' Telesfor an' Joe go in. Why don't you go with 'em?"

"Why don't you go?" Carlisle countered.

"Because there's nobody waitin' for me," Rusty answered bluntly. "We can hold this herd tonight without your help. You go in an' see Ellen."

Carlisle flushed. "You're sure . . . ?" he began.

"I'm blame' sure she wants to see you," Rusty said forcefully. "By damn, if you don't go I've got a notion to . . ."

"To what?"

"Aw, hell," Rusty growled. "Go on. You're wastin' time."

Carlisle grinned, turned and walked to his horse. "I'll be back tonight," he called after he had mounted. "I'll stand my guard."

"You come back tonight an' I'll fire you," Rusty promised. "Get out of here now."

Turning his horse, Carlisle started toward town, and before he had gone a hundred yards the horse was loping. Rusty watched him go then walked back and spoke to Joe Deems.

"There's one of these Kansas boys that claims he's a cook. Why don't you go to town an' let him prove it?"

Deems grunted. Rusty walked away, leaving the old cook digging into the wagon for his ancient saddle.

With Deems, Telesfor and Nugget gone, Rusty sat down beside the wagon. There were other men in camp, but somehow Rusty felt all alone. It was not a cheerful feeling. Sitting there in the shade of the wagon, he rolled and lighted a cigarette. Tomorrow he would be done, through with all this responsibility he had assumed. Rusty shook his head. He would not be through with it. There remained an unfinished matter, a thing that he had not begun but that he would finish. He stared through the smoke, his eyes vacant, not seeing the country that stretched before him. With a shake of his head he discharged the thoughts that possessed him and turned to other channels.

About now Leonard Carlisle would be meeting Ellen. About now Ellen would be putting her arms around Carlisle's neck and kissing him. That was all right. Carlisle was fit for Ellen now, fit to be Ellen's man. He was a lot different from the spoiled youngster that had started up the trail. And Rusty had fulfilled his promise. He had brought Carlisle back; brought him back to Ellen and to Marcia.

Marcia! Carlisle and Ellen were forgotten as Rusty recalled the girl. Marcia's voice and the words she had spoken on the honeysuckle-covered porch at the Secáte ranch were a poignant memory. All along the trail, through the days and nights, through the trouble, the fighting, through it all, Marcia had been with him. And now she was close — only a few miles distant — and the thought frightened him. He loved Marcia Carlisle. Rusty knew it with certainty. But he was afraid.

There had been promise in her voice back there at the Secáte. Rusty could hear her now, hear the words she spoke. But time had passed and perhaps she had changed. Moodily Rusty puffed his cigarette alive. Suppose she had changed, or suppose she had wanted him to come to her when her brother was safely back, simply that she might thank him? Rusty shook his head at the thought. He didn't know. Here he was and there she was, just five miles away. He could climb on Big Enough and in thirty minutes he could see her. And what then? Rusty Shotridge, afraid of no man, master of himself and circumstances, winced at the question. Suppose she smiled and thanked him and turned away? Or suppose it was the other way? Suppose she had really meant what she said back there in Texas? If she did, who was he, Rusty Shotridge, to consider himself worthy of a girl like Marcia Carlisle?

Rusty flung away his cigarette and looked at Big Enough tied to a wagon wheel. Big Enough was a mighty good horse, just plenty of pony; but Big Enough could be outclassed. How would Big Enough look in the company of thoroughbreds?

"Yeah," Rusty drawled, and Big Enough cocked an ear to listen. "You an' me, Big Enough. We could get out of our class pretty easy, couldn't we?"

Big Enough brushed a fly from his belly with a black hoof and brought his leg down with a stamp. Mechanically Rusty began the fashioning of another smoke. He had postponed his meeting with Marcia, but he could not avoid it. That meeting must occur and Rusty was afraid.

"When yo're through dreamin' you might get up an' shake hands," a familiar voice drawled just back of Rusty. Rusty came to his feet. Tom Flanders was standing there grinning at him. Rusty's fingers gripped Flanders's outstretched hand.

The greetings over, Flanders held Rusty off at arm's length and commented forcefully and unfavorably on his appearance.

Rusty in turn accused his friend of getting fat on soft living, then they sat down to talk.

"I rode out to see you," Flanders stated. "I knew that you'd come in with the steers an' I heard somethin' about what had happened to you. Have you seen Bud?"

"He's right behind us," Rusty answered. "I saw him a couple of days ago. He ought to be in tomorrow."

"Ad Marble went out to meet him," Flanders commented. "There's been considerable talk about the quarantine since you got through it."

"What do the drovers say?" Rusty demanded eagerly. "Are they going to stick to the lane?"

"Most of 'em are," Flanders replied. "There's a couple that think they own the world an' don't need to pay attention to anybody else, but they'll see the light."

"I've got to talk to them," Rusty said. "I promised."

"You'll have a chance tomorrow," Flanders assured. "I'll go with you. Now tell me what happened, kid. Tell me about the trouble you had an' how come you lost some cattle."

"I didn't exactly lose 'em," Rusty returned. "Maybe I'm some to blame though. If I hadn't been so stubborn an' had made a friend of Carlisle, we likely could have found out what was comin' before we crossed Red River. I'll tell you what happened."

He began his tale then, describing the events of the trail. Flanders listened without interruption, and when Rusty concluded the peace officer grunted.

"You couldn't help it," he said, giving judgment. "It wasn't your fault, kid. It's goin' to be hard on Colonel Watrous though. He was nearly broke last year, an' this will just about put on the finishin' touches."

Rusty made no comment, and after a moment Flanders spoke again. "I hate to have Smith an' Honey Yates get away with it."

"They ain't got away with it . . . yet," Rusty said quietly.

Flanders glanced sharply at his friend but made no reply. Rusty was staring thoughtfully at the toe of his boot stretched out in front of him. "Tell me what's been happenin' to you, Tom," he requested after a moment.

"Nothin's happened to me," Tom Flanders answered. "Dodge City is quiet. I think this is the last year for Dodge. The railroad's goin' on west. They're buildin' now."

Rusty nodded. "It won't be long," he drawled, "until there 'll be no more cattle driven up from Texas. This is about the end of it."

"Just about," Flanders agreed. "A year or so more will see the finish of the trail."

Flanders stayed the remainder of the afternoon. When evening came he departed, his duties in town calling him. He would see Rusty, he promised, in the morning. Rusty watched his friend leave and then, taking his horse, he went out to the cattle.

Telesfor, Deems and Nugget returned about midnight. Colonel Watrous had given them an advance on their wages, and the three had investigated the delights of Dodge City. All three were freshly shaven, had had their hair cut and wore new clothes. They were clean and just a little drunk, and Rusty envied them. Deems crawled under the wagon and went to bed. Telesfor sought his own blankets, and Nugget, after a cup of coffee, went out to relieve a man on guard.

Morning broke clear and bright. Shortly after breakfast Watrous and Carlisle with the steer buyers arrived from town, and now the final stage of the journey began. Before noon the steers were in the stockyard, and when the last animal was through the gate Rusty rode over to his employers for orders. Carlisle and Watrous were talking to the buyers, and as Rusty dismounted the men shook hands.

"That settles it then," Watrous said and, turning to Rusty, explained that he had sold the remuda to the men who had bought the steers.

The horses delivered, Nugget, Telesfor and Rusty loaded their saddles in the wagon and climbed on. The Kansas hands mounted their own horses, and the caravan started toward town. Watrous was to meet them all at the Drovers' Hotel and pay off.

Riding the wagon into town, Rusty watched the dust puffing up from the wheels and wondered what was coming next. Carlisle, Watrous and the steer buyers were in buggies, and these had gone on, not waiting for the slower-paced wagon. The Kansas hands, too, had left the wagon, following after the buggies. Rusty, Joe Deems, Telesfor and Nugget were alone.

"What you goin' to do now, Rusty?" Nugget asked, staring curiously at his companion. "Go home?"

"Not just yet," Rusty answered shortly.

Deems clucked to the mules. "That high wheeler's gettin' lame," he commented. "Guess I'll have to get him shod again."

"*We* won't have to shoe him," Nugget growled. "Leave it for somebody else to do."

"*Yo creo . . .*"Telesfor announced and then

stopped.

"What 'd you think?" Nugget growled.

"I theenk," Telesfor said in his careful English, "that tonight I get draunk."

There was silence for a moment and then Deems growled: "It ain't a bad idea."

Deems wheeled the wagon up in front of the Drovers' Hotel, and its occupants alighted. In the lobby Carlisle and Watrous were standing together, and as Rusty came through the door the last of the Kansas hands, paid off, brushed past him with a grin and a word. He would, the man said, see Rusty around. He promised to buy Rusty a drink. Rusty nodded and smiled and went on toward Carlisle and Watrous. As he came toward them Ellen Watrous and Marcia Carlisle appeared, so that while Rusty approached from one direction they came from another, and all five — Watrous, Carlisle, the two women and Rusty — converged in a single compact group. For a moment after the meeting no one spoke. Then Ellen smiled brilliantly at Rusty and placed her hand on his arm. "Thank you, Rusty," she said, "for keeping your promise."

Rusty grinned at the girl. "That's all right, Sorrel-top," he answered. Carlisle's hand was placed possessively upon Ellen's shoulder, and Rusty, noting the hand and the look in Carlisle's eyes, knew that everything was all right between them. Colonel Watrous broke in then with a word, and the group drifted to chairs against the lobby wall.

As they talked Rusty could not keep his eyes from Marcia Carlisle. She was even more beautiful than he had remembered her, and there was a certain gentleness in her manner, a subdued temperance that Rusty did not remember at all. Things had been happening to Marcia, Rusty judged. He could not keep staring at her constantly, for Rusty was not rude, but twice when he turned his eyes quickly toward her he caught her covertly watching him.

Watrous finished with his questions and comments and brought out a handful of money. "I'm paying you the wages I paid McBride," he announced. "From the time you left San Marcial until you reached Dodge. Here." He counted off bills.

"But that isn't right, Colonel," Rusty protested. "I hired on as a hand. All the wages I've got comin' are rider's wages."

Watrous shook his head. "You've got this comin'," he announced forcefully. "Take it."

The colonel would not listen to further protestations and, perforce, Rusty accepted the bills. "An' now," Watrous said, "you'll probably be headed home soon, Rusty?"

"Not for a while," Rusty answered. "I'm goin' to stay around here for a little while."

Watrous smiled and nodded. It was natural that a man coming off the trail should wish to sample Dodge City.

As they talked a drover — a stranger to Rusty — joined the group. Rusty made awkward excuses and started to leave. Watrous called him back. "I nearly forgot," he said. "Here's some mail for you." He gave Rusty two letters which Rusty accepted, and, again making his excuses, he left the party. Out on the porch of the hotel he found a chair and, seated, opened his letters.

One, short and terse, was from Dan Shotridge. Things were all right at the ranch. As laconically as though talking, Dan Shotridge reported to his son. Rusty finished that letter with a grin on his face. It was hard to read love and sympathy and pride into Dan's letter, but all three were there. The other letter, from his mother, was longer and in more detail. Rusty finished reading that letter and sat holding it in his hands, musing, his mind far away. A light step beside him caused him to glance up and then scramble to his feet. Marcia Carlisle was standing beside his chair, smiling.

"Sit down, won't you?" she said gently.

Rusty drew another chair over beside the one he had occupied, and, when the girl was seated, resettled himself. For a time Marcia did not speak, then turning, her eyes bright and frank, she met Rusty's gaze.

"You've come back," the girl said, watching Rusty. "You kept your promise to Ellen and me. Did you see how happy they were, Rusty?"

Rusty lowered his eyes from her bright scrutiny. He had seen how happy Ellen Watrous and Leonard Carlisle were. No one could help but see. "Yes," he said.

Marcia's voice was musing. "I hated you at first," she said. "You were taking Leonard away from me and I hated you for it. Then I saw that you were right. You told me that I was bad for Leonard and that I had spoiled him. He isn't spoiled now, is he?"

"No." Still Rusty would not look at the girl. He was afraid to meet her eyes.

"Leonard told us about the trip," Marcia's voice went on. "He told us all the things you've done. He thinks . . ." She broke off and then continued: "Leonard thinks that you are grand."

Rusty looked up now. Marcia's face was turned so that he saw only her cheek and the soft hair that covered her ear and the side of her neck.

"I did what I had to," Rusty said. "There wasn't anything else I could do. I had to get the cattle through an' . . ."

"And you'd made a promise," Marcia interrupted softly. "I told you once . . . You make it hard for me, Rusty."

Now she turned and met his eyes. There was a light in her own, a light such as Rusty had never seen. Warm it was, and soft and promising. His big hand, tightly clenched, opened now and moved toward the girl. Then abruptly the movement checked. Rusty's voice was hoarse and low as he spoke. "I . . ." he began. "I've thought about you all along the trail. Nights I'd dream about you. I . . ."

A smile, small, fleeting, appeared on Marcia's lips. She leaned toward Rusty. "And now I'm here," she said softly. "And you, Rusty, you're here. I . . ."

The speech stopped short. Marcia saw the emotion that twisted Rusty's face, tearing at him. His big hand dropped to his side and hung limp.

"Rusty!" There was alarm in the girl's voice. "What is it? What is the matter?"

Words ground out of Rusty's torture, harsh, rasping, carrying his emotion: "I can't! I've got a job! I can't." He came to his feet and stood there, looking down at her. Gradually control returned. Gradually his features smoothed. Marcia stared up at him.

"Rusty!" she said again.

"I've got a job," Rusty said. "You wouldn't understand, Marcia. I can't tell you, but I've got it to do. Good-by, girl!" Without another word he turned and strode toward the steps, and Marcia Carlisle, angry, afraid and uncomprehending, sprang to her feet and watched him go.

Going down the steps, Rusty tried to clear his head and think. Up there on the porch he had remembered just in time, recalled the task he had set for himself. There were things to do here in Dodge City. There was his promise concerning the quarantine to keep. There was his meeting with Flanders and Sigloe. There were preparations to be made. He shook his head angrily. He had a job to do. But first he must find Flanders and accomplish these minor things.

It was not hard to locate Flanders. He was in the marshal's office down the street from the Drovers' Hotel. Observing an ordinance against carrying fire-arms in Dodge City, Rusty left his gun in the office, and with Flanders beside him the two went out on the street. They talked as they strode along, talked concerning the lane through the quarantine. Flanders took Rusty to a saloon and introduced him to several men there. One of these was a drover who had failed to see the beauties of the lane through the quarantine. Rusty talked forcefully to that gentleman and at the end of their conversation had convinced the man that to prevent loss and keep the peace the two herds the drover had coming up from Texas must follow the corridor through the quarantine. The two men shook hands pleasantly at the end of the short conference, and the drover made a statement:

"I'll have three herds coming up next season, Shotridge. If you are looking for a job then come and see me and I'll give you one of them to handle."

Rusty spoke his thanks, refused a drink and with Flanders left the saloon.

"That's the last of 'em," Flanders announced when they were on the sidewalk. "Marble an' Watrous have got the rest convinced. What do you want to do now, Rusty?"

"Get cleaned up," Rusty answered promptly. "Then I've got a little business to look after."

"Bud will be in town tonight," Flanders

said. "He sent in word. You ain't forgot our party?"

"I'll come back to your office as soon as I get cleaned up," Rusty promised. "I haven't forgotten. We'll have supper together an' then you can show Bud an' me the sights."

"I know 'em all." Flanders laughed. "I'll show 'em to you."

"Have you heard any more about Colonel Watrous?" Rusty asked.

"Not much," Flanders replied. "He got thirty dollars a round for his steers is all I know; but the talk is that he owes some money from last year an' that he can't pay off."

Rusty nodded thoughtfully. "I'll see you *poco pronto,*" he announced. "Now I want to get some dirt off me." Flanders grinned and the two friends parted, Flanders returning to his office, Rusty swinging off down the street.

In succession Rusty visited stores where he purchased clothing, boots and a hat; and then a barbershop where a bath, a haircut and a shave worked wonders in his appearance. He was leaving the barbershop when he encountered one of the two men who had bought the Watrous cattle. Hailing that man, Rusty entered into conversation with him, and at the conclusion of the interview money changed hands. The steer buyer folded the bills and put them in his pocket. "What you goin' to do with the horses, Shotridge?" he asked curiously.

"Nothin' right away," Rusty answered. "You have 'em delivered to the livery barn, an' I'll go over there an' tell the hostler to expect 'em."

The steer buyer nodded. "That sorrel is a good horse," he said. "I kind of had him marked for myself but I'm glad enough to let you have him. I'll see that they're brought in for you."

Rusty said, "Thanks," and the two men shook hands and parted.

Back in Flanders's office Rusty waited until his friend should be free. It was plain that Flanders was popular in Dodge City, and it was equally plain that the marshal's office was not too busy. Men came in and visited; they did not come to make complaints. Bud Sigloe made his appearance about five o'clock, shaved to the quick and resplendent in new clothing. Flanders spoke to the deputy he left in charge, and together the three friends went out on the street.

That was a night to remember. The three ate supper in the dining hall of the Drovers' Hotel, and following the meal, with Flanders as a guide, they took in Dodge City. They built a high, keen edge as the night wore on, and their progress from bar to bar, from gambling hall to gambling hall, became a procession. Tom Flanders's money, save across the gambling tables, was not good in Dodge City, consequently his friends were also guests of the various places they visited. Gray dawn was breaking in the east before the final round of drinks was taken and the men parted. Sigloe, a little unsteady on his feet, found his horse and mounted to ride back to his camp, and Tom Flanders and Rusty stood in the street and watched him ride away.

"An' now," Flanders announced, "we'll go to my place an' sleep. Come on, Rusty."

Rusty found Flanders gone when he wakened the next morning. The deputy in the marshal's office told Rusty that Flanders had been called to investigate a killing at the edge of town. Left to his own devices, Rusty drifted from the office on down the street. He was of two minds. He wanted to go to the hotel and see Marcia. He wanted to talk with her, but he was afraid that if he did his resolution would weaken.

A block from Flanders's office he entered the livery barn. Big Enough and Toughy, the two horses Rusty had purchased, were at the barn, and the hostler showed Rusty where they were stalled.

"They'd carry you back to Texas right now," the barn man said. "That where yo're goin' with 'em?"

"Maybe," Rusty answered.

When he left the livery he went on down the street, nodding to men, acquaintances made by Flanders's introductions, and still debating with himself. Leaving the street for the coolness of a saloon, Rusty stepped up to the bar and, before he could order, felt a hand on his arm. Turning, he saw the grinning face of Telesfor, and behind Telesfor were Joe Deems and Ben Nugget. These three — horse wrangler, cook and hand — were beginning their celebration anew, and they insisted that Rusty join them. Nothing loath, Rusty walked on back to the far end of the bar where a bottle stood.

"We got tired of buyin' by the drink," Deems explained. "This here is our bottle. Bring another glass, barkeep!"

The bartender obeyed the command, and Rusty, filling the fresh glass, lifted it toward his companions. "Here's how," he said briefly.

They stood there at the bar end after that first drink, Telesfor, Deems and Nugget pleased and a little awed by their companion; Rusty moody and introspective. Telesfor suggested another drink and poured the liquor, but before the drink was taken a stranger, coming along the length of the bar, accosted Rusty.

"Yore name Shotridge?" the stranger asked.

"That's right," Rusty agreed.

"I got a message for you," the stranger said. "It's kind of private."

Rusty excused himself and, accompanying the stranger to a booth, sat down. The stranger took a seat opposite him.

"This message I got," the stranger said, "is from some friends. They're friends of mine too."

"Yeah?" Rusty drawled.

The stranger leaned forward and lowered his voice. "Kansas asked me to bring you word," he announced. "I met him a way down the trail. Kansas said to tell you that Smith struck out west from where he was and would be headed for Colorado. Kansas said you'd know what that meant."

Rusty nodded, his eyes fixed upon the speaker.

"An' he said to tell you that him an' Red an' Gus an' Chico was headed in that direction." The stranger lounged to his feet, and suddenly he grinned at Rusty. "I'd of liked to be along on that trip you boys had," he announced, his voice warm. "Kansas told me about it. Good luck, Shotridge. You'll be seein' Kansas, I reckon?"

"I'll be seeing him," Rusty answered flatly and took the extended hand. "Thanks a lot. If ever I can . . ."

"Never mind the thanks." The stranger relinquished Rusty's hand. "You just tell Kansas you got his message. So long, Shotridge, an' good luck."

"So long," Rusty said absently. He lowered his eyes and for a long minute examined the top of the table in the booth. When Rusty looked up again the stranger was gone and Joe Deems stood in his place.

"Yore drink's poured," Deems complained. "You wasn't there, so I drunk it. Come on an' I'll buy you another."

"Joe," Rusty said quietly, "there's a packsaddle in the wagon, isn't there?"

"Sure." Deems looked his surprise. "I allus carry one. Can't tell when yo're goin' to need it. What's on yore mind, Rusty?"

Rusty did not look at Joe Deems. He was staring at the door. Telesfor placed his hand on Rusty's arm with the affectionate gesture of the maudlin inebriate. *"Amigo mio . . ."* Telesfor began and paused to hiccup.

"I'm goin' to borrow that saddle, Joe," Rusty said.

293

"Sure," Deems agreed. "But what you goin' to do with a packsaddle, Rusty? Where you goin'?"

Rusty looked down at the old cook and smiled tightly. "You an' Telesfor an' Ben have a drink on me," he commanded. "Here," reaching into his pocket and producing a bill, "drink on this."

Joe Deems took the bill without looking at it. His eyes were fixed on Rusty's face, curiosity filling them.

"Where you goin'?" Joe Deems persisted. "What you goin' to do?"

Rusty's smile was grim, and his narrowed eyes were blank, no recognition in them as he looked at Joe Deems. "Why," he said, his voice a drawl, the tone such as a man might use to explain a simple thing to a child, "I'm goin' to cut trail, Joe. Yeah, that's it. I lost some cattle so I'll cut the herd an' get 'em back."

Chapter XVII

Leonard Carlisle, sitting beside Colonel Watrous in the lobby of the Drovers' Hotel, watched his companion affectionately. "It won't make any difference, Colonel," Carlisle objected. "It's all in the family anyhow. If we hadn't lost those cattle out of this herd we'd have made some money. We made a little, as things stand, and I haven't entirely given up the idea that we'll get those cattle back. Surely a man can't lose a trail herd. If we write to the various markets and inform the officers there concerning our loss, they'll see that Smith is caught. I think . . ."

Colonel Watrous shook his head vigorously. "You don't understand, Leonard," he interrupted. "Smith has our cattle marked with his own road brand now. And there's no question but that he has a forged bill of sale. If I hadn't been foolish and consented to road-marking the cattle by grubbing an ear, we'd have had a chance. Now we would have to go to law even if we found Smith — which is doubtful. And in a court we'd have to spend money that I can't afford to spend."

"But I've told you . . ." Carlisle persisted.

"I know, my boy. I know." Again the colonel interrupted with a wave of his hand. "You and Ellen are to be married and you say 'it's all in the family'; but I don't do things that way. The debts I contracted are my own and I . . ."

It was Carlisle's turn to break in. "You and I formed a partnership," he announced. "I put in some money and you put in the experience. That partnership still stands. I think . . . Hello, Flanders."

Tom Flanders, with Bud Sigloe a half pace behind him, had paused before Watrous and Carlisle. Flanders nodded and returned the greeting. "Good mornin', Carlisle. Good mornin', Colonel."

Watrous made a gesture. "Sit down, won't you?" he invited.

Flanders did not heed the invitation but stared at Watrous and Carlisle. "Bud an' me are lookin' for Rusty Shotridge," he announced. "Have either of you seen him?"

Watrous shook his head. "Not since yesterday," he answered.

"I haven't seen him," Carlisle proffered. "I thought he was with you."

Marcia Carlisle and Ellen Watrous, seated a short distance away, looked toward the men and, seeing the women for the first time, both Flanders and Sigloe removed their hats. "Rusty ain't been with us since last night," Flanders stated. "He slept at my place. I had some business this mornin' an' didn't see him. We've looked for him an' couldn't find him."

"What is it, Leonard?" Marcia asked. "Is anything wrong?"

Carlisle shook his head. "Nothing," he answered. Marcia leaned back in her chair again.

"He'll turn up somewhere," Watrous assured. "Joe Deems and Ben Nugget and my horse wrangler were having a celebration yesterday. Rusty might be with them."

Flanders glanced at Sigloe and then spoke to the colonel again. "That's right," he said. "We'll hunt them up."

"When you find him tell him I want to see him, will you?" Carlisle requested as Flanders turned away.

"Sure," the officer agreed.

He and Sigloe walked of toward the hotel door, and Carlisle turned once more to Colonel Watrous. "I'm trying to convince you, Colonel," he said, taking up the argument where he had dropped it. "Both of us stand to make some money if we stay together. There's no use in your being obstinate about it."

Watrous shook his shaggy head and repeated his objections. The talk went on. They were still at it half an hour later, when Flanders and Sigloe returned. The two men crossed the lobby, stopped, and Flanders spoke without preamble. "Rusty's pulled out," he announced. "He had two horses at the livery barn an' he took them this mornin'. We were told that he rode west."

"But why . . . ?" Carlisle began.

"We found Deems and the others," Sigloe

rasped. "They'd been celebratin', all right. Rusty was with 'em yesterday for a while. Then some fello' they didn't know spoke to him, an' they talked a while. The fello' pulled out, an' Rusty give Joe some money to buy some drinks an' asked if there was a packsaddle in the wagon. Joe asked him what he wanted of it an' where he was goin', an' he said he'd lost some cattle an' was goin' to cut trail."

Sigloe stopped. Carlisle exchanged a startled glance with Watrous. "What do you think he meant?" Watrous demanded.

"My guess is," Flanders drawled, "that the fello' that talked to Rusty had some word of Slippery Smith. I think Rusty's gone to find Smith an' get your steers back. That's what I think."

"But why didn't he tell us?" Carlisle demanded. "Why didn't he . . . ?"

"Yeah." Sigloe's voice was aggrieved. "You'd of thought he'd told Tom an' me anyhow. Hell . . . excuse me, ladies!" Bud Sigloe flushed red. Ellen Watrous and Marcia, alarmed by the tone of the talk, had left their chairs and approached the group.

"What is it, Leonard?" Marcia demanded.

"Rusty is gone," Carlisle answered. "Mr. Flanders thinks he's heard where Smith's herd is and has gone to find it."

"An' that's just what he's done," Tom Flanders stated positively. "Losin' those steers has stuck in his craw. I could tell it. He's pulled out."

Ellen, standing beside Carlisle, looked anxiously at the man. Watrous was staring at Flanders. Carlisle looked up at his sister and then at Ellen.

"But . . ." Marcia said. "Alone?" She looked from one to another of the group. "He couldn't have! They'll . . . If he finds them they'll kill him!" Here now was the explanation: the reason why Rusty had dropped his hand when he reached toward her, the reason why he had not spoken, answering her. Marcia knew why now. All the anger against Rusty, all the shame she had felt for her boldness, fell away and there remained only the woman in love.

"He ain't goin' to be alone very long," Bud Sigloe promised grimly. "Tom an' me are goin' after him. We know he went west an' we'll catch him before he reaches Smith."

Flanders nodded soberly. "We just came to tell you," he announced. "Come on, Bud."

"Wait!" Marcia commanded. Flanders and Sigloe stopped. The girl was not looking at them; rather her eyes were on her brother's face. What she saw there satisfied her. Leonard Carlisle wheeled from his sister and confronted Flanders.

"I'm going with you," he said quietly. "When are you leaving?"

Flanders and Sigloe exchanged quick glances. "Just as soon as we can," Flanders answered. "We've got to get organized. We'll be at the livery for a while."

"I'll join you there," Carlisle stated definitely.

Flanders nodded and he and Bud Sigloe tramped off across the lobby to the door. Carlisle turned toward Colonel Watrous. "While we were *talking* about getting the steers back," he said, bitterness in his voice, "Rusty was doing something about it. I'll ask you to look after things here, Colonel. I don't know how long I'll be gone."

"Of course," Watrous said. "I'll take care of things, Leonard."

"Leonard!" Marcia's voice was quick. "You . . ."

"You mustn't try to stop me, Marcia." Carlisle faced his sister. "I've got to go."

"But I want you to go. I want . . . Bring him back, Leonard?" Surprise flooded Carlisle's face. For an instant he stood, uncomprehending, and then with one swift step he reached his sister and took her in

300

his arms. Marcia buried her face against his chest, and a sob shook her shoulders. Over her dark hair Leonard Carlisle's eyes met Ellen's. There was compassion in the girl's face.

"Of course I'll bring him back," Carlisle assured. "Of course I will, sweet. I didn't know you felt that way. Of course I'll bring him back to you."

Rain struck Rusty the second day out of Dodge City. The fall storm came slowly at first and then with increasing intensity, cold and penetrating, the wind blowing the rain down the collar of his slicker, drenching him. He went on through the rain and camped that night beside a swollen stream. As he hobbled Toughy and turned his two horses out together he noticed that even the short rest and the easy stages of his journey had freshened them and let them put on a little flesh. Unable to find dry wood for a fire, Rusty philosophically unrolled his bed in the shelter of a cottonwood thicket and turned in, totally unaware that some twenty miles behind him three of his friends cursed the wet wood that refused to burn and the rain that had washed out the tracks they followed.

The next morning Rusty went on toward

the west, not hurrying, not pushing, but traveling steadily. There was a half-formulated plan in Rusty's mind. The word had been that Kansas and Gus, Chico and Red, were following Slippery Smith and his herd. Somewhere in the west Rusty would find Slippery Smith. When he did that he would scout around the herd and eventually encounter Kansas and his fellows. That they would help him, Rusty had no doubt at all. When that liaison was accomplished, with his companions helping, Rusty would cut the Hackamore herd. The details of his plan were unperfected because they would depend on circumstances; but the plan itself was there, definite and unchangeable. Rusty rode on, serenely confident, unworried, certain of his task. That he would meet danger, that death was possible, he knew and disregarded the knowledge. Neither death nor danger deterred him. Rusty Shotridge had made up his mind. He had taken too much from Slippery Smith and Honey Yates, and it was time to level, time to have an accounting. A new Winchester rode in the scabbard of Rusty's saddle; about his middle his Colt was strapped, and in his mind was that fixed determination, that cold, set purpose that only a strong man can feel. Slippery Smith and Honey Yates had lived too long. Perhaps they felt the same way about Rusty Shotridge. Somewhere ahead in Colorado or Wyoming or Utah the three would meet and the dice would be thrown. Somebody would come riding out of it.

Behind Rusty — the distance greater now because of the storm and uncertainty — Tom Flanders and Bud Sigloe held consultation with Leonard Carlisle.

"Mebbe we'll find him an' mebbe we won't," Flanders stated bluntly. "It's like lookin' for a cow track in a marble quarry. There's a lot of country yonder" — he nodded toward the west — "an' Rusty's just one man in it. We had a chance while we could follow his tracks. Now we've lost 'em. What do you fello's think?"

Sigloe did not answer but looked at Carlisle. This was a far different man than the youngster who had started up the trail from San Marcial. Carlisle's skin was tanned to the color of an old squaw's, and his eyes were wrinkled at the corners from looking into distances. The line of his jaw was clean and firm and definite as were his words when he answered Tom Flanders.

"Maybe we'll stumble onto his trail," Carlisle said. "Anyhow, we'll find Smith. Rusty will be looking for Smith, and we'll look too. It ought to be a lot easier to find a herd of cattle than to find one man."

Bud and Flanders exchanged glances. Now they had the answer to a question that they had asked themselves. Both had wondered how far Leonard Carlisle would go.

"And I hope that we find Smith before Rusty does," Carlisle completed.

"Yeah," Bud drawled. "So do I."

The three rode on toward the west. At ranches where they stopped Tom Flanders asked questions, always the same questions, and always he received the same answers.

No, there hadn't been a trail herd through. Slippery Smith? Never heard of him. No, nobody had seen one man traveling with a pack horse. Won't you fello's light an' stay the night with us? What's the news over east around Dodge City?

Now they dropped into the Dry Cimarron and traveled up its length. Flanders was familiar with the country, and Bud Sigloe had once taken a herd north over the Goodnight trail.

"If Slippery Smith has gone to Colorado he'd have to use one of two passes. Either he went through Trinchera, or the Raton Pass," Sigloe stated definitely. "So we'll find him at one place or the other."

Flanders nodded his agreement, and

Carlisle added a word. "I hope," Carlisle stated, "that we're ahead of Rusty. That's what I hope."

Both Flanders and Sigloe nodded agreement. They joined with Leonard Carlisle in his wish, but they were afraid, afraid that Rusty was ahead of them and that they would be too late when they found Slippery Smith and the Hackamore herd.

At the end of the wide valley of the Dry Cimarron the three turned north. Climbing the long slope of Trinchera Pass, they dropped down the other side. There, below them, was the little village of Trinchera and, hoping against hope, they rode toward it.

Trinchera sprawled in the fall sunlight. There were horses at the hitch rails and dust in the single street.

"Mebbe" — Tom Flanders turned to his companions — "we'll get word here. We'll ask at some of the stores. Rusty would have had to stock up, an' anyhow, they'll know if Smith come through the pass." He swung his horse toward a hitch rack and dismounted, and beside him his two companions wearily climbed down.

In the first store part of Flanders's question was answered. The storekeeper had stocked a wagon for a trail herd just the day before. The Hackamore wagon, the storekeeper said. Yes, the cook had definitely named his outfit. No one, said the man behind the counter, had come to town except the cook. To Flanders's second question the merchant answered "no." He had not see one stranger in town, one man traveling alone. There were four strangers in Trinchera, all in a bunch, and, oddly, they had asked the same questions. The storekeeper looked at Flanders, curiosity showing in his eyes. Flanders wheeled to consult his companions.

"Four men," he said. "Now I wonder . . . ?"

"Does it make any difference?" Carlisle demanded. "We know that the Hackamores have been through here. They're north of us. Rusty hasn't been in this town. It's too small for any stranger to get through without being seen. I wish . . ." A nameless dread showed in Carlisle's eyes and was likewise reflected in the eyes of his companions. The Hackamore herd had come across Trinchera. Had Rusty Shotridge met the Hackamore below the pass? Had he?

"Let's get out of here," Flanders said suddenly.

They left the store and, standing in front of it, held a consultation. There were two other stores in Trinchera, and on the chance that Rusty had patronized one of these, investigation was indicated. In a group the three men walked on to conduct their search.

Their inquiries at the other two stores brought no results, and once more they talked together. "We'll go on," Carlisle announced. "We know that Smith has been through here and we know that Rusty hasn't. Either we're ahead of him or we're not. If we're ahead of him . . ." Carlisle broke off. Four men, a lanky individual in the lead, were approaching the three along the walk. The quartet stopped, and the lanky man drawled comment: "Folks say that yo're lookin' for the Hackamore herd. That right?"

Flanders's eyes were sharp as he surveyed the questioner. "Yeah," he answered. "What of it?"

Carlisle spoke quietly. "Hello, Kansas. How are you boys?"

Sigloe and Flanders relaxed. Kansas, advancing, extended his hand to Carlisle. "We're fine," he said. "Are you lookin' for Rusty too?"

Carlisle nodded.

"So are we," Kansas said needlessly. "I sent him word in Dodge City. Did he get it?"

"He got it," Carlisle answered. "Tom, I want you and Bud to meet these men. This is Kansas . . . Red . . . Chico . . . Gus . . . Mr. Sigloe and Mr. Flanders."

Hands were shaken gravely. Kansas looked Tom Flanders up and down, and a slow grin broke across his face. "You needn't worry about Rusty," he drawled. "He ain't reached the Hackamore yet. Not up to last night he hadn't. We been watchin' 'em an' lookin' for him too. Let's get someplace where we can talk."

CHAPTER XVIII

Brooding eats the heart out of a man. Brooding may make him mad. Honey Yates brooded as day stretched endlessly into day. He had no weapon of his own, and about him armed men rode. He had no defense and daily he was subjected to torment. No man falls so low as one who has occupied a peak. Honey Yates, known and feared from the border north, had fallen. Constantly he was the butt of the rough humor, the rawhiding of his companions, but it was the malicious lash of Slippery Smith's tongue that drove him to the brink of insanity. Never a day passed by but that Smith applied that lash; never a night fell but that

308

Yates harbored some fresh cut in his mind.

Once he rebelled, snatching out his pocket-knife, flashing it open and springing to the attack. That attack stopped short before the muzzle of a Colt and Smith's hard laughter. It gained Yates nothing save the loss of his knife.

Other, lesser, men would have quit. Other men, riding on guard about cattle in the night, would have turned their horse and spurred away. Not Honey Yates. Hatred held him up. Hatred seared him but strengthened him. Honey Yates, brooding, was filled with an idea. There were two things he must do, two things he would do: kill Slippery Smith and when that was accomplished find and kill Rusty Shotridge.

It is difficult to understand such a man as Honey Yates. He had from youth lived by death. A boy of eighteen, he had killed a man in a cow camp east of El Paso. He had run from that killing. The next year, working in the territory, he had killed again. The protection of his employer had kept him from flight, but he had purchased that protection by another murder. The taste of blood was in Yates's being. His career, founded on death, had continued. He was a wolf loose in a sheep pen, a rabid dog loosed among lambs. How could Honey Yates do other than kill? It was his one answer, his one retort.

Slippery Smith knew these things and chose to play with Yates. There are some men who will torment a crippled rattler, enjoying the rage of their victim, enjoying the tortured coiling of the snake and its crazy lunges, enjoying the very idea of the death that lurks in the fangs. Slippery Smith was such a man, but, like the tormentor and the snake, he intended to kill his plaything in the end.

Slippery Smith's cattle, including six hundred and ninety head of big steers, their right ears grubbed close to the head, a hackamore burned across their noses and bearing a big LM on their left flanks, moved west and then turned north. The crew, bribed by a promise of a division of spoils, was content and even happy. There was entertainment in the camp, a constant play, and their savage natures enjoyed it. They were fascinated by the play. Someday, somewhere along the trail, Honey Yates would die. That was the play and the fascination.

Driving north, the herd reached the Dry Cimarron and crossed it. Through the long pass that the natives had dubbed Trinchera the cattle took their way. Above the pass they went on north, approaching a possible market, and as the end of the trail came closer, so, too, came the end of the drama. There was no question of it. Smith's tongue grew more rasping, his words more hateful. Under them a man must break, and when Honey Yates broke the drama would be finished. Every man with that herd knew it; every man anticipated it, including Honey Yates. And Yates not only knew it, he looked forward to it. There was a guard about him; watchful eyes were always on him. On the third day above Trinchera Pass that guard relaxed fractionally, and on that day, late in the evening, Honey Yates acquired a weapon.

The incident that led to Yates's acquisition of a gun was an accident. The country above Trinchera was rough. Crossing an arroyo, the chuck wagon lurched, struck a rock and broke a wheel. The wagon went over on its side, for the front wheel at the time was cramped sharp to make a turn in the ascent. Food, beds, cooking utensils, all the thousand and one things with which the wagon was loaded, came tumbling out.

Honey Yates was in the drag of the herd. He did not see the catastrophe but he heard the cook yell. With Sam accompanying him he left the cattle and loped over to see what had happened to the wagon. He was on the ground, helping straighten things out, when Smith arrived.

Slippery cursed the cook and pitched in to help effect repairs. A pole was brought and lashed under the rear axle and to the front axle after the wagon had been set up and lifted until the bed was level.

With the pole acting as a wheel the crossing of the arroyo was completed, and Smith loped back to the still-traveling herd while Sam and Honey Yates helped the cook reload.

It was now that opportunity knocked for Honey Yates. He helped Sam heave the beds up to the cook, and in handling the beds Honey felt the hard outline of a gun through a canvas tarpaulin. He managed to leave that bed until last. The cook called Sam to give him a hand, and while Sam was gone Honey reached into the loosely lashed bed and acquired the pistol.

Of all the men in the crew, Yates was the only one that wore chaps. He had clung to them throughout all the journey. Now he was thankful. There was a pocket in the chaps, and into it Yates thrust the gun before Sam returned. The flap of the chaps effectually hid the pocket and the gun was safe.

With the loading completed, the two riders left the cook to his own devices, and as they rode the gun rubbed comfortingly against Honey's leg, and his eyes were narrow with savage satisfaction. Now, when opportunity presented itself, he would settle with Slippery Smith. He would not make that settlement openly and boldly, but as occasion offered. Honey Yates had set himself a task and he would not jeopardize one portion of it at the expense of the other. He wanted to kill Smith and get away so that he might kill again.

The Hackamore outfit camped that night close to a piñon thicket. The cattle were bedded and the camp made by sundown. As usual Slippery Smith found occasion to lash out at Yates, and as usual Yates took the cursing. Routine was in force at the Hackamore wagon. By dark the men were ready for bed and the cook had finished with the dishes. Honey Yates pulled his bed well away from all the rest. He took off his chaps and his hat and turned in. Under his thin pillow the gun lumped wickedly.

For a long time Yates remained awake. He hoped that the night would bring the opportunity he wanted. It did not. Smith was restless. He was up and out with the cattle most of the night. Only — and here grim humor played a part — he did not visit the herd while Yates was on guard, and when Yates came in the foreman was on the way out with the relief. So all during the night there was no chance for Honey to use his weapon. He did not worry. His revenge was not averted; it was simply delayed. Returning from his guard, he went to sleep.

In the morning the Hackamore outfit moved as usual, the cattle strung out, the wagon and remuda paralleling the line of the herd. Slippery Smith rode at one point, Sam at the other. Behind Sam, in the swing, Honey Yates held his position. All that morning they moved, and at noon the cattle spread out to graze. In midafternoon the march resumed, and once more the riders fell in place. The sun sloped west toward the Spanish Peaks, and the evening breeze was cool as the cattle followed up a long, piñon-flanked hollow. Noting movement among the piñons, Slippery Smith rose in his stirrups; then with a surprised grunt he dropped back into his saddle and, his hand rising, touched the butt of the gun at his waist. There was a man coming out of the piñons, riding deliberately down the slope. Slippery Smith recognized the rider. It was Rusty Shotridge!

Rusty had missed the way. Unfamiliar with

the country, he had struck too far north after the rain in place of following the easy passage of the Dry Cimarron. Striking the north fork, he followed along it, stopping occasionally at ranches and small crossroad stores to ask casual questions, identifying the country through which he traveled, locating himself and learning that there had been no herds through. He learned, too, that there were but two passages on the western trail: Trinchera and Raton. Through one of these the Hackamore outfit must come.

At a Block ranch line camp on the Chiquaque, Rusty spent a night and there received his first definite information concerning the Hackamore herd. There was another stranger stopping at the camp, and from him Rusty learned that the Hackamore outfit had come through Trinchera Pass the day before and was moving on north. Leaving the line camp the next morning, Rusty rode west. Somewhere close to the Hackamore herd he would find Kansas and his companions. Deciding upon Trinchera town as the most likely place, Rusty made for that little village.

He reached Trinchera in the morning, having made a camp between the Block ranch and the town. Riding in, Rusty stopped by a hitch rack, dismounted, tied his horses and began his discreet questioning. Knowing Kansas and his companions, Rusty sought out the bartender of Trinchera's principal saloon.

The bartender responded to Rusty's cautious pumping. A saloon in that Western country was a club, a newspaper and a meeting place. Whatever went on in the town or in the country about was sooner or later retailed at a saloon, and Rusty's bartender gave information. The Hackamore trail herd had been through Trinchera, the bartender said. It had passed the town — the bartender paused and pondered — two, no, three days ago. Rusty nodded his satisfaction and pursued his inquiry.

The bartender eyed Rusty curiously. He had seen some strangers in town, the bartender said. Four of them. Rusty brightened. Come to think of it, the bartender continued, those four strangers had been asking about one man, traveling alone.

"They were lookin' for me," Rusty announced. "Are they still in town?"

The bartender shook his head. "They pulled out," he announced. "They was in here an' there was some other fellows showed up. Officers, I guess. I didn't see 'em, but from what I heard that's what they were. I guess those four that were lookin' for you didn't want to meet the others. Anyhow they left." The bartender's eyes were very bright as he examined Rusty. Rusty nodded, spoke his thanks and left the saloon. That bartender, Rusty knew, thought that he, Rusty Shotridge, was on the dodge. The bartender thought that Kansas and his friends were on the dodge too. It would not take the bartender long to get hold of an officer. Rusty walked out to the hitch rail and untied his horses. He wanted no difficulty with the law in Trinchera and he wanted no delay. Kansas, Red, Gus and Chico were not in town. They were gone. Rusty wondered who the other men might be? They could be and probably were officers following Kansas and his friends. That was entirely logical. Rusty stepped up on Big Enough and, leading Toughy, headed out of town toward the north.

As he rode he considered his predicament and his plan. The men he had counted on for help were gone. They were, Rusty surmised, looking after their own hides. But north of him was the Hackamore herd, and with that herd were Slippery Smith and Honey Yates and five hundred big LM steers carrying a grubbed ear for a trail brand. And here was Rusty Shotridge. He had come a long way to cut the Hackamore herd. Rusty's jaw firmed. He'd cut it!

All the remainder of the day Rusty traveled steadily, keeping Big Enough at a steady saddle gait, covering country. No use to save his horses now; he was almost at the end of his journey. No use to hold back. Rusty stayed to the east of the trail plainly marked in the grassy country. He passed the camps and the bed grounds that the Hackamore had made and, unknowingly, he passed his friends. West of the trail Tom Flanders, the recognized head of the group, led his followers. And Flanders had no more idea that Rusty was to the east than Rusty had of Flanders's presence west of him. So as the day drew to an end Rusty Shotridge marked the thin line of dust — emblem of marching cattle — and, swinging west, came across the line of march. And so, too, as day closed, Tom Flanders spoke to his men.

"We'll pass 'em in the mornin'," Flanders said. "Then we'll come ridin' down an' cut the herd." All about Tom Flanders grim-faced men nodded agreement with the plan.

"I want the horses fresh an' I want to surprise 'em," Flanders drawled. "They're not two miles ahead of us now. We'll camp tonight. Tomorrow will be soon enough."

Again the grim faces showed assent, and

Carlisle spoke. "We can look 'em over this evening when they bed down," he said. "That will give us some idea of what we're up against."

"Let's ride on a little then," Flanders commanded.

The party moved along, horses walking, men lounging in their saddles. Ahead of them the dust rose up from the trail herd, close, just across the low hills.

"We might . . ." Bud Sigloe began. "Hey, wait a minute! What was that?"

The men reined in. Faint across the distance came a sound, low, reverberating, rolling.

"That's a shot!" Tom Flanders snapped. "I . . ."

"There's another!" Sigloe shouted the words and spurred his horse. Behind Sigloe the others lifted their mounts from walk to run.

"I hope to God that ain't Rusty," Sigloe shouted. "Come on, Tom. Come on!"

Rusty came steadily down the slope toward the leaders and Slippery Smith. Across the thin line of cattle he could see Honey Yates spurring forward. The sight of those two men swept away the last vestige of caution from Rusty's mind. Here were the men he had come to find, the men who had tricked him, who had tried to kill him, the men who had lived too long. This was the end of the trail, this little piñon-clad valley where the dust of the herd rose up. Rusty dropped Toughy's lead rope and Toughy, freed, stopped, watching Big Enough carry his rider on. Smith was coming out from the herd toward Rusty, and circling across in front of the leaders came Sam and Honey Yates. Yates passed Sam, and Smith was close. Rusty reigned Big Enough to a stop.

"Hello, Smith," he said casually.

Slippery Smith stopped his horse. Yates had pulled down from run to trot and was close behind Slippery Smith now. Rusty watched him. It would not do to let these two separate. He must keep them together where he could watch them both.

"What's on yore mind, Shotridge?" Slippery Smith drawled. "Yo're quite a ways from Dodge City, ain't you?"

"Quite a ways." Rusty's drawl was as smooth and soft as that of Slippery Smith. "You've got five hundred LM steers of mine, Smith. I've come to cut yore herd."

Yates had reined in now close to Slippery Smith, and Rusty's swift glance noted the snarling mask of hatred on Yates's face. Yates's hand was hidden on his right, and

Rusty, knowing what was coming, caught Big Enough with rein and spurs and swung him to the left. As the horse moved, Rusty's hand went up to the gun at his hip. It had come, then. This was the showdown!

Yates's hand rose from concealment. Smith was reaching for his gun, and Sam was pulling his horse to a halt and also reaching. Yates's hand came out and up and, from across his body, he fired one shot.

Honey Yates was not three feet from Slippery Smith when he fired. The lead plowed through ribs and lungs and heart, and Smith pitched down from his frightened horse, his right foot catching in the stirrup. The horse whirled and ran, dragging the body, kicking to free himself from his gruesome burden, and Honey Yates, swinging the gun around, screamed at Rusty Shotridge.

"You get the same, damn you!"

Yates's gun was up and level. Rusty could not hope to beat the shot even though his own weapon was in his hand. He was out of position, out of line. Lifting Big Enough once more with spurs and rein, the sorrel came around, throwing his head high, and as the horse swung Yates's gun exploded.

It was Big Enough that took the slug. His head had come in line, and the bullet crashed into the blaze of the sorrel's face. Big Enough went down like a poleaxed steer, and Rusty, dropping with the horse, thrust out his feet and struck upon them, the horse squarely between his forked legs. Yates had gone on by, and Sam was shooting, his horse whirling and fighting his rider. From along the frightened cattle men were coming, their horses running full out. Rusty, wheeling, turning the torso of his body, followed Yates with his weapon. Once, twice, three times the heavy gun bounced and dropped level again, and Honey Yates, flinging his arms wide, reeled on his running horse and pitched free of the saddle.

Dropping the Colt, Rusty reached down, snatching the Winchester from the saddle boot, and jumped free of Big Enough as the horse went over on his side and lay, kicking. As Rusty came up with the carbine a shot struck him, whirling him half around as it smashed into his left shoulder. Rusty dropped down to his knee, brought up the carbine and fired once. Sam had emptied his weapon with his shot, and with Rusty's bullet singing by his ear he turned his horse and fled. The other riders were rapidly approaching, and the steers, frightened by the shooting and the sudden action, were streaming past at a lumbering run. Rusty flung a shot from the carbine after Sam, levered the gun and sighted again. Once more he fired, and a horse, running hard, broke stride as though tripped, pitched down on head and neck, and his rider went sailing.

A Hackamore rider reined in beside the fallen horse. Others fanning out at a distance came on. Rusty levered the Winchester again and raised it, taking careful aim. Seven shots in the Winchester and he had used three of them! He was on the ground, hurt, but a fighting man, and toward those circling riders he flung his defiance.

"Come on, you! Come on!"

Back beside the fallen horse the Hackamore rider yelled. Shots pattered about Rusty, singing close, vicious and whining as they ricocheted, and then the circling riders broke and wheeled away, and beyond the cattle Rusty saw men streaming down a slope, their horses running full out, the men shouting as they came.

Rusty surveyed the apparition through red-rimmed, dust-blinded eyes. Surely he knew those riders. Rusty shook his head and lifted his left hand to his eyes, disregarding the pain the movement brought. That man in the lead, that man sweeping down toward him, was Leonard Carlisle. It could not be true, but it was. Carlisle! What was he doing here? And there was Kansas and there was Tom Flanders and Bud and little Chico and Gus and grinning Red. Rusty lowered the carbine and took a step. His toe struck an obstruction and, looking down, Rusty saw Big Enough's sorrel hip. Weakly he sat down upon that hip while Flanders and Sigloe and Red went streaming by. And then Leonard Carlisle slid his horse to a stop and leaped from his saddle, and Carlisle's voice was harsh and filled with anxiety as he called:

"Rusty, are you all right? Are you hurt?"

There on sorrel Big Enough's unmoving flank Rusty looked up uncomprehendingly at his questioner. "He killed Smith," Rusty said, his eyes wide. "Just pulled his gun an' shot him."

"Easy, Rusty," Carlisle ordered. "You're hurt. Here comes Bud, and Tom is right behind him. Easy now. Let me look at you."

CHAPTER XIX

They camped that night beside Slippery Smith's wagon. Save for Rusty, not a man had been hurt. The Hackamore cattle were scattered over half of Colorado, so Bud Sigloe said, and it would be a chore rounding them up. There might be other chores, too, he intimated and looked grimly at a man tied to a wagon wheel.

Of all the Hackamore outfit only that captive was left. The others, even the cook, were scattered to the wind. The charge that Tom Flanders had led had been too much for the Hackamore. With Slippery Smith dead, with Honey Yates down, with Sam gone, fleeing pell-mell from stuttering, vengeful guns, the Hackamore had no stomach for more fighting or iniquity. Two of their number they had left upon the field: one dead, the other unhorsed by Rusty's shot.

Rusty Shotridge camped in peace that night and despite the wound in his shoulder slept the long hard sleep of exhaustion. Not so the others. They sat around the fire and talked, low voiced, now and again glancing at their sleeping comrade, awe and respect in their eyes.

"He was goin' to handle it by himself," Kansas said once, nodding toward Rusty. "All by himself."

"He about had the job done too," Sigloe commented. "He was down mebbe, but he was a long ways from bein' finished when we come in."

The others nodded soberly. Over by the wagon wheel the captive spoke his defiance: "We'd of got him. If it hadn't been for you fello's . . ."

"You'd of got hell!" Tom Flanders snapped, and the captive lapsed into silence.

In the morning Carlisle and Sigloe rode to Trinchera. They were back before evening, and with them came a lanky, tobacco-chewing deputy sheriff. The deputy got down, shook hands with Flanders, Rusty and his fellows and strode over to the Hackamore man. It was immediately apparent that cow thieves were no more popular in Colorado than they were in Texas.

Under the deputy's persuasion the Hackamore rider talked. Nay, he more than talked; he babbled. And when the rider's story was done the deputy turned to Flanders and nodded thoughtfully.

"I reckon that settles it," he drawled. "The boss 'll be out from Trinidad tomorrow, an' he'll have some questions to ask, but I reckon I got the answers for him."

In the morning the sheriff from Trinidad did arrive and, as his deputy had foretold, had questions to ask. Once more the Hackamore rider told his tale, and again Rusty, abetted by Flanders, Carlisle, Sigloe and the others, answered questions. The Colorado sheriff listened gravely and pronounced judgment.

"Too damned bad," the sheriff stated,

"that you didn't get 'em all. I reckon that was too much to expect though."

Under the sheriff's orders the work of rounding up began. The sheriff had brought two men with him, and these helped in the task of gathering Hackamore cattle. Rusty, with Chico — who admitted that he could cook a little — remained at the camp, Rusty in charge of the remuda. For three days the work went steadily forward, and on the fourth day the sheriff was satisfied.

"I guess we got 'em all," he pronounced. "Now what did you want to do?"

It was Rusty who answered that. "I came this far to cut 'em; that's what I'm goin' to do."

The sheriff, after a long survey of the speaker, nodded agreement. Like a good many officers he was both the law and the court. "Cut 'em then," he directed.

So with the sunshine bright upon him and the fall air crisp, disdaining the ache in his wounded arm, Rusty cut the herd. Kansas helped with the cutting, and the others held the herd and the cut; and when he was finished Rusty rode out and reported to the sheriff. "They're clean."

There was much still to be done. Every man there knew it. While Kansas and his friends, in company with the deputies, held the cattle separate, the sheriff talked with Carlisle, Tom Flanders, Rusty and Sigloe. A plan was made and agreed upon.

"Likely it ain't legal," the sheriff said doubtfully, "but it's sense. Let's get at it."

The plan was not lawful but it was sensible. A court would tie up the Watrous cattle as well as all the rest. That was the thing they all sought to avoid. So Carlisle accompanied the sheriff and his prisoner when they departed for Trinidad, and Rusty and his companions stayed with the herd.

Carlisle was gone a day and two nights. When he returned there was a local ranchman with him. The local man inspected the Watrous steers, a bargain was struck and a bill of sale and a draft exchanged.

"You can drop 'em here," the local man directed. "This is my range, an' I'll have my riders shift them where I want them. There 'll be no kickbacks on this deal, Carlisle?"

"No kickbacks," Carlisle assured, and the local man was satisfied.

According to the sheriff's wishes, the remainder of the Hackamore herd was shifted nearer Trinidad. Three days were used in accomplishing that movement, and at the end of the third day the sheriff came out again to meet the cattle. Drawing Flanders apart, the two rode together while the herd moved slowly, and when camp was made the sheriff made a proposition.

"I've got to hold these cattle here until the court does something with 'em," he announced. "I can't spare any of my reg'lar deputies for the work an' I've got to hire some men. I wonder where I could get 'em?" He glanced guilelessly at Kansas. Tom Flanders, too, was watching the lanky man, as were Carlisle and Rusty.

Kansas began to grin. He looked at Chico, at Gus and Red and then at the officer. "You'd need about four?" Kansas asked.

"About four," the sheriff agreed, his face expressionless.

"I guess we could accommodate him, couldn't we, Chico?" Kansas asked, and Chico nodded.

In the morning there were good-bys. Kansas and his friends were staying with the cattle; Rusty and his companions were going to town with the sheriff. Rusty shook hands all around. There was no way to thank these men, his friends. They had come to him when he needed them most and they had gone through.

"You boys," Rusty said to Kansas, "will do to ride the river with. That's all I can say. I reckon . . ."

"Aw hell," Kansas blurted, and his voice,

too, was strained, "you ain't so bad your-self."

So they parted, Rusty riding away with his friends toward the west, Kansas and Red, Gus and Chico, remaining with the herd.

Rusty looked back when they had gone a hundred yards, and Kansas, beside the wagon, lifted his arm in good-by. Rusty answered the gesture and then turned away. The sheriff, riding beside Rusty, drawled slow speech.

"There's cow thieves an' cow thieves," he stated. "Them boys ain't wanted here in Colorado, an' I'll keep 'em busy till spring comes round. You'll see 'em again, son. They'll look you up. You can't lose them kind of friends."

In Trinidad there was more detail to attend. Before a justice of the peace Rusty, Flanders, Carlisle and Sigloe made statements that were notarized. Tom Flanders's reputation smoothed the way and made things easy, and the sheriff talked with the county attorney. Back east of Trinidad, north of Trinchera, there were three graves. Honey Yates lay in one, Slippery Smith in another and a nameless rider in the third. The statements before the justice explained those graves. There was law in Colorado and in the West, but there was a certain philosophy too. "Good riddance of bad rubbish," the West said and shrugged its shoulders.

So finally the legal labyrinth was solved and there was nothing more to hold the men. They bade good-by to their friend the sheriff, promising that they would see him again and urging that he visit them, and a full two weeks after the swift action that had finished Honey Yates and Slippery Smith the four rode out of the little town beside the Picketwire River.

Over Raton Pass they went and then east, across the Chico hills, and as they rode Rusty Shotridge was moody and distraught. His shoulder was almost healed and pained him but little, but his mind was not at rest.

They rode steadily east, sometimes making camp beside a stream, sometimes utilizing the hospitality of a ranch house or line camp, and as they traveled on his companions watched Rusty, sensing his mood and not able to explain it.

One by one they tried to help him. Flanders spoke quietly of his job in Dodge City and intimated that he could still use a good deputy. Rusty gave Tom no answer. Bud Sigloe, in turn, suggested that Ad Marble could use another trail boss, or that, should Rusty wish, he could take a place in Sigloe's crew. Rusty spoke his thanks. Then

well along the road to Dodge City Leonard
Carlisle took his turn.

There was a bond between Rusty and
Carlisle now, an unbreakable tie. They had
fought and hated each other, but each had
proved himself a man. Carlisle, riding beside
Rusty, blurted out the thing that was on his
mind.

"What's wrong?" Carlisle demanded.

"Nothing," Rusty answered. "There's
nothing wrong, Leonard."

That was not true and Carlisle knew it.
Still he did not refute the statement. "I've
held off talking to you," he said. "I wanted
Colonel Watrous to tell you about this, but I
guess I'd better do it myself."

"Tell me what?" Rusty demanded.

"Colonel Watrous and I are partners,"
Carlisle said. "We've made some money on
this herd. We'll stay in partnership."

Rusty nodded, wondering what was coming next.

"I've got another idea," Carlisle continued. "I think that we can make more money
if we raise our own cattle. I think we need a
breeding ranch and I'm prepared to put up
the money to buy one."

Rusty looked at his companion with surprise. Carlisle was talking sense, but Rusty
wondered where he himself fit in. Why was

Carlisle telling him all this? Carlisle smiled quietly.

"We'll probably pick a place in Colorado or New Mexico," he announced. "Texas is crowded with cowmen, and we'll need more room than we can find there. Next year we'll be trailing stocker cattle to a new home."

There was a pause and then Carlisle continued: "I want you to bring those cattle up the trail, Rusty. And I want you to run the outfit that we'll buy. No, wait a minute!" He held up his hand, checking Rusty's speech. "We'll make you some kind of a proposition, the colonel and I. We want you with us, Rusty, as a partner. How about it?"

For a long instant Rusty did not answer. Then, meeting Carlisle's eyes fairly, he spoke: "You don't want me, Carlisle. I . . . You don't want me."

"Why not?"

"Because . . ." Rusty said. "I . . . Marcia . . ."

A slow smile spread over Leonard Carlisle's face, becoming a wide grin of delight. "So that's it?" he exclaimed. "We all wondered what had got into you. Here you pull off a stunt that would make any man proud, and you've been going around glum as an ox. So that's it!"

"I'm in love with her," Rusty said stubbornly. "I'm not in her class. One time I thought . . ."

Leonard Carlisle's hand came down on Rusty's injured shoulder and closed. Rusty did not even feel the pain for Carlisle was speaking.

"Marcia sent me after you, Rusty. She sent me to bring you back to her. Do you understand?"

The trail was long now, for Rusty was eager. Day crawled into day, and the miles were no longer miles but distances that had no end. Still, long as was the trail and endless as were the miles, there came a day when as they rode the four men saw smoke against the sky and under the smoke a black clump that, growing nearer, resolved itself into buildings.

"Dodge City," Tom Flanders said and urged his weary horse to a swifter pace.

The smoke came nearer and the buildings grew larger. Presently they were riding through streets. Beside the Drovers' Hotel they stopped and dismounted, tying their saddle horses and pack animals to a convenient hitch rack. Stiffly, as men move who have spent a long time in the saddle, they rounded the corner of the building.

Colonel Watrous was on the porch, smoking. His feet were on the porch rail; his chair was tipped back and his hat lowered over his eyes. The ashes from his cigar dropped on his vest, and the colonel languidly brushed them away. He had just completed the gesture when he saw the travelers. The colonel's feet struck the floor with a thump and he sprang up, his voice an inarticulate bellow of greeting.

The quartet paused just below the hotel steps. Watrous came charging down the steps, his hand outstretched. He caught Carlisle's hand, reached for Rusty, and words came tumbling from his lips, inarticulate in his eagerness. Ellen Watrous appeared in the doorway, and Carlisle, freeing himself from the colonel, went to her. On the porch he held her in his arms, all the world forgotten, and Ellen's red hair was pressed against his breast. Rusty, watching, was happy for his friend.

Watrous had released Rusty and gone on to Sigloe and Flanders. He was pummeling them, almost overwhelming them with his greeting. Behind the two on the porch there was movement. Marcia Carlisle appeared in the doorway of the hotel and paused. Rusty took a step forward and stopped. There she stood, the girl who had been constantly with him, the girl who, no matter what happened, would be with him all his life. He could not go to her. He stood waiting.

For an instant Marcia stood in the doorway, her eyes, dark as Rusty remembered them, searching the porch, the steps, the scene before her. Then, moving swiftly, she passed her brother and Ellen and reached the steps, and her arms were widespread and her voice was glad as she cried one word: "Rusty!"

She ran down the steps toward him.

ABOUT THE AUTHOR

Bennett Foster was born in Omaha, Nebraska, and came to live in New Mexico in 1916 to attend the State Agricultural College and remained there the rest of his life. He served in the U.S. Navy during the Great War and was stationed in the Far East during the Second World War, where he attained the rank of captain in the U.S. Air Corps. He was working as the principal of the high school in Springer, New Mexico, when he sold his first short story, *Brockleface,* to *West Magazine* in 1930 and proceeded to produce hundreds of short stories and short novels for pulp magazines as well as *The Country Gentleman* and *Cosmopolitan* over the next three decades. In the 1950s his stories regularly appeared in *Collier's.* In the late 1930s and early 1940s Foster wrote a consistently fine and critically praised series of Western novels, serialized in *Argosy* and Street & Smith's *Western Story Maga-*

zine, that were subsequently issued in hardcover book editions by William Morrow and Company and Doubleday, Doran and Company in the Double D series. It is worth noting that Foster's early Double D Westerns were published under the pseudonym John Trace, although some time later these same titles, such as *Trigger Vengeance* and *Range of Golden Hoofs,* appeared in the British market under his own name. Foster knew the terrain and people of the West first-hand from a lifetime of living there. His stories are invariably authentic in detail and color, from the region of fabulous mesas, jagged peaks, and sun-scorched deserts. Among the most outstanding of his sixteen published Western novels are *Badlands* (1938), *Rider of the Rifle Rock* (1939), and *Winter Quarters* (1942), this last a murder mystery within the setting of a Wild West Show touring the western United States. As a storyteller he was always a master of suspenseful and unusual narratives.

We hope you have enjoyed this Large Print book. Other Thorndike, Wheeler, Kennebec, and Chivers Press Large Print books are available at your library or directly from the publishers.

For information about current and upcoming titles, please call or write, without obligation, to:

Publisher
Thorndike Press
295 Kennedy Memorial Drive
Waterville, ME 04901
Tel. (800) 223-1244

or visit our Web site at:

http://gale.cengage.com/thorndike

OR

Chivers Large Print
published by BBC Audiobooks Ltd
St James House, The Square
Lower Bristol Road
Bath BA2 3SB
England
Tel. +44(0) 800 136919
email: bbcaudiobooks@bbc.co.uk
www.bbcaudiobooks.co.uk

All our Large Print titles are designed for easy reading, and all our books are made to last.